JORDAN'S KISS

By the Author

In Helen's Hands

Arrested Pleasures

Jordan's Kiss

JORDAN'S KISS

by

Nanisi Barrett D'Arnuk

2021

ISBN 13: 978-1-63555-980-4

This Trade Paperback Original Is Published By
Bold Strokes Books, Inc.
P.O. Box 249
Valley Falls, NY 12185

First Edition: September 2021

_____

Credits
Editor: Barbara Ann Wright
Production Design: Susan Ramundo
Cover Design By Tammy Seidick

Dedication

For Ti, my muse

Chapter One

Pianist Morgan Sparks handed her band's business card to the young man who had just introduced himself. He was planning a party for his parent's thirtieth wedding anniversary next month, and he wanted her band to perform at it. His parents had come to this restaurant many times and really liked their music. The trio, or occasionally a quartet, had been playing there for a couple years. Everyone knew, if you wanted to hear good music that wouldn't bust your eardrums, The Dam Restaurant, just outside Boston, in Newton, Massachusetts was the place to be. It was on the Chestnut River, just below a dam. On their menu and in their advertising, they boasted, "Best restaurant by a dam site."

"Give me a call this week, we can discuss time and place, and if there are any special songs that mean a lot to your folks, or songs that they really like, let us know, and we'll try to include them."

He nodded happily, thanked her and shook her hand. As he walked away, she felt someone at her shoulder and turned to see Robbie Nelson, the band's drummer, standing there with a big hopeful smile on her face.

"I've got a good friend that's here, and she wants to sing a song with us," Robbie told Morgan.

"We're in the middle of a gig, hon. She can audition later tonight after we finish, and the place starts to clear out, or I can hear her tomorrow," Morgan replied. She really didn't want a new singer in the group, especially one she hadn't heard before.

"No, no, not to *audition* for us. She's really good, and I'd love to hear her sing just one song. Actually, she didn't ask. I suggested it," Robbie admitted. "We went to college together. We both studied music. I'll vouch for her. She's real good. She's been singing with her own band out in California."

Morgan looked at Robbie with a raised eyebrow.

"Oh, c'mon, Morg. She's *really* good. I think she has a recording contract with her band there." Robbie continued trying to persuade Morgan.

Well, if Robbie's friend was truly visiting, it was nothing to worry about. Morgan hated to deny her coworkers anything. She'd gone out of her way to take a truly mediocre song that their bass player had written and rework it into a fairly good piece they had added to their repertoire. She'd let Robbie do some of the set-ups and pick new material. Actually, although she had the experience and the training, it wasn't her band. Robbie and Lori were the ones who organized it…then left it in her hands. But now, another someone she hadn't heard? Well, to keep her fellow band-members happy. After all, it was only one song.

Morgan focused back on Robbie's persistent pleas. She interrupted with, "What does she want to sing?"

"I'll ask." Then Robbie hurried off to the other side of the room.

A few minutes later, as Morgan had just gotten up to the piano, Robbie came back. "I'm sorry if this is an inconvenience," Morgan heard over her shoulder.

Morgan turned. A stunning brunette stood beside Robbie. Average height for a woman, but her eyes had a glow in them that was hard to look away from. Morgan's breath caught in her throat.

"It's no inconvenience," she barely got out. "What do you want to sing?"

"Something slow. Any oldie. Something from mid-last century. Your call. 'Over the Rainbow,' 'Unforgettable,' 'Who Can I Turn To,' something like that." The timbre of her voice sent chills up Morgan's back. It was low and very sultry. Morgan felt a warm feeling down below her belly.

"'Rainbow' sounds good. Original key?"

The new woman nodded and reached to shake Morgan's hand. "Thank you for this," she said. "You didn't have to. Robbie just wanted to hear me sing again."

Morgan smiled. "What's your name so I can introduce you?" she asked.

"Jordan Phelps."

She repeated the name to herself so she wouldn't forget it, although she wasn't sure she'd ever forget this stunning woman in front of her. "Second in the next set."

"Thank you." Jordan smiled at her, and Morgan's insides melted.

As wonderful as this one looks, I shouldn't do this. She'd better be worth it.

She beckoned to Lori, their bass player. "New singer, friend of Robbie's. We'll do 'Over the Rainbow' second in E-flat."

The opening two notes of that song were extremely difficult; few could do them well. It would have been a dynamite audition test. Morgan couldn't wait to hear how that went. She hoped Jordan was up for it, especially with no warm-up.

They got back onstage and prepared for the next set. They played one lively number to get the audience back in the mood. When the first song was over, Morgan pulled her microphone closer. She had to make this sound good so the audience would be enthused.

"Hey, everyone. We've got a treat for you tonight. A friend of Roberta's, our drummer, is visiting from California and she's gonna sing a Judy Garland hit that was named Number One Song of the Twentieth Century. Ladies and Gentlemen, singing 'Over the Rainbow,' Ms. Jordan Phelps!"

Jordan hurried up onto the stage and took the mic from Morgan. Morgan and the band started the song with an enticing introduction.

Jordan's voice slid into the song so very easily, it was as smooth as velvet. The opening octave jump was like butter, not even a skip or short break into the second note. Morgan could feel her own eyes open in wonder as she watched person after person turn to watch and listen to Jordan, smiles on every face. The soft notes seemed to caress each ear gently, but the long ones soared. Jordan was a very talented performer. She knew how to get the most out of each note, and Morgan found herself almost melting again.

Jordan looked at individual members of her audience and seemed to draw them in. All through the song, they were mesmerized by her voice. As Jordan finished, the crowd erupted into wild applause. There were even a few on their feet. Yes, Jordan was a gifted singer.

She bowed to her audience and acknowledged their applause. She returned the mic to Morgan, waved to the audience again, and hurried back to her table.

Morgan immediately switched to the next tune. She had to get that song out of her head. Had that woman cast some sort of spell on her? *Concentrate, Sparks.* She couldn't think of anything else. *Concentrate. Concentrate.* She had a hard time getting through the rest of the set. There were only a few more pieces, and then the set ended.

"Thank you all for listening tonight," Morgan said, still playing the closing number, "and for welcoming our friend, Jordan Phelps. Wasn't she great?" She waited until the applause died. "We'll be back next week, Wednesday through Saturday, same place, same times. Have a great week, and don't forget to tip your server. From Lori Richards-Brand on bass, Roberta Nelson on drums and me, Morgan Sparks, this is Stone Cold Perception giving you a giant thank you and signing off for the week." She finished the ending song, and the music stopped. The room got very noisy as some patrons got ready to leave, servers finished serving their last diners, and others cleared the emptying tables.

"So, what did you think?" It was Robbie as she was closing up her kit. She had just put a tarp over her drum set and strapped it down. She didn't have to take it down unless they were going to rehearse before Wednesday. The set could stay there. The management would assure that no one disturbed it. Robbie took her sticks, cymbals, and smaller instruments home with her.

"Very beautiful," Morgan said.

"Yah, but I mean her voice." Robbie snickered.

"That's what I was referring to." Morgan grinned at her.

"Were you?"

"She has a very nice tone and a great style." Morgan didn't want to mention that she'd noticed what an outstanding backside Jordan had when she turned to sing to the audience. It wasn't hard to watch her through the song. Jordan looked great from head to toe…back *and* front. And yes, she'd noticed the front, too. Great curves, astounding tits. Nothing that looked less than perfect.

"I knew you'd like her. If she's moving near here, can we use her?"

Morgan gazed at her. "I thought you said she was just visiting?" she asked warily.

"Well, it seems she's looking for a new place to move to."

Morgan leaned back. Had that been a scam? Did Robbie want to include Jordan in their band? A fourth member? She had sounded wonderful, and she looked great. It would take a little bit of responsibility off her shoulders, not that she didn't like being the front person of the group, but it wasn't a necessity to her ego. Did they need to add another member to the band? They already had a sax player that they could add if they were doing parties or larger, louder gigs. A singer would add a lot, though.

The restaurant owner wouldn't have to increase the pay, but would he? Or would he say, *you hired her, you pay her*? "Are you willing to give up a quarter of your pay?"

"Oh, come on, Morg. We don't make that much. We still have to have day jobs. This gig just gives us extra to put back to buy something special from time to time."

That was true, but the more Morgan thought about it, the more appealing it became. *Include the entire band, smartass. You can't make an executive decision with this.* "We should get Lori's input."

She turned to look for their bass player.

"Yo, Lor," Robbie called across the room.

It looked like Lori was coming back from the ladies' room. She walked over to them.

"What?" she asked as she picked up her backpack from the stage.

"What did you think of Jordan?"

"She's way cute."

The other two laughed.

"Good, Lor. Musically," Morgan said.

"Oh." Lori thought for a moment. "She was in tune, and her timing was good."

"How good? Do you think she'd fit in with us?"

"Fit in with us?"

Robbie looked into Lori's eyes and grinned.

"Earth to Lori. Did you just sneak a hit out back?"

"Sorry. My mind's somewhere else. I'm having a fight with Mel. She wants to go to this gathering tomorrow, and I want to stay home."

"And she can't go without you?"

"It's with her family, at her sister's house. If I don't go, her mother will spend the afternoon bitching and ripping me to shreds."

Morgan and Robbie nodded. They both knew the mother-in-law from hell.

"You'd better go. That's one of the drawbacks of married life, sweetie."

Lori was always talking about how her mother-in-law had it in for her: that she didn't have the education Mel had, that she didn't spend enough time with Mel, that she couldn't make enough money to keep her daughter happy, even though Mel's job brought in a whole lot more than hers did.

Robbie and Morgan were single. Morgan didn't even have a steady girlfriend.

"So what should we do about Jordan?" Robbie asked.

"Is she staying around here? She sounds really good." Lori asked as she looked from Robbie to Morgan. "I think she'd add a lot to the group. Can you work with her?" she asked Morgan.

"I'll have to see what else she's got. If she has some good stuff, maybe I'll ask her to come back one day next weekend. Are you both willing to give up a quarter of your pay for a night?"

"That's no problem for me. She'd be good on Friday or Saturday. That's when the most people are here. That's when people can be kind of raucous," Robbie said.

"Makes no never-mind to me," Lori said. "This job is just extra so Mel's mother can't say I'm lazy. I think she might be good on those hard nights."

Good. "I'll talk to her."

"Well, I gotta run home if I'm getting up tomorrow to go to this debacle. It's a good thing her sister likes me," Lori said as she leaned down to heft her bass. Her electric bass was locked in its case and stashed behind her amplifier. The stand-up bass would go home with her. "If you feel we need to rehearse anything, give me a call. Otherwise, see you next Wednesday."

Lori got all her things together and then left. Robbie made sure all her equipment was safe, then looked over to where Jordan was sitting and waved that she was done there.

Morgan turned away from the audience, straightened her music into a neat pile, and put them into her big messenger bag. Well, another week, another few nickels. These gigs didn't pay much, but it gave them a chance to perform. Maybe some name would hear them sometime. At least, it gave her something to do after work.

"Morgan?" The voice was low. "Thank you so much for letting me sing tonight." It was Jordan, of course, who'd come up behind her.

"You're welcome. You have a very fine voice. It should take you far." She had been surprised when Jordan had started. She'd expected an average amateur performance, maybe pleasant at best, like so many others who'd auditioned for her. But Jordan's voice was sensual, and her long notes floated and curled around you like honey. "I'm surprised you're not performing somewhere."

"Thank you. That means a lot to me. Robbie said you had the best ears around."

"Well...maybe not quite," Morgan said, a little embarrassed. "I'd like to talk with you, maybe tomorrow? Do you have a card?"

"Not right now. I'm moving so I'm staying at a hotel for now. I could give you my cell number." She reached into her purse.

"You're in a hotel? How long are you going to be in town?"

"I'm not sure. Until I find a place to live, I guess." She took a small notebook out of her bag, jotted on it, and tore a piece out.

"Here in Boston?" Morgan continued to question.

"I haven't decided. Can I call you? Robbie gave me *your* card." She handed Morgan the paper. Morgan skimmed the writing on the jagged piece of paper. *Well, now I have her number.*

"Sure." Morgan refocused. "Either way would be great. We'll have to be in touch."

"Hey, Jordey," Robbie said, using the nickname they'd used in college, "why don't you stay with me for a while? It's silly paying for a hotel." Robbie had come up beside the piano. "I haven't got a big place, but the couch is comfortable."

"Well...we'll talk."

"Did you eat here, or do you want to go get something?" Robbie asked. She looked around as if to make sure there was no management nearby. "There's an all-night diner not too far from here," she said softly, "and it's a lot less expensive. I always get hungry doing these gigs. Come with me?"

Jordan nodded.

"Want to join us, Morg?"

"Not tonight. You two must have a lot to catch up on."

"Let me go check out the ladies' room. I'll be ready in a minute." Jordan walked over to where the restroom signs were pointing.

Robbie leaned over the piano. "See? I told you she was wonderful."

"Yes," agreed Morgan. "She does have a beautiful voice."

"I'm going to find out why she's not still in California." Robbie said.

Morgan added, "And find out how long she's planning to stay here. Just in case we decide we want to use her long-term in the band." She quickly accentuated to prevent any suspicion she had any attraction to this new member.

Robbie continued without a hitch. "She said she was resettling but didn't say why. Something must have happened. The last I heard, around Christmas, she was teaching in a private high school, her girlfriend had moved in, and her band was cutting a demo."

"That doesn't sound like a time to move across the country." *No, it wasn't a time to cut-and-run.* They talked for a few minutes about how Robbie knew Jordan from college and the mischief they'd gotten into while they were there.

"She was one of my roommates there. We've stayed in touch, but I have no idea why she's here now."

Finally, Jordan walked back, her coat over her arm. She slipped it on. "Ready?" she asked.

"Always," Robbie answered. "I'm parked out in the back. I'll meet you around front. I have the red SUV."

"All right, I'll see you in a minute. I'm in the beige Acura."

Robbie grinned. "The only car in the lot with California plates."

They both said good-bye to Morgan and headed to their cars.

Morgan sat back. She almost wanted to play another song while the staff was clearing up some of the empty tables. She did most of her thinking while she was playing. And the situation might need a lot of serious thought. She should just go home.

Whoa...what is happening? She knew why she was feeling itchy, and the thought disturbed her. She hadn't had a reaction like this to another woman in years. Every nerve in her body was on alert. Her heart had been beating wildly, and she barely controlled her breathing or the feeling down below. It had been like that since Jordan started singing. She almost sounded like...*no!* She put her head down. *Don't go there. That was almost fifteen years ago.*

"Morgan?" The owner, a gray-haired older man, stood behind the piano. "Are you thinking of adding a singer to the group?"

"I'm not sure yet, Paul. What do you think?"

"She sounds good, and she's real pretty. She might add a lot."

"Are you saying we're not pretty?"

"No, I wasn't saying that at all." He might have wanted to, but she was sure he wasn't going to insult the entire band with a comparison right now. "But face it, there aren't many as pretty as her."

Morgan grinned. Yes, she'd noticed that. "What about money?" she asked. Hopefully, he liked Jordan well enough to add something. This wasn't a high-paying gig, but it was steady and gave them a place to perform.

He paused to consider it. "I can give you another two-fifty, but not more than that."

"A night?"

He laughed. "Right," he said sarcastically. Then he clarified his offer. "A week."

"Even if I use her only on Fridays and Saturdays?"

For several seconds, he chewed his bottom lip, his eyes looking through her as he considered it. "Sure. That would be fine."

"Okay, thanks." Morgan said and he walked away.

Now, how do I meld her into a set? Morgan continued her thoughts. *Jordan's sound is special. Like she should be on center stage somewhere, carrying an entire show. Why is she here? Shouldn't she be in New York on Broadway, or at some high-end club where record companies, movie producers, or people with the right connections would hear her?*

She looked around the club. It was emptying out. She'd call her tomorrow. No. If Jordan was serious about this *she'd* call. Yes, she should wait and see if Jordan called her. Then she'd know if this was serious.

By then, she'd figure out just how serious she herself was. She knew why she had reacted to Jordan's singing. She sounded very much like Suzanne, but that affair had ended years ago. Why was she still carrying it with her? She'd spent several years in therapy to get over it. Now was not the time to start it up all over again with someone new.

CHAPTER TWO

Robbie and Jordan had spent several hours talking and laughing at the diner last night. There was a lot to catch up on, or at least a lot for Robbie to share. Jordan still hadn't revealed all her plans or why she was looking for a new place to live. When Robbie had asked about Jordan's girlfriend, all Jordan had said was, "Her parents got involved. They don't like me very much."

Eventually, Jordan had gone back to her hotel, and Robbie had gone home.

Robbie had originally made plans to spend Sunday with Chelsea. She actually spent every Sunday with Chelsea. They had talked about driving down to Carson Beach just south of the city. Although it was still too cold to go swimming, just sitting in that sweet little coffee shop overlooking the water near there would be great. It was called a coffee shop, but they served more food than that national coffee chain or the other coffee shops around the city. They would spend the entire afternoon there, and then go back to Chelsea's for the evening and... well...

Chelsea was such an incredible woman, far better than others who had previously been in her life. Even after they'd been dating for almost six months, there was still that spark between them. It hadn't even started to fade. It might even have grown. Robbie would go to work on Monday morning still tired, just like all the other Mondays in the last six months.

This morning, after too little sleep, Robbie had called Chelsea to see what they should do today. Driving to the beach didn't really appeal to either of them this morning. It was too cloudy today, and the fog over the ocean would make viewing the area far less pleasant than they had anticipated, so she suggested this place that Chelsea loved in Boston's North End, so they could get some of their special ravioli.

Robbie was worried. She wasn't sure how Chelsea would react to the idea of another woman being in her apartment, but she had to bring up the subject of asking Jordan to bunk in with her until she could find her own place.

"She was my roommate and best friend in college. She's great. You'll see when you meet her, if she can find this place."

"She will. It's probably a parking space she can't find."

Robbie sat back as the server set cups of coffee in front of them. Robbie reached for a couple sugar packets, and Chelsea opened just one container of creamer. The idea of helping her college friend while keeping her lover as a top priority was hard. She wasn't sure how she was going to do it. She didn't want Chelsea to feel insecure at all, but she wanted to help Jordan save money.

"There's nothing to worry about," Robbie told Chelsea as they stirred their coffee.

"You only have one bedroom. Will she be sleeping in your bed?" Chelsea asked.

"No," said Robbie, right away. "Of course not. She'll sleep on the couch. It's comfortable enough for a couple weeks or so. It's just until she finds a place of her own." She turned a little bit more toward Chelsea. "There's no way Jordan and I will sleep together. We tried that in college, but we weren't right for each other. We're only friends now."

"Well," Chelsea said, while staring out the window. "If it's just while she looks for an apartment…"

Robbie couldn't understand why she was asking Chelsea's permission to share her own apartment with her own long-time friend, but she was trying to do the right thing in this relationship. It was almost a first for her. Was she getting too serious about this woman? The others in her past hadn't questioned her like Chelsea. And she'd never even thought of getting their opinion. Was she just growing up, or was there something growing in this relationship? She knew she liked Chelsea a lot more, but was this love?

The door to the little restaurant opened, and Jordan walked in and looked around. A hostess walked up to offer her a seat, but she shook her head and pointed to where Robbie and Chelsea were sitting. Robbie waved at her. She came over and took the seat Robbie offered.

"My college roommate, Jordan Phelps, meet my, uh, girlfriend, Chelsea Manchester." The two reached across the table to shake hands.

"Have trouble finding this place?" Chelsea asked.

"Nope. My GPS brought me right to it. This is a colorful little neighborhood."

"It's the Little Italy part of town," Robbie said. "Lots of great little restaurants."

"This one has the best mushroom ravioli around." Chelsea said.

"That sounds good." said Jordan. "Are you vegetarian?"

"No, but I try to eat healthy on the weekends. The weekdays are so busy for me that I usually grab whatever is close. Not always the best thing." She cut her eyes to Robbie. "And your friend here is no help. She'll eat anything." The three laughed at that thought.

Chelsea studied Jordan. Robbie hoped Chelsea didn't feel intimidated. Her chest was at least a cup-size smaller, but she shouldn't feel inferior. Robbie and Jordan were not right for each other. "So, what brought you to Boston all the way from California?"

"Looking for a new place to live. I tried St. Louis and Indianapolis, but they didn't seem right, even though I knew Indianapolis quite well, so I kept driving. I've always heard Vermont is beautiful."

"And she figured, seeing we hadn't seen each other in a few years that she'd stop and say hi." Robbie said.

"And you're looking for an apartment in Boston?" Chelsea continued.

"I may try somewhere in this general area. I was only going to stay a few days, but Robbie convinced me last night that this was the place to be, musically."

"Jordan has a great voice," Robbie added. "You should have heard her last night. She sang "Over the Rainbow," and it was as good as Judy Garland ever sang it. She had people on their feet."

"That's impressive, especially in that restaurant."

"Well, I think the piano player, Morgan, can make anyone sound good."

"Yes. Morgan is the best." Their appetizer, a platter of fried calamari, came, and the server offered Jordan a menu. She ordered the ravioli and a cup of coffee, and the server walked away. "Help yourself," Robbie said, putting the plate in the center of the table. Each took a portion.

"If you two went to college in Illinois, how did you end up on different sides of the country?" Chelsea asked while dipping her calamari into the spicy marinara.

"I think a better question is, how did we both end up in Illinois?" Robbie said with a chuckle. "I'm from Maine, and Jordan is from Texas.

"I grew up just outside Fort Worth and was so ready to get out of Texas that I applied to a lot of colleges far, far from there. I think my first choice was BU, right here in Boston. But Urbana-Champaign gave me the best scholarship."

"I think my reason was about the same," Robbie said. "I just drifted back here after we graduated. I knew it would be hard to compete with the drummers from Berklee, but I had to try."

"But you could have taken that teaching job," Chelsea added.

"Oh sure." Robbie sniffed at the thought, "A hundred twelve-year-olds and one small marching band. Definitely not my thing."

"Really?" Jordan said sarcastically. "Those would have been your peers." She tried to hide her smile, but her eyes gave her away.

"Whoa. Are you calling me a twelve-year-old?"

"No, a small marching band."

Robbie placed her fists on the edge of the table and said in jest, "Well, at least when I open my mouth, I'm not the entire choir."

Jordan raised herself a few inches in her chair, using her palms on the edge of the table to keep her balance and leaned toward Robbie with a glare in her eyes and a half-tainted grin. As Chelsea looked on in embarrassment, Jordan said, "At least I've got tone and tune and not just tap and tempo."

They stared each other down for a few seconds. Chelsea turned her head slightly as if to see how many customers just heard this battle of the musicians. Jordan and Robbie burst into laughter. They always came at each other to add a bit of humor whenever they were together. The more they insulted, the better they felt about their friendship. Chelsea eased back in her chair and joined the laughter.

"Another one of those best-deals-available, wasn't it?" Jordan said. "I sent my resume everywhere and got a teaching job in California. I had two choruses and several classes. I was there almost ten years."

"I still can't figure why you quit mid-year."

"It had become a place that wasn't right for me," was Jordan's explanation. She seemed to try to get the focus off herself. "Why are you working as someone's file clerk when you should be in an orchestra somewhere?"

"I'm not a file clerk. I'm an administrative assistant.

"Is there a difference?"

"Yes, the name-plate on my desk is much wider," Robbie boasted half-heartedly.

Jordan laughed at her. "But why?"

"Because there's no pressure, and I have my weekends and evenings free to do what I want. There's no overtime unless I want it. Besides, I like the music we do at the Dam."

"Your band has a great sound. Lori plays some mean bass, both on electric and stand-up."

"She started out in the orchestra in middle school and just advanced from there. It was luck that we found each other. I met Lori at a lesbian bar, and we started talking. I don't think we'd ever considered cruising each other. It was more of a shoulder to cry on 'cause neither of us was getting lucky that night." She saw the look on Chelsea's face. "That was years before we met, honey." She gave her a light kiss on the cheek. "Anyway, we ended up talking all evening, along with drinking the same brand of beer. We knew we both wanted to start a band of some kind, but we needed a keyboard player or a couple guitars. Then, when Lori was looking for a new house, she just happened to mention it to the realtor. The realtor said she used to play piano and really missed it. Said she would like having a night job. So we met, and here we are."

"Wow. So Morgan is a realtor?"

"Yes, Morgan is a real go-getter. She's even gotten us jobs playing at private parties. That's where the money is for something like we do. I think she was talking to someone last night about playing an anniversary party."

"She's not that old, though, is she?" Jordan asked.

"A little older than us. Somewhere around thirty-eight or nine."

"She's so tall and such a good-looking woman. Is she straight?"

"Nah. She's had a few brief affairs, but she doesn't date much. I'm not sure what her story is. I tried to set her up a few times, but nothing really stuck. She may have had a second date once or twice, but that was it. She won't let anyone get close." Robbie was sure that Morgan would be a wonderful girlfriend for someone if she'd just let someone in.

"You've been playing with her for five or six years, hon. You must know something else," Chelsea said.

"Her name is Morgan Justine Sparks, but don't you dare call her Sparky. She hates that and will walk out on you." They laughed. "She grew up out in Lexington, I think. I know she used to live in New York City."

"Really?" Jordan asked.

"She played with someone really well-known, but she never says who. I know they went on tour to Europe or Africa, but the competition is real rough in New York."

"I'm not sure I'd want to live in New York City," Jordan said, "but it's always an exciting thought to dream on. Imagine all those big-name performers that live in New York."

"Morgan played back-up with someone. In fact, she was hired while she was still here at Berklee. She dropped out of school for that."

"Why did she move back?"

Robbie shrugged. "Burnout, I think. She's talked about doing a lot of drugs while she was there. That may have contributed to it.

There also must have been a lot of competition. I know some of her arrangements were recorded, though."

"But you don't get money from arrangements. It's probably one of the hardest and least paid of all the careers in the business. And in New York, there must be twenty musicians on every block."

"Yeah, you have to be really tough-skinned to work there. There's a lot of burnout. New Yorkers can be brutal."

They all shook their heads. Jordan seemed lost in thought. When Robbie touched her arm, it seemed to startle Jordan back into reality. "Are you going to call Morgan and see what can happen at the club?"

"Ah, yes. I'll call her tonight."

The server brought their entrees, and they started to eat. They talked and laughed well into the afternoon.

That evening, after checking out of the hotel and moving her things into Robbie's apartment, Jordan called Morgan. They made an appointment to meet on Monday evening at Morgan's house. Jordan would bring all the music she had with her.

"You know, the way you and Morgan sounded last night," Robbie said, "I bet you'll fit right into the band," *And maybe that's what Morgan needs. The two of them look very good together. Morgan's height and Jordan's looks balance each other. Maybe I shouldn't stick my nose in, but it is a thought.* It might be just what they each needed.

Chapter Three

"Wow, you've got quite a repertoire," Morgan said as she sat back. She and Jordan had just gone through almost twenty songs Jordan knew perfectly. She had brought a pile of arrangements with her from California. She had a distinctive style that set her apart from a lot of others. Her arrangements were well-done, too. Morgan knew they hadn't been done by an amateur. She began to wonder what *her* arrangements would sound like coming out of Jordan's mouth.

"Did you do these arrangements?" Morgan asked.

"No. I paid to have them done."

"They must have cost a lot. They're very professional."

"I had started doing this professionally when I lived in California, but I haven't been able to find the right group since I left there."

"You were doing well there?"

"Very. I sang with a small jazz group and also a rock band. I also did some solo gigs at parties and weddings with just a pianist. I had a job almost every week."

"Why'd you leave it if you were that successful?"

"Personal reasons."

Morgan felt her close down the discussion. What was she hiding? *Should I keep pushing? No, leave it alone, she'll get comfortable in time.* "I'm sorry. Well, whatever the reason, I'm glad you're here."

"Thanks, Morgan. I appreciate any help you can give me. I know nothing about the music business in Boston, so I'm on my own."

"There's a lot happening here."

Jordan nodded her agreement.

"I wish I could offer you more, but all I can promise is the two nights like we discussed."

"Thanks." She stood as if in a hurry to leave.

The attraction Morgan started to feel on Saturday was blossoming even bigger, being this close in a closed place. In fact, she wanted to lean over and kiss her, but that would be so unprofessional.

"I'd better get going, though," Jordan said. "I've got a job interview tomorrow morning, and I want to be prepared."

"Good luck. I'll see you Friday night?"

"Definitely."

"I think that arrangement 'I Want Money' will get you a bit *more money*, too," Morgan said quickly

"I hope so." She picked up her music and left.

Morgan took a deep breath and watched her leave the house. There was so much she wanted to ask Jordan. With a voice like hers, it seemed unimaginable that a record company or major group hadn't picked her up long before she moved here. The way she'd shut down the discussion about California also kicked up some questions in Morgan. Something had happened there that Jordan didn't want to talk about. She'd have to check the internet and see if anything was there. But…if it was a romantic breakup, it wouldn't be on the internet, unless she had posted it on her personal page. *Though, I had left New York for reasons that no one knew about, so you never can tell. Some things are better left unreported…like Suzanne.*

"I'm not sure I can do this," Jordan thought as she slipped into her car to drive back to Robbie's. If she had stayed at Morgan's, she wasn't sure she'd be able to keep from kissing her. *Every time I look at Morgan, my stomach tightens up, and my panties get wet. She's such an attractive woman, and Robbie tells me she's not dating anyone. Please don't do this to me. I can't get involved with anyone ever again.*

Morgan was the type she'd always wanted to date: tall, thin, almost androgynous, but with just that spark of femininity that prevented anyone from assuming right away that she was a butch. And she was beautiful, with mesmerizing dark blue eyes, and she was talented and intelligent. *Oh my God. Stop this.*

She had lied about the interview the next day. She didn't have one, but she couldn't sit with Morgan any longer. No, Morgan was too much. Jordan had been attracted to the piano player since she walked into the restaurant Saturday night. Hearing and watching her play only increased the attraction. Morgan's praise of her voice had cut into her heart, too. Yes, she was glad her singing was pleasing someone, but she didn't want Morgan to be attracted by it. She'd have to leave.

She glanced at the pile of arrangements on her passenger seat.

What a waste. If I had all that money back, I could pay rent on a good apartment for the next few months. I wouldn't need to worry about finding a new job right away. And these weren't the only arrangements she had. There were a dozen or so more in those boxes she'd left at Blaine's. She shook her head, remembering when she had a job, a lover, a home, a future, and money. Then, *that* night had happened. Now: no lover, no career, and scrounging for a place to live. At least she had had enough to pay for a week at the cheap hotel. It was fortunate that Robbie offered her couch. Now she didn't have to worry and take the first thing she saw. She would have enough to put a deposit down on a small apartment if she found one. She could pay her rent for the next few months and get the minimum amount of furniture and appliances she'd need, but after that, it would be hard. She'd have to bite the bullet and look for a low-paying job at some fast-food joint or convenience store just to eat.

Maybe I'd get a job in a good restaurant so I could sneak a little bite here and there, she thought as she drove back to Robbie's. Of course, this two-night gig would help a lot to begin with.

But maybe that was a mistake, too. Why put herself in front of Morgan two nights a week? Was this the torture she'd have to put herself through to pay for California? Why not just stay on the road and head to Vermont or Maine like she had originally planned? She could find a small place there and fade into the woodwork...or the actual woods. She needed a place where there were no other women and no distractions to cloud her head. She might even be able to get back to her own writing or find a new teaching job. But how did one become unattractive and androgynous so no one would be drawn to her, and she would not be pulled to someone else? Oh God. She definitely couldn't do it if she was going to sing.

Tuesday afternoon, Robbie had called Chelsea, who'd agreed to meet her and Jordan at the all-night diner that evening. She said she'd be there in about a half an hour.

"So come with us to the party on Sunday," Robbie told Jordan as they sat there waiting. "You'll meet a lot of new people, and you never know, you might meet that one you've been looking for all your life."

Robbie wanted her to get out more, and now that they were living together, maybe they could do that. She remembered that when they were in college, Jordan had lived with someone for a while but had moved out when that relationship had failed. She had shared a place with Robbie and another woman in their class. She'd dated from time to time, but there was never anyone she was that interested in. Maybe the cosmos was just holding someone off so Jordan would meet her when the time was right.

"I've already met a few of them. I'm still looking for her, but I don't think you get more than one good chance in this life to find the real one."

"Damn, I've already met fifteen or twenty of mine. It was just convincing *them* that they were the right ones." She'd dated one after another since she returned to the east coast, but no one seemed to be a perfect fit.

Jordan laughed. "Even Olivia?"

Olivia was a crush Robbie had had in college; they'd dated for a while, but Olivia was never as serious as Robbie wanted. Their parting wasn't all that friendly. "No, not the Big O. That was my mistake. We were too young."

"What about Chelsea. Think she's the one?"

"She might be. She's put up with me longer than anyone else." And Robbie was tempted by her every time she saw her. Chelsea was definitely one, maybe not *the* one, but certainly *a* one.

"Then treat her right and hang on to her."

"I'll try, but what about you? You never seemed to find the right one."

"They're few and far between, as the old saying goes."

"But if you don't look around, they can pass you right by."

"Robbie, I'm just not in the space to go out looking for someone."

"What the hell happened in California? The last thing I heard, you were doing really well and were about to get a recording deal. You were teaching at a great school, the woman you were dating was going to move in with you, and you were as happy as shit. Then, you show up here, and it's like your world has imploded."

"Yes. It was something like that."

"Your band was working for thousands a night. Now you accept a hundred-and-a-quarter a night for a two-night-a-week gig? What happened?"

"Life," Robbie thought she heard her say. "Sometimes it works, most times it doesn't." Jordan's lips slammed together tightly. She shook her head and looked away as if pleading with Robbie not to push. "The recording contract was withdrawn, unfortunately."

"That's no reason to give up. You might have gotten one with another company."

"No, I think that was it."

"If you want to talk about it, I'm here," Robbie urged her.

"I know." Jordan took a deep breath and didn't look back.

Robbie watched her silently staring off into the distance. What the hell had happened to her? Jordan should be on her way to stardom. "Do you want to go look at apartments again?" Anything to get her out of this mud-hole she was wallowing in.

"Is that a nice way to say I've overstayed my welcome?" Jordan turned back with a devilish grin on her face.

Robbie chuckled. "Of course not, you can stay for months. I'm just not used to seeing you hanging back doing nothing. I want to see you smile."

"I'll smile when I'm onstage."

"Then we'll get you more gigs." *Maybe that was the solution.* Robbie began to ponder.

"I'm still wondering if I shouldn't go to Vermont or Maine."

"Why? What's Vermont got that you can't find here?"

Jordan took a deep breath and seemed to think about it. "Space, for one thing. Clean air and colorful trees, nature and seclusion."

"Did you get your heart broken in California? Is that why you left there?"

"Something like that."

Robbie studied her as she looked down. Something like that? What was Jordan running from? Then Chelsea walked in, gave Robbie a soft kiss, and sat. "Hi, Jordan, how's it going? Have you found a job yet?"

"Just the two nights at the restaurant. Something will come up, even if I have to hawk fast-food." She seemed to force a silly smile and said, "Do you want fries with that? Thank you, drive through."

Robbie and Chelsea laughed. "I may have found you a place to live that you'd like," Chelsea said. "I've got friends over in Cambridge who have rented a house. They have a fourth bedroom that they want to let out. The cost is pretty good, and the utilities are split between them. That's if you don't mind sharing a house with a man. There are three people there already: Carole, Kathy, and Bob. We all met at MIT."

"Three? All separate or do two share a room?"

"They're all friends. There are no romantic attachments. You'd have your own room but have to share a bathroom and the kitchen."

"That sounds good."

"You'd have to bring your own furniture for your bedroom."

"I sold all my furniture when I left California, so I'd have to buy a bed. I'll have to buy that anyway, I guess. All of the beautiful furniture I loved had to be sold because I could only keep what would fit in my car. At least I got some of my money back, enough to buy some stuff."

"But you won't need to buy any cooking stuff. The rest of the house is fully furnished."

"Yes, that's a perk."

"I can take you over there tonight if you want. There's no pressure."

"I guess I should go look. I appreciate your keeping an eye out for me."

"It's no problem, hon."

Robbie hoped Jordan didn't feel like Chelsea was tired of having her at Robbie's place, but this was probably a good deal that she wouldn't find again.

❖

The house was on a side street, not hard to find and it was in good shape, although it was an older two-story house with a third-floor attic that was Bob's room. The bedroom they wanted to rent was on the back corner of the second floor. There were two windows, one overlooking the backyard and the other, the house next door. It was an average-size room with a small closet that had several shelves added. The upstairs bathroom was next to it and had a washer and dryer. On the first floor, there was a large kitchen, a dining room, a half bath, and a living room. The rest of the house was sufficient, though a lot of the fixtures hadn't been upgraded since the sixties. It was better than what Jordan had lived with in Texas but not quite as good as her California digs. It could be okay until she came across a job that paid more, and she could afford better.

Carole seemed to be the leader of the group, or at least the most friendly and talkative. Kathy and Bob were nice but didn't say much.

"Jordan just got here from California. She'll be singing with Robbie's band out at the Dam Restaurant in Newton," Chelsea told them. "You've got to hear her. I'm going out next Friday night. You should come with me."

"I can't," Bob said. "I've got a date."

"Bring her with you," Chelsea suggested.

"Him. And he's deciding where we're going."

"Then, you'll have to bring *him* out on Saturday or next week. Hopefully, I'll be singing with them for a while," Jordan said with a smile. She felt better knowing that the man in the house was gay. "Come out any Friday or Saturday."

"Did you come all the way out here to sing in her band?"

"No. I came to look around. It was just time to get out of California."

"I've heard everything is outrageously expensive there."

"It is. Is this room the average rent price for something like this?" She waited until they nodded. "In California, if you could find a place like this, it would cost five times that much."

Kathy snickered. "Then maybe we haven't charged you enough."

"This is just about what it costs around here. Actually, it's a little lower because Kathy knows the owner."

"Yes," added Kathy. "My father did business with his company."

"Well, it looks like a nice place. Do you think I'd fit?"

"Sure. You'll probably fit right in if you want." Bob said.

"When can I move in?"

"Anytime you're ready." Carole said, all business-like. "We just need the first month's rent and a month's security."

"Not a problem. I just have to go to an ATM."

"Then we'll expect you whenever you get here."

"I have to find some furniture, too. I sold everything I had when I left California."

"There are some second-hand stores around that have good prices. I can take you to one of them tomorrow night if you want," Kathy offered. "I'll take you to the one where I bought my dresser."

"That sounds great, Kathy. I really appreciate it." It felt nice to have someone care enough to help her.

They made plans for the next night, shook hands, and Jordan went back to Robbie's with the thought of a new home...or at least a semi-permanent place to stay.

"That fell in line very easily. It must have been the right thing to do, at least for now." Jordan said to Chelsea.

"Yes. I think you'll like those three. They can be a lot of fun."

Jordan wasn't looking for companions, just a place to sleep and hang her clothes. She felt they wouldn't push anything but would be around if she needed someone.

❖

Robbie stopped Morgan after the gig on Wednesday night. "Chelsea found Jordan a place to move into," Robbie said. "I guess Chel was still jealous that she was staying with me."

"But there was nothing going on between you and Jordan was there?" Not that she was worried, but Robbie seemed to want almost every woman who came into view.

"Nah, we tried that in college. It wasn't right."

Morgan chuckled. "I guess you can't have them all." In the five years that she'd known Robbie, there must have been at least twenty women Robbie had sworn were *the right one.* Most had lasted just three, four months at the most. Chelsea had actually lasted the longest.

"I rehearsed with Jordan on Monday," Morgan said. "She's got quite a repertoire. She even has some original things that are very nice." Morgan led them over to the bar and took a seat on one of the stools. The bartender looked at her in question, and when she nodded, he poured her a glass of scotch and opened a bottle of beer for Robbie.

"She was doing really well in California. The whole band was doing great. Jordan had a fantastic job, a steady lover, and they were approached by a recording company to cut a demo. Then she comes here. She won't talk about it, but something happened, and she ended up here with her car packed tight. It doesn't make sense."

Morgan nodded. "I looked her up on the internet."

"And you found something?" Robbie's eyes were wide. She twisted toward Morgan.

"I hated to go behind her back to look for these things, but I thought we should know, just in case something came up. Remember, nothing is private these days. Things get across the country instantly. There was a police report and quite a discussion on Facebook."

Robbie took a deep breath. "Police report? What did you find?"

"It seems there was a fire at a club, and someone was burned pretty badly. Jordan was arrested and charged with attempted murder."

"Attempted murder? I don't think she'd do anything like that."

"It was a BDSM club."

"A Leather club? I've been told that everyone who's into BDSM is there completely voluntarily. Everyone knows the risks, so it's usually the safest place you can be, or so I've been told."

Morgan looked at Robbie's eyes. How did she know that?

"I dated someone once who used to do that stuff," Robbie explained. "I went with her one time, but it wasn't for me."

Morgan pulled up the news listing on her phone and let Robbie read it. After Robbie finished, Morgan said, "The charges were eventually dropped, but I imagine the damage had already been done."

"She was teaching in a high school. If it was in all the media, I imagine there was a lot of backlash. No wonder she won't talk about anything. She lost her job and had to move," Robbie said.

Morgan agreed. "She should be touring. She's too good to be singing here two nights a week."

Robbie frowned. "Well, so are you. You should be doing a whole lot more, too."

"But not like her."

"Morgan, if you took your arrangements to a record company, they'd snatch them up and have you working full-time. Your piano playing is wonderful, and I can hear the horns and guitars in your playing. You could be the next Quincy Jones."

Morgan wasn't convinced. "I have a full-time job." Yes, back in the day, she'd have been thrilled to be compared to Quincy, but now that was years gone by.

"Is it in music?"

No, Morgan worked for a real estate agency. The only music she heard there were the phones dialing, and her sole keyboard was on the computer. She took a deep breath. "This wasn't about me. I was asking about Jordan. She's beautiful, has a great voice, and can connect with her audience. She should be out there recording and touring."

"That I agree with. How do we let her know we know that and that we still support her?"

"That's why I wanted to talk to you. You're her friend. You know her better."

Robbie thought about it for a moment. "You're right. I should be the one."

Morgan was relieved. That was the last thing she wanted to talk to Jordan about. She had dreaded bringing something like that up to her, especially since she had feelings for her. *It has to be someone close to her, who knows how she will react.*

❖

Thursday night, Jordan went into the restaurant during the next to last set just to get another feel for the space so she'd be comfortable performing there. After the final set, Morgan said something to Robbie, then turned and walked out of the restaurant. Robbie waved good night to Lori, then went up to Jordan.

"Are you going anywhere now or do you want to go catch a bite?" Robbie asked.

"That sounds good. I had a little something earlier, but could eat something now." Jordan wasn't sure what she wanted, something to eat or just something to drink. Her stomach was roiling.

"And I think we need to talk."

"What about?" Jordan studied her.

"I know about California," she said softly.

Jordan felt herself pale. Robbie no doubt saw the fear and horror lurking there. Jordan turned away. The air leaked out of her as her shoulders slumped.

"Come on, hon," Robbie said. "You can't keep this bottled up inside you. Please, talk to me. Tell me what really happened. I didn't want to believe what little I read."

"What did you read?" Jordan asked.

"That you were arrested for attempted murder when someone got burned at a Leather club."

"Does everyone know?"

Robbie shook her head. "Just me and Morgan. We're concerned about you."

"There's nothing anyone can do except keep quiet about it. You told Morgan?"

"No, she found it and told me."

"Damn." She didn't need this. Morgan was the last person she'd want to tell about her past. "I don't need to explain it."

"Really? Is that why you're not talking? So that no one will find out? Well, it's not working. It's on the internet for anybody to see."

Jordan turned to stare at her. "What do you want?"

"Tell us what really happened. We're on your side." She seemed to be waiting for a response, but Jordan said nothing. "Listen, Morgan wanted to get us some bigger gigs and invite some reviewers and agents to come listen, but if you can't expose yourself, then why bother. At least let us know what the score is so we won't be blindsided." She surveyed her. "You should be doing better than this. If you keep it locked inside, it will never get better."

Jordan nodded. This was not what she wanted to do, but at least she could tell someone. She had been holding it inside her for so long. Since Blaine, there hadn't been anyone to talk to. No one knew what she'd gone through, what she had in her heart. "All right, but just you and Morgan. And not here."

"Any preference?"

"Just somewhere very private where I can get a drink."

"What about going to Morgan's? She's got a full bar there. We can be comfortable."

Jordan nodded.

"All right, sounds good," She wrapped her arms around Jordan and hugged her tightly. "You'll feel better once you get it out. I know it. I'll call Morg." She flipped her phone on.

Jordan went outside to her car. How was this going to affect her friendship with any of the group? Would they still want her around? Would they think of her as the "kinky bitch" like they did in California? What about Morgan? Would there be any chance to start a relationship? It was better to get it out before she got too involved. Jordan sat back in her seat and watched the scenery pass as her thoughts raced in her mind.

CHAPTER FOUR

They settled in Morgan's living room, and each had a full glass in front of her. Jordan studied Morgan and Robbie. They were good women. Why shouldn't she trust them? She'd never told anyone the story, not since that first day. Maybe she'd feel better if she got it off her chest.

She pictured the scene in her mind. She still had difficulty thinking about it. It had all happened so fast and fallen totally apart within just a few hours.

"This happened early last month," she started. "Six weeks ago, to be exact. It had started on a Monday night, a slow night at a very private club, The Furies Loft, a popular BDSM Playhouse on the edge of the city. The weather was not too bad for March, but only nine or ten other people were there, not the hundred or hundred and fifty who came out on the weekends. In fact, that made it better. It kept it a little more anonymous for those of us whose jobs weren't that accepting of this lifestyle. Of course, it didn't really matter once you were inside because no one would say anything, but you always ran the risk that someone would see you going in or out. It was also a good night for me because I didn't have any morning classes on Tuesday."

Jordan remembered it clearly, perhaps too clearly.

"Lacey had moved in with me just a month or so earlier, right after New Years. We were not really lovers, just playmates. I loved her in a way, but we weren't romantic with each other. Close friends, most of all.

"We wanted to play that night because on Mondays or Tuesdays, most of the private rooms were available. There were only six on the second floor. One room had just a single bed in the middle of the floor and a table on one end. There was also a bunch of equipment hanging on one wall. We had negotiated at home, and Lacey wanted me to do some wax play with her, so we had brought a few candles and their candlesticks to set up around the room. I never worried because I was so used to doing wax play. Perhaps that is where I got tunnel vision and let down my safety training.

"I stripped Lacey's clothes and laid her down on the bed and ordered her onto her stomach because I wanted a bigger canvas than her belly.

"She said, 'Then we should have done this before Christmas. My belly was a little bigger then.'

"We laughed at that. Her belly used to be a lot bigger, but she'd been exercising, dieting, and losing weight. In fact, she'd lost twenty-five pounds since the beginning of the year and was really proud of it.

"So Lacey rolled over, and I handcuffed her arms to the posts at the top of the bed and tied her long blond hair over her shoulder to clear her back of any obstruction. I began to massage her back to give us a few minutes to get back into the mind space to begin.

"I finally took a hank of thick rope from my bag and started to tie her legs to the posts at the bottom. I used thick rope because it was stronger and wouldn't leave marks like a thinner rope would. This wasn't Japanese bondage, but I tied several intricate knots of my own to each leg. It took me a while to complete it. I was so happy with it 'cause it looked so good. We were going to have such a good time.

"I said, 'Now, I have you in my clutches, and you can't move to spoil my picture. I can do anything I want to you, can't I?' in a very severe voice.

"'Yes, Mistress,' she murmured. We always started like this to get into the mood.

"I slapped my hand hard on her rear. I was really happy with the large red hand print that sprang up on her butt cheek and asked, 'Am I going to have to spank you?'"

Jordan couldn't interpret the look in Morgan's eyes. Was she turned on or totally disgusted by what Jordan was telling them? She was having a reaction, but it was hard to tell just what that reaction was.

Jordan continued. "'If you must, Mistress,' Lacey answered.

"My hand came down on the other cheek just as hard. I was having fun now. I set up candlesticks with long colored candles across the table, at the foot of the bed in a rainbow array, and then lit them. I took one and let a large drop of molten wax fall on Lacey's butt. She was silent, but the muscles in her rear clenched.

"'What? You're not thanking me?' I said. 'I thought you wanted this.'

"'I'm sorry. Thank you, Mistress, Thank you, very much.' Lacey said.

"I walked around the side of the bed and let another drop fall on her shoulder. Drop after drop fell across the length of her torso. She thrashed for a few seconds if the pain got too bad. I was really enjoying it. I dripped speck after speck of wax down on her, switching the candles to change the color of the wax. Soon I had a beautiful, intricate design beginning. Almost like a mandala. The wax was getting thicker and thicker.

"'This will be so beautiful,' I told her. 'I'll have to take a picture of it so you can see.' Lacey hadn't said anything for a while. 'Are you still here?' I asked.

"It took her a moment to respond.

"She was in the zone. A place the mind goes to when pleasure or pain gets to an override limit. It is further than orgasm, trust beyond trust, euphoric pleasure. She wasn't fully there, and I was really enjoying moving back and forth creating my design on her."

Jordan smiled at the memory. It wasn't part of the horror she was about to tell.

"Maybe twenty minutes later, one of the candles fell from the candlestick and landed on the bed. The mattress went up like a pile of dried hay.

"We both screamed, 'Oh my God. Fire. Fire. Help. Fire!'

"I ran out into the hall, calling for help. I was frantic and screaming as loud as I could. I ran back into the room, unlocked first one handcuff, then the other. My hands were shaking so badly, I almost dropped the key a couple times.

"Lacey was fully awake now, screaming, 'Help me, Jordan.' The flames were lapping at her feet. I reached for the knife in my jacket to cut the ropes. The smoke was beginning to choke us both. It was blinding me. I took off my jacket and tried to smother the flames.

"Lacey's screams of fear turned to screams of pain and terror.

"Harry Lynch, the manager of the club, raced into the room, his sub, Jack, right behind him. He took the knife from my hands and slashed the ropes with more force than I could ever manage. Lacey instantly curled into a ball.

"Other members of the club also ran in and attacked the flames to smother them with a blanket. It stopped the flames from spreading but didn't put them entirely out. There were sparks still glowing, ready to jump into flame at any moment.

"Lacey continued to scream and cried as her feet glowed where they had been burned. I held her in my arms. We were both still coughing and gasping from the smoke.

"I said, 'I'm so sorry, baby, we'll get you fixed up in just a moment. It will be all right. It will be all right. Hold on, baby.'

"Smoke was thick in the building. Everyone was coughing, choking. We could barely breathe. Harry pushed me out of the way, lifted Lacey, and carried her out of the room. I was right behind them. Lacey was crying, coughing, and screaming from the pain. Harry carried her outside and set her gently on the grass in front of the building. The skin on the outside of her left foot was singed, red, white, and black. I was horrified when I saw her leg.

"Oh my God, oh my God, was all I could think.

"I held her in my arms as I placed small kisses all over her forehead. Harry stripped his shirt off and placed it over Lacey's shoulders to cover her. It hadn't even dawned on me that she was naked. I tried to pull the shirt down and straighten it to hide her.

"Soon, we heard a siren, and a fire truck screeched to a halt right in front of the building. Some of the Loft members pointed the firefighters to the room where the fire had started. There continued to be a lot of smoke inside. Two medics came over and put oxygen masks on us, then started examining Lacey's legs. She wouldn't let go of my hand. I watched the medics treat her. She was crying and screaming.

"'It shouldn't have happened,' I kept saying over and over to Harry, who stayed beside us.

"'She's going to be all right,' he said again and again, trying to soothe me and probably himself.

"The fire chief came over and wanted to know how it happened. I explained about the candle as the medics started an IV and put special wraps around her legs. Harry explained everything else, so I kept my eyes on Lacey. One of the medics was on his phone. The others lifted Lacey onto a gurney. Every movement caused her to cry out. They strapped her onto the stretcher and started to roll her away and said they were taking her to the Grossman Burn Center in West Hills.

"She held her hand out and screamed for me, and I said I had to go with her. Harry's boy said he'd bring my car. I tossed him the keys, then hurried behind the gurney and got into the ambulance, holding Lacey's hand. She wasn't fully awake but tears were still running down her face. I was afraid she was going into shock. The ambulance sped away."

Jordan took a deep breath and a long quaff of her drink.

"Oh, honey, that was a terrible happening," Robbie said.

Jordan looked up with a scowl. "And the worst, for me, hadn't even started. At Grossman, Lacey was taken into a treatment room. I went into another room to have the smoke and soot washed from my face and hands. A nurse made sure I hadn't been burned and assisted with more oxygen.

"Harry brought my stuff and sat with me and a couple other Furies Loft members and explained everything that had happened to a police officer. I admitted to tying Lacey up and told him about the candle falling. The others contributed their memories. We were both well-known at the club, and everyone swore how safety-minded we were. Harry had even brought a copy of the rules and regulations of the club that everyone had to sign before they were allowed inside.

"One person reported that the scene room was burned but not gutted, mostly smoke damage. The old mattress was mostly in ashes, as was my jacket, and the other blankets they'd used to smother the flames. Aside from the damage the firefighters had to do to make sure there were no live sparks in the ceiling or walls, not too much had been destroyed. Smoke damage was the major harm to the building. They would be able to reopen in a week or so, once everything was aired-out, washed, and repainted. Everyone seemed to agree that it was a tragic accident."

Jordan shook her head and rubbed her forehead. This was the hardest part. She had felt so hopeful at the time, but then it happened. Her breath caught in her throat as she started to tell them what had followed.

"I called Lacey's parents, and they came to Grossman, but Lacey was still being treated in another room. She had been sedated so she wouldn't feel the pain. The wax design had been removed from her back.

"A police officer and I sat with Mr. and Mrs. Sumner for a while and explained, as best we could, what had happened. Mrs. Sumner's angry eyes bore into me the entire time. She looked like she wanted to say something but was holding it back. It was apparent that Lacey had never told her parents about her lifestyle.

"Lacey was finally transferred from the treatment room to a hospital room on the burn unit. She was unconscious, her legs wrapped in large white bandages and suspended from sling supports so they didn't rest on anything. Her left leg and most of her foot had second-degree burns to just above her knee. Her foot had a third-degree burn near her little toe. They were keeping an eye on her little toe, which was the worst. Her right leg had first-degree burns to her calf. She'd been treated for smoke inhalation.

"Mr. Sumner, Lacey's father, sternly told me, 'I think you can leave now.'

"'I feel responsible for this,' I said. 'I want to know she'll be all right.'

"'She's getting the best treatment they have here,' he said. 'There's nothing more you can do.'

"Their expressions told me I was neither welcome nor wanted there. I finally drove home. I had hoped that when Lacey woke up, she'd tell her parents her side of it, and they'd see I wasn't at fault, that it was an accident."

Jordan sat back and drank some more of her drink. She almost wanted to just down the whole thing and get this over with in a drunken stupor. But now she had to tell them about the terrible next day.

Chapter Five

Good heavens, Jordan," Robbie exclaimed. "What a terrible, terrible night that was."

"And that was just the beginning," Jordan said. "The worst was yet to come."

"Are you sure you want to tell us the rest?" Morgan asked.

"Might as well. You've heard this much." She took another sip. Her glass was almost empty.

"Before you continue, do you want me to freshen that for you?" Morgan asked.

"No. I'll never be able to drive home."

"You can always stay here. I have a guest room," Morgan told her.

"No. I have the feeling I may cry all night. I should be alone." She didn't feel that Morgan was condemning her for any of this, but she still needed to be alone in her own space.

"But you don't have to be."

"Thanks, but it's still so raw." Jordan paused but decided to go on. "When I got home, I threw all my clothes into the washing machine with lots of baking soda. Then I took a long shower and got into a T-shirt and pajama pants. I had to lie on the couch. The bed, without Lacey in it, seemed much too empty.

"At four a.m., just a few hours later, I was awoken by two police officers who told me they had a warrant for my arrest. I thought they had to be kidding, but they said it was for attempted murder of Lacey.

Attempted murder? I couldn't believe it. My insides were shaking wildly. And my nightmare was just beginning.

"I was handcuffed, my hands behind my back. They asked for my identification, and I nodded toward my purse. They took it, and I was brought downtown, still in my pajama pants and T-shirt. I didn't even have shoes, a bra, or even panties on. They asked if I wanted to call someone but, my family was in Texas. Who could help me there? So I called Blaine Jones, my best friend and the guitarist in the band I sang with. She said she'd call Max Denton. Max was the manager of the band. They would find a lawyer for me. Blaine asked what else I needed. I told her how I was dressed. She came to the police station and got my keys, then went to my place with a police escort to get some decent clothes.

"I sat in a holding cell for six and a half hours, worrying and crying. What would people say about me? Who would be on my side? How did I get out of this? What happens next? The questions swirled around in my head faster than I could process them. And my stomach ached and churned at the thought of being charged for attempted murder of someone I would never dream of harming.

"Max finally got there with a lawyer, John Stanfield. I answered some questions for them. I explained what happened, that it was an accident, and that I would never harm anyone, especially Lacey. 'She's been collared to me for over a year,' I said. 'We live together, for God's sake.' I wanted to pace. I wanted to slap something, I was so upset. I felt like a caged animal, but I sat there, nervously tapping my foot on the floor.

"My lawyer said it didn't sound like it was intentional and at the very most, they could only charge me with reckless conduct or endangerment. He said the judge was going to hear my bonding at eleven-thirty that morning.

"The only thing I felt I was guilty of was stupidly not securing the candle back in the candlestick better. I panicked and told my lawyer, oh my God, the media. Were there photographers and reporters hanging around the ambulance? I taught at a school. My principal would *have* to fire me.

"He tried to ease my fears by telling me to go to the school in person and talk to the principal before it came out in the media.

"An hour later, I was arraigned. The charge of attempted murder was dropped and replaced by mayhem. I was released on my personal recognizance. A second hearing was scheduled for a week from then.

"My lawyer did the best he could to comfort me after the hearing. He asked if there was anything I needed before I went to talk to my boss. At that moment, all I wanted was a shower, but it would have taken too long to drive all the way out to my apartment and back again.

"Max also tried to console me, but I knew this would have an effect on the band. I told him he would probably end up firing me to keep this from tarnishing the band. But Max being Max wouldn't talk about it then and just told me to handle the school and we would talk about the band later.

"I left the jail, and it seemed like a lifetime drive but took only about fifteen minutes before I walked into the administration office of the school. This was a private school which had grades six through twelve. I was in charge of all the vocal classes and the choruses. There was another teacher who taught band and orchestra. Usually, Principal Wright had a very busy schedule and could only be seen by appointment, but I guess when the secretary saw how red my eyes were and the condition of my clothes, she got me in right away.

"I remember just blurting out, 'I need to warn you before you read it in the news or a parent calls in, Mrs. Wright. I was arrested this morning, and I've just come from the courthouse.'

"Her expression was surprised but not angry, and her only reply was, 'Heaven, no. What happened?' I began to explain how Lacey Sumner was my roommate, and she and I had been involved in the BDSM and Leather community for several years, but kept it quiet. As far as I knew, no one knew about it except the members of Furies Loft, who would never tell. I also explained what happened and Lacey's parents' reaction to it.

"I watched her reaction as she chewed on her lip. Ethyl Wright had been a mentor and a friend, and she was studying me at that moment without saying a word. I couldn't stand the tension, so

I broke the silence and told her that if she would give me a piece of school stationary, I would write my resignation and sign it. She could then write whatever she chose later. She didn't even address my resignation at that time. She was more concerned with my emotional condition and asked how I mustered the strength to walk in and confront her with this horrible news. She asked where Lacey was and if she understood what was happening. I told her that Lacey was at the burn center, and she was sedated and probably didn't know much about what was going on.

"I was so set back at what she said next, though. She said she knew nothing about BDSM firsthand but had read about it. She said that educators are encouraged to know about these things should they ever come up with the students, but she never thought it would come up with one of her faculty, yet she couldn't see why not. She asked if it was consensual, and I replied yes. I also replied, my eyes down, tears flowing, 'And totally accidental and with witnesses.'

"In a regretful tone of voice, she said the words I didn't want to hear: 'I hate to do this, but I fear I must accept your resignation.' But then she added, 'Hopefully, it will blow over, and I can rehire you.' It was then I could look her in the eyes.

"We both sat there for a few moments as she pushed a box of Kleenex toward me and let me get my composure. Then she began again, 'I really don't want to lose you,' she said. 'You've brought such joy to this school and to the students' lives. Unfortunately, I think the parents are going to believe otherwise.'

I replied, 'Sure. No one wants their kid to be taught by a known pervert.' And do you know what she said?"

Robbie and Morgan looked at each other and then shook their heads.

"She said, 'I'm sure some of the parents aren't as innocent as all that, but in relation to their youngsters, it is something for them to complain about. If I were in your shoes, I'd probably go home and down a full bottle of gin.' That made me grin a small bit. 'I'm so sorry this is happening to you,' she said. 'You've been such a great part of this faculty. I'm not sure we'll ever get anyone who can do what you did with the kids, I mean, look at the trophies your choirs have won.'"

Jordan downed the rest of her drink. "I thought coming face-to-face with my boss was the hardest part of this nightmare until the knock came on the door of her office. It was her secretary. The phone calls had started to flood her desk. It was parents who had read the paper, demanding I be fired. I was completely horrified that Mrs. Wright would have to face an angry mob of parents over what should have been my private sexual choices. Now it was all in the open for the world to see. I would be forever marked. But Mrs. Wright stayed calm and told the secretary she was handling it.

"After the secretary left, I told Mrs. Wright that all of my lesson plans and ideas for the rest of the year were in my office and could help the next person she hired. I gave her my keys, looked around the office I had come to love. Mrs. Wright clutched my hands for a moment before I turned and walked out.

"Before I could get to my car, some high school boys came by and said, 'Kinky, Ms. Phelps. Too bad it backfired! Back*fired*. Get it?' They laughed and laughed at me.

"An item appeared in that night's news, in print, on the internet and on TV. It is sealed into my memory; I'll never forget it." She closed her eyes and recalled:

High School Chorus director arrested after BDSM debacle.

Monroe Middle and High School music teacher, Jordan Phelps, was arrested early Tuesday morning after a fire broke out at the Furies Loft Monday night. The fire seriously burned Ms. Lacey Sumner, who had been chained to a bed being used in a BDSM scene. The bed had caught on fire from a fallen candle. Police and medics responded to the fire alarm, and Ms. Sumner was rushed to the Grossman Burn Center in West Hills for treatment, where she was diagnosed with second and third-degree burns on her legs and foot. Ms. Jordan Phelps was identified as the person allegedly responsible for chaining Ms. Sumner and, lighting the candle. She was taken into custody, at her home this morning. She was seen by Judge William Sanchez, who charged her with mayhem, and she was released on her own recognizance. Furies Loft is a BDSM club in the Angledale district of the city.

Jordan summed up the article, then said, "That night, I was inundated with calls and texts, some supportive but most not. A group of people had gathered outside my apartment building with signs, chanting, 'This is the home of the kinky bitch.' I had to call the police to get them to leave."

"Good God, Jordan," Robbie said. "No wonder you left there."

"That wasn't all. I'd stopped at the hospital on the way home from the school, but Mrs. Sumner had screamed and made quite a scene when she saw me there. I thought it best to stay away until I was sure Lacey's mother wasn't there. There was no way for me to see Lacey face-to-face with her mother present. So I went home, and Blaine came over to commiserate with me.

"The next day, Max came by with the news that the recording company had rescinded our contract because of all the negative publicity. They said they'd review the band in six months as long as I wasn't a part of it."

"Bastards," Morgan grumbled.

"Yes, that was a big disappointment for everyone. So the next week, I met with the judge. My lawyer had gotten a recorded deposition from Lacey saying it wasn't my fault and ranting about all the things that had been done to me, so the charges were dropped."

"Oh, Jordan." Robbie had tears in her eyes. "Did you ever get to see Lacey again?"

"I finally got to see her when her mother wasn't there. We agreed that I had to get out of the area. It felt like I had the kiss of death or was the black widow."

"I thought that, by now, everyone had read that *Fifty Shades* book and wouldn't think twice about a little kink," Morgan said.

Jordan felt good hearing Morgan's thoughts about the situation. "Most wouldn't care if it was adults in my class, but I was teaching children. Early high school is such an impressionable age. Think what a real pervert could do with kids that age," Jordan said bitterly.

"It still shits," Morgan said.

"Oh, and I went back to Furies Loft to thank Harry and Jack. They'd gotten all the subs to paint and wash the place and redo the upstairs. One of the guys had wanted to place a sign on that room we'd

been in and name it 'Mistress Jordan's Memorial Bonfire Room.'"
Morgan and Robbie chuckled with her. "I sold or packed everything.
I left what wouldn't fit in my car in Blaine's garage and drove across
country, hoping to find a place that felt safe. I had to get off the west
coast. I stopped to see Olivia in St. Louis. She's doing really well."
She glanced at Robbie, but there was no reaction. "Then, I went up
through Urbana and checked with a couple people there. I spent two
days in Indianapolis. Nothing there seemed right, either. Now, I'm
here to see you, Robbie." Jordan felt relieved at finally finishing her
story. "And that's the end. I'd heard that Vermont was beautiful and
thought I might settle down there. If there's nothing around here, I'll
go down the east coast and see what's in Virginia or the Carolinas. I'll
check out Nashville, although I'm not that good with country music.
I can still rely on my Texas twang."

"I'm glad you didn't get there," Robbie said.

Morgan nodded. "I agree."

Jordan eyed both of them apprehensively. "So now that you
know my story, still want me around?" Now that she'd bared her
whole life to them, it seemed on the edge.

"Of course," Morgan said. "It sounds like you were just the
victim of a mother who didn't want her own reputation tarnished. It
doesn't sound like it had anything to do with Lacey."

"I don't think so, either. I think her mother was more concerned
with what her friends were going to say about the way she'd brought
up her daughter than about Lacey's injuries," Robbie said.

"So that's it," Jordan said.

"That was *that* story. We're still living in *this* next one, and I
think it's going to be a lot better," Morgan said.

"It couldn't be worse."

"Don't even think that. Somehow things can always get worse."

Robbie got up and pulled Jordan to her feet to give her a tight
hug and a little kiss. Morgan did, too, but the kiss lasted a little longer.
They looked into each other's eyes for a moment. Then Morgan took
a step back, took a deep breath, and looked away, almost seeming
embarrassed. Why had she let the kiss last that long? Was she
interested? No, Jordan wouldn't trust that.

Morgan sat down as if nothing had happened. "By the way," she started, "I was going to update our website last night and didn't know if I should add you."

Jordan took a very deep breath as she sat back down, considering it.

"Do you want me to keep you off it? It's up to you."

Jordan was undecided. "I'll have to think about it."

"Why don't I keep you off for now? I can update it anytime. We can rethink it later. This does go across the net, so anyone looking for you can see where you are."

"Yes, please keep me off it for a while. Let me see what's happening back home. Home..." She stopped herself. *It's not home, anymore, Phelps. Stop that.* "Back in California," she corrected. "I keep in touch with Blaine, and she lets me know if anything comes up. Things seem to have died down now that I'm not there, but you never know who'll remember something."

"All right, you're not on the website, for now."

Jordan was a little disturbed by her reaction to Morgan's kiss. She didn't have space in her life for that now. *Don't get into that now. It's neither the time nor place for a new romance. You don't want to fall into that trap again.*

Chapter Six

The next day, Jordan made her debut at the restaurant. This was new to her. She'd sang in concert with choirs and rock bands, but up close and personal with diners who might or might not be listening to her was new. She felt secure with Morgan and Robbie behind her, but she'd have to fight for the whole room's attention. She took a deep breath and waited for Morgan to introduce her.

"Ladies and gentlemen," Morgan announced, "this woman was received so well last Saturday after just one song, we've arranged for her to come back every Friday and Saturday to entertain you. Starting tonight, please welcome Jordan Phelps."

"Starting Here, Starting Now" was the first thing she sang. It was an older song, a Streisand song, but she blew it out of the water. The audience seemed to love it. Jordan made her way around the room, going in all directions. She sang three songs in a row, then took a break while Morgan played the next.

They finished that set, took a break, and started the next. Jordan did a good "up" number, then a love song. She loved that the audience ate up everything she sang.

"This next song is an audience participation song," Jordan announced before her big number. "So dig out your wallets and let's get this one on the road."

Robbie started with a big roll, then a crash. Morgan started the intro.

"You asked for my heart, but you wanted my soul," Jordan sang. "Agree to my offer and you can have it all. I want money."

The band responded with, "Give her money, lots of money."

"Give me money."

"Yes, just money, money, money," the band sang.

"A penny or a dime or a dollar is good, but a twenty will make me give you more than I should."

There was a musical interlude. The rest of the band was having a good time with this. Jordan had started the song well, and the band was floating on the wave of the audience's approval.

"They say you can never ever capture a heart," Jordan sang. "That you'll need something diff'rent to get that part. You'll need money."

The band responded, "Give her money lots of money."

"Give me money."

"Yes, just money, money, money."

"A penny or a dime or a dollar is good, but a twenty will make me give you more than I should."

The band took over while Jordan strutted from table to table with her hand outstretched. Little by little, they handed her bills. She put the first in her pocket. The next was from an older man, so she kissed the bill and put it in her bra, then she kissed her hand and put it on his bald head and winked at him. The audience loved that as the others at that table kidded the man and clapped him on the back. The audience was really getting into it. When a woman gave her a bill, Jordan bent down and kissed her on the cheek.

"Well, they say I'm no angel and times are hard, so please plant some greenbacks in my backyard." She slapped her butt as the audience roared. "I want money."

The band responded, "Give her money lots of money."

"Give me money."

"Yes, just money, money, money."

"A penny or a dime or a dollar is good, but a twenty will make me give you more than I should."

She stuffed the next handful into her cleavage, which caused whoops and cheers, and even more bills waved in the air. Some she shoved into her back pocket. By the end of the song, Jordan's pockets and bra were overflowing with green.

The audience cheered as the song ended. Jordan ran backstage to empty her pockets while the band played another song, then came back and did a love song. After the evening was over and the restaurant was clearing out, Jordan walked up to Morgan.

"Well, what did you get?" Morgan asked.

Looking at the currency she'd taken on the desk, Jordan answered, "Fifty-three ones, a five, and two twenties." *Yes, this was a good choice that will add a few dollars for my living expenses.*

"That's more than some strippers get," Robbie said.

"How do you know?"

Robbie just winked.

"Fantastic. I told you it would work," Morgan said.

The owner, Paul, walked up. "Nice show. Does that mean I don't have to pay you tonight?"

"Of course not, those were just tips, Paul," Morgan told him.

"Damn right. I had to work for that," Jordan crowed.

"It was a good show," he said to Jordan. "Glad you're on board."

Jordan smiled. "Thanks."

It felt like a good beginning. Yes, Jordan was glad she'd stopped here.

CHAPTER SEVEN

Chelsea studied Robbie's face. "That really happened to her?" Chelsea gasped, looking into Robbie's eyes. They'd sat in bed and talked for almost an hour. Robbie had just told her all about Jordan's predicament.

"I know. How can that happen? I mean, she had to resign from her teaching job," Robbie groused.

"And you said the kids were all making fun of her?"

"Yes. They thought it was really something that their teacher was a Leather Domme. They called her the Kinky Bitch." Robbie shook her head in amazement. Some kids were so rude. How did someone put up with that?

"You'd think that wouldn't be a big deal these days."

"I imagine a lot of the parents envied her at first, then realized what a role model she was presenting to their kids, and they couldn't have that, the hypocrites."

"Maybe it's a California thing. Would that happen here in Massachusetts?"

Robbie stopped in thought. "I can't picture it, but you never know. Remember this state was founded by Puritans, and this is where the Salem Witch trials happened."

"Right, maybe we're not that progressive. I'm glad you're not involved in something like that."

"And if I were?" Robbie raised her eyebrows.

"I'm glad you're not." Chelsea seemed final on that.

"No, honey, I'm not." She leaned in and kissed Chelsea on the cheek.

"You haven't wanted to be, have you?"

"Well, I've thought about it from time to time, but I haven't wanted to really try. I can't imagine myself hurting anyone. And I would definitely not want it done to me."

"What have you imagined doing to someone?" Chelsea leaned a little closer.

"Well, there are a few girls I would have loved to spank but not out of love."

"And?"

"Well, we could get a little closer..." She wrapped her arm around Chelsea and pulled her closer.

Chelsea turned and brought her hand to Robbie's neck. "How much closer?"

Robbie took a deep breath. "How close do you think we are already?"

Chelsea stopped. "What do you mean?"

"How far do you see us going with this?" Robbie wanted to know what Chelsea was thinking. If Chelsea wanted to get closer, then perhaps they could have a good relationship and not just a Sunday, every week one. Maybe they could have a real togetherness. She wanted to invest a lot more in this relationship, but she hadn't always made the best decisions about things like that.

"How far do you see?" Chelsea asked in return.

"No fair. I asked first."

"Okay. Well, I really like you and I like being with you. We've been together over half a year, and we seem compatible."

"Do you want to take this further?"

Chelsea looked into her eyes, "Yes, I would."

Robbie returned the look into Chelsea's eyes. "Me, too." She pulled Chelsea in and kissed her deeply on the lips.

"Do you love me?" Robbie asked.

"I could, but I'm stopping myself so I don't get hurt if you break up with me."

"Do you want me to break up with you?"

"Robbie! Of course not. Why are you asking all these questions? Where's your head?"

Robbie sat there with her lips clenched. She'd been considering this for a couple weeks but was scared to bring it up. *Damn, I should just go for it.* "Do you want to move in with me?" There it was. She'd asked. She'd finally put herself out there.

Chelsea sat back. "Are you serious?"

Now Robbie was worried. Had she blown it? Should she not have asked yet? "Well, if you don't want to, you don't have to. I was just suggesting. You can forget I said it, if you'd rather."

"Robbie, no, I will not forget you said it." She clasped Robbie's face. "I just need to know if you're really serious."

"Well, I *was*...unless you don't want me to be."

"You drive me crazy. Just come out and ask."

"I thought I just did."

"Be serious about it."

"Uh, okay. Will you move in with me?"

"I've been waiting weeks for you to ask something like that."

Robbie raised her eyes in shock. "Really?"

"Oh, Roberta Nelson, you shouldn't need to ask. I've wanted us to be closer for so long. I was just waiting for you. I know you were a player, and I didn't have hope that you'd ever settle down."

"A player? I'm not a player." Okay, so she dated a lot but not just to play around. She'd been trying to find the right woman.

"But you dated so many women before we met."

"Yes, and none of them were right. I wasn't just going around from one to the next. I was looking for the right one. I guess I was looking for you."

Chelsea pulled her in and kissed her hard. "Now you've found me."

"So do you want to move in with me?"

"Will I have to sleep on the couch like Jordan did?"

"Absolutely not."

"Where will I sleep, then?"

"Right here, in my arms, in this bed."

"In that case, yes. Yes, I'd love to move in with you."

Robbie tackled her and lay her flat on the bed. "Shall we seal the deal?" She willed her eyes to bore into Chelsea's.

"Absolutely."

CHAPTER EIGHT

The band continued to play each week, and a lot of people seemed to look forward to Fridays and Saturdays when Jordan was singing. That seemed to make Jordan's ego feel pretty good. There turned out to be a lot of return followers. Jordan's roommates, Carole, Kathy, and Bob would come out every now and then.

Jordan and Morgan planned each show and rotated it around so that each week was different. This felt right. Morgan was happy Jordan hadn't gone to Vermont. In fact, she was really pleased with the way things were going. Seeing Jordan three times a week felt good but was slightly disturbing in that she was enjoying it. She'd sworn to herself that she'd never get involved again, so she'd have to check her feelings so she didn't get sucked in. No, she couldn't do that again. Even Paul seemed happy because they had a full house every weekend.

One Saturday, Robbie rushed in at seven fifty-seven for the eight o'clock show. "Sorry I was almost late. I was helping Chelsea move."

"Okay," said Morgan. "Where's she moving to?"

Robbie hesitated as though she was embarrassed. "In with me."

"What? Did I hear you right?"

"I don't know. What do you think you heard?"

"Is Chelsea moving in with you?"

Robbie nodded.

"You're sure about this one?"

"Yes, I am."

"Well, congratulations. Have you told anyone?"

"Lori knows I was thinking about it."

Morgan motioned over to Lori. "Has the sun exploded? Chelsea moved into Robbie's place."

"What?" Jordan exclaimed from the other side of the piano. "Congratulations!"

"Yup," said Lori as she played a riff on her bass. "Another one bites the dust."

"Well, Morgan. That leaves you."

Yes, that leaves me. And it always will. If they want to settle down, let them. I tried it once, and it didn't work. I definitely don't want to try it again. Morgan shook her head. "Nope, did that, didn't work."

"You just had the wrong one."

Yes, she definitely was the wrong one, but I'm not going to try it again. It hurt too much the first time.

Jordan's eyebrows rose as if she was curious.

Morgan tipped her head to brush that off and hit the first song. The evening was underway.

The next day, Robbie, Chelsea, Morgan, Jordan, Lori and Mel met for lunch to celebrate Robbie and Chelsea moving in together. Lori and Mel were enthusiastic about it. Morgan seemed hopeful, but Jordan was reserved. She was happy for Robbie and Chelsea but still didn't know what to do about Morgan. There was clearly something in Morgan's background that had hurt her badly. Why hadn't she let go of it?

Jordan had been bewildered when Morgan had kissed her that night. She'd confessed to herself that it had confused her. Something had passed between them. She had felt it, and she knew Morgan did too, but then Morgan acted like nothing was there. There hadn't been a word about it since and no acknowledgment of it any other time. What should she do?

Maybe I should just forget it, I swore I wouldn't get involved again, and it sure sounds like Morgan doesn't want to either. Why even consider what might happen when I'm questioning getting involved. I need to curtail my emotions about Morgan. Hell, she's beautiful and sexy, and that kiss wasn't just a kiss of sympathy but a kiss of compassion. I felt it. My body felt it. But I can't risk this gig, I need the money.

The two nights at the restaurant each week would cover the gas to get back and forth to the restaurant, Jordan's car insurance, and half the rent at the house, but it left her hungry and without clean clothes. Her savings were dwindling quickly with the bed and dresser she'd had to buy. Sheets, blankets and pillows had added up, too, and this was frosty New England, not sunny California. Fall had arrived, and she realized she didn't have the right clothes for a Boston winter. She checked around her neighborhood, but all the jobs, both full and part-time, were filled. This was Boston and Cambridge, the home of hundreds of schools and colleges, so all the minimum-wage jobs were taken. Carole, Kathy, and Bob said they'd look, but they didn't know of any openings, either.

She finally asked Paul if he could use another employee on the nights she wasn't singing. He thought it over. "I'm getting too old to do this every night, and my daughter wants to do it twice a week at most, so would you like to be a hostess? You won't get tips, but the pay is steady, and it's not as backbreaking. I'll pay you hourly and for an eight-hour shift, from four till we close, and you'll get the same as the nights you're singing. The hosting usually stops well before midnight. I'd need you Tuesday through Thursday. We're closed on Monday, and we close early on Sunday so that's not hard for me to handle."

Jordan didn't have to give it a lot of thought. "I'll do it," she said. It was definitely not the teaching job she had, but she wouldn't have to correct papers, prepare lessons, and advise students, so in the long run, although the pay wasn't great, it gave her a lot more time for herself.

She started the next week, and within just a little while, began to recognize the regulars. Those who had heard her sing were enthused that she was the hostess, too. There was a poster in the entrance that advertised, "Friday and Saturday nights, Stone Cold Perception includes singer Jordan Phelps!" Paul had taken a snapshot of her singing and included that in the advertisement, too.

The photo was cute. Not as good as the professional ones she'd had done in California, but at least she was smiling. She looked happy to be singing for people. She was comfortable with this band, always comfortable performing, and she trusted Morgan to complement her sound.

Her roommates also came in every other week to hear her sing. It was going well. The band had decided to do the money song only on Saturdays, and Jordan made almost a hundred dollars every time. With her pay there, she was able to replace some of the savings she had spent on furniture and still had money for a winter jacket and heavier boots. She'd have to save for snow tires now, too.

Every other week, she'd call or get a call from Blaine. The California band had found a new singer, but according to Blaine, she wasn't as good as Jordan. Some in the band liked her, but she was still settling in. Their recording contract hadn't been renewed.

Jordan rehearsed new music with Morgan every Sunday, the one day they both had free.

Jordan sat in Morgan's living room now. They'd been rehearsing for the past two hours. She was comfortable working with Morgan like this. She had the urge to reach out and hug Morgan, to kiss her, to be kissed and hugged by her. *Why can't I stop drawing her into my thoughts?*

"Your voice is totally incredible," Morgan said. "You surprise me every single week."

"Not as incredible as your piano playing. Why did you never do it professionally?"

"I did at first, but it didn't work out. I mean, look what we're making at the club."

"Yes. But there are much more lucrative places to play."

"Then I got the job at the real estate office, and real money started coming in. I could never have afforded this house if I was playing piano somewhere. I mean, I was making fairly good money in New York, but the things I had to sacrifice for it weren't worth it in the long run. Now, with my real estate job, I can save enough to afford things like this house."

"You own this place?" Jordan looked around the room, surprised, and remembered the quaint apartment she'd had in California.

"Well, I have six more years on the mortgage, but after that, it's mine."

"Even with my teaching job, I could never have bought a house."

Morgan nodded. "I imagine nothing in California is affordable. It's being in the right place at the right time. I picked this piano up at an antique shop. It had been there for quite a while, and no one ever looked at it. It was taking up space, so the owner was happy to accept a grand just to get rid of it."

"A grand piano for a thousand dollars?"

"Right place, right time. Yes, it needed a tuning and a little repair, but it was well worth it."

"That was my mistake in California: wrong place, wrong time."

"It'll change, hon. Something will happen." She pulled the cork out of the bottle she just brought up and poured two glasses of rosé.

"But with your playing, you could have been making a lot more money than what we get at that restaurant.'

"The things you have to relinquish for it makes the money really not worth it."

"You really think so?" Jordan asked.

"Well, that's what I found. It may be different for some, but the things I gave up to be a success really weren't worth the hassle."

"I'm sorry you had that experience." Jordan studied Morgan's eyes, her hands, her smile. She was unlike anyone Jordan had ever seen. *How could anyone let her slip by?*

"Who knows? Maybe your experience will be different. I think we've both been through the worst. Maybe next time will be better."

"Something already has been better, I think," Jordan mumbled. "I met you."

Morgan took a sip of wine. "Yes, but we don't match. I don't do BDSM."

"BDSM isn't about sex or love. It's a power exchange. Giving it up or taking it all."

Morgan shifted in her seat. "And that's not sexy?"

"It depends. Sexy is what you do with it. Lacey loved pain. It turned her on. Actually, the body reacts exactly the same way to pain as it does to pleasure. It's the same hormone that's released. If I provided the pain, then she was ready for sex. She couldn't get off without the foreplay."

"That's not all it is."

"Of course not, but it takes two people to provide the lift. Yes, I loved being in charge and I enjoyed being sadistic but not all the time and not with everyone. It's no fun being sadistic to someone who doesn't enjoy being masochistic in return."

"You've always been the aggressor?"

"Not at the beginning. I was very submissive to my first two Mistresses. The first one trained me in all the techniques. It was hot and heavy for quite a while. Unfortunately, it didn't last. We weren't *in* love."

"So you can't do BDSM without love?"

"Oh, of course you can but not in the long run. Without love, almost any sexual act is just a sexual *act*. With BDSM, I can do it for a while in a new relationship. But you know how it goes when the fire dies down, and you don't have any fuel there to stoke it back up. It just sits there in ashes. Any manual or emotional manipulation can be done without love, but why bother?" Jordan looked into Morgan's wide eyes, so inquisitive, so longing to find out what she was thinking, what she was feeling. "I think Lacey and I would have burned out in a little while. Lacey and I weren't *in* love. We cared about each other, and we had a dynamite friendship and play ethic, but in the long run, it wasn't romantic love. I can't really explain it. I couldn't get off just kissing her. I can sometimes enjoy BDSM without some kind of love, but I also totally enjoy sex without BDSM. It's a strange dichotomy. It's the power exchange that turns me on."

"Is everyone like that?"

"I doubt it. Some make BDSM equal to love. Others are just players, never having the impetus to settle down, never falling in love, and never equating the two. Yet, I know two guys who have been together for over forty years. They're married now, but they have always had a daddy-boy relationship, and they're definitely in love. It's sickening to watch how lovey-dovey they can get."

"Are women like that, too?"

"Well, the few that are into the age play describe themselves as Fem-daddies with their girls. I imagine there are many mommy-girl relationships, too, because it's like gender roles. They slide all over the spectrum. I know some who are mommy to their little bois...that's b-o-i."

"And where are you?"

"Wherever you want me to be, Morgan." Jordan knew she'd do anything Morgan asked of her, be it BDSM or vanilla, and now she had thrust her feelings out in the open. Over the past few weeks, seeing Morgan five times a week, she'd let Morgan drift into her heart and mind every moment they were together. She was unlike any other person Jordan had ever known. Morgan was the exact person she'd always wanted, whether *she* knew it or not. Jordan had never had this feeling for anyone, not even Amy. And certainly not Lacey. She wanted to touch Morgan, to draw her close, to kiss her, to hold her, and was willing to fit into Morgan's life any way Morgan would let her.

Morgan looked taken aback.

Jordan took a leap. "I'm falling for you, Ms. Sparks, harder than I ever thought I could. I can be as vanilla as you want, just tell me what turns you on, and I'll do it." There hadn't been many loves in her life. She didn't need them. She had focused all her emotions into her music, but there were two women who had made an impact on her, and Morgan was one of them.

"Jordan..."

"If you don't want me at all, say so. I'll never bring it up again. Like I said before, you're the boss. I'll be wherever you want me to be."

"Jordan," Morgan said in a firm voice and then took a deep breath. "Believe it or not, I don't do *relationships*. They don't seem to work out for me."

"I don't understand."

"It's just the way it is."

"Someone hurt you badly."

"That's not in the conversation. It's not you. I could be very attracted to you, but I don't get close to anyone."

"But why?"

Morgan stood. Jordan could feel her towering over her. "Because I don't," she stated with finality. "I'll see you at the restaurant. You can let yourself out." She turned and hurried upstairs.

Jordan watched her go. Stunned by the abruptness and embarrassed that she had released her emotions when she vowed she wouldn't, she gathered her music off the piano.

Because why? Was Morgan hiding a physical disability? If so, she sure hid it well. Was it an emotional disability? Definitely, but what had caused it? Perhaps there was a previous lover? *Probably.* So was that why she came back from New York? *Again, my guess is probably. How do I get her to open up about it so it could be fixed?*

Jordan felt Morgan's hurt in her heart. She also felt the deep pain of rejection. The sudden shut down of emotions. Her heart was bleeding for her. Her mind was filled. *My God, but I want her. Not as a sub. I want to kiss her, make love to her, hold her in my arms, and taste her. Am I crazy? It's happening all over again.*

Wednesday, the band came in to play as they usually did. Robbie and Lori were friendly and bantered with Jordan before and between sets. Morgan was all business. Distant when she was away from the piano but open and vibrant when she was playing. The difference was very noticeable.

Chelsea came in that night to have a drink and wait for Robbie.

"Want to go out for a bite with us after we're though?" Robbie asked Jordan.

"Sure." She could use someone to talk to.

Later, they settled into a booth at the all-night diner. "Morgan seemed a little down tonight," Jordan finally said to Robbie.

"She can get like that. Sometimes it will last for a week, sometimes much longer, sometimes a little shorter. You never know."

"How do you get her out of it?"

"Just let her work whatever is bothering her out of her system. If you pry, she'll get even more distant."

"I think she's hurting inside." Jordan thought back to the night Morgan had rejected her offer. *She's running from something. There's a deep-seated pain, far deeper than just a sexual relationship. And it has to do with BDSM. Was she hurt? Oh God, did Morgan suffer at the hands of another like me?*

"If she is, she's been hurting for years," Robbie said. "She'll work her way out of it. She always does."

"Does this happen often?" Jordan continued to probe. *I have to reach out to Morgan again. I have to persuade her that I would never hurt her, that all I want to do is love her. It's not about the lifestyle. It's what I feel for her, what I have longed for. What I have found and what I am not going to let be taken from me.*

"No. And it's not seasonal. I don't know what triggers it."

"Maybe she needs to get laid." Chelsea giggled.

"Yes. I used to think that, too, but even when I set her up with someone hot, she didn't change."

"So what's her problem?" Chelsea asked. "She's a fine-looking woman. Is she still grappling with her sexuality?"

"God, no," Robbie said. "She's been a dyke for thirty years. There's no question there. She just doesn't get into relationships."

"Only one-night stands?"

"Seems that way, when it happens, but unless she has a secret life no one knows about, it doesn't happen often."

"What a waste," Chelsea murmured.

Jordan didn't want to, but she had to tell Robbie. "I think I may have triggered this latest one. I told her on Sunday that I was attracted to her. She told me she never got involved in relationships, and I could let myself out of her house. Then she went upstairs."

"That was rude," said Chelsea.

"No, that was Morgan." Robbie looked at them. "She keeps away from even discussing serious relationships like the plague."

"What can we do?"

"I've been asking myself that for the past five years. That is the twenty-million-dollar question."

❖

The rest of the week was much the same. Morgan was the perfect entertainer when she was onstage, but when she wasn't in front of the audience, she barely spoke to anyone. Finally, Jordan had to make a move.

Sunday's rehearsal at Morgan's house was ending. They'd worked on three new songs to add this week. Before she turned to leave, Jordan said, "Morgan—"

"No," was the response.

But Jordan had had enough. She wasn't going to sit back and watch this happen when she knew she should try to do something about it. "Don't tell me no. You don't even know what I was going to say."

"I'm not your submissive."

"I know you're not because I would never allow a submissive to behave as you do. You're driving me crazy."

Morgan stood there looking at her.

"I don't know who's responsible for this, but I will not take the fallout. Talk to me, damn you. Don't treat me like some shit off the street."

"I won't do this," Morgan stated and went upstairs.

This time, Jordan followed. She went into the second room, a smaller bedroom that had the electric keyboard, a desk, and a lot of recording equipment set up. Morgan sat at it.

"Come on, Morgan, we can't keep on this way. The music won't take it. I need to connect with you. Otherwise, it's like we're doing karaoke. There's no connection between our instruments. The music will only be better if we communicate. Even a soloist with a full hundred-piece orchestra communicates with the conductor."

Morgan stopped. She looked at Jordan. Their eyes met, but neither spoke. Finally, Morgan said, "I'm sorry. You're right."

"Where do you go? I haven't felt you around here all week."

"I don't know."

"Don't give me that. You do know. Do I have to be super-Domme and demand you tell me?"

"I won't do Domme-sub."

"You don't have to. Just tell me where your mind goes when you run out of here." She paused for a moment, but Morgan didn't respond. "And you don't have to do any power exchange. I told you before, I'm flexible. I can do this any way you want, but I will not take being ignored. We have to communicate. If we talk to each other, it doesn't have to be one or the other of us in charge…or on top." She grinned at Morgan, hoping she'd smile, too.

She did. Then she took a very deep breath. She clamped her lips tight. Jordan waited to see what was going to come out.

"I don't do BDSM because I was in that sort of relationship when I was younger. I was still in college. She was older and very well-known. It wasn't physical BDSM. It was emotional BDSM. I fell in love with her, and I thought she did me. But she reminded me constantly of the things I had done wrong or how my former lovers had left me because of how I ignored everyone and how I always fucked things up. I merely had to walk into a room, and she'd find something wrong with the way I was walking, with the way I was carrying something. I would be working on an arrangement, and she'd complain that I never helped with cleaning around the apartment. I'd never helped with cooking or the dishes, that I'd never listened to her, or that all I ever did was sit there and scribble on music paper. It didn't matter that I was doing something that would make us money. I wasn't paying enough attention to her. I was ignoring everything. Whenever we argued it always became my fault, and she twisted the logic to make it look that way. I could barely function on my own. After a while, I couldn't do anything right or wrong. For quite a few months, I was in a place so dark that it took me quite a while to find my way out of it. People wondered why I came back from New York. I came back because if I had stayed, I would have committed suicide. I swore I'd never get into another relationship like that again, so the minute it feels abusive, I'm gone."

Now that made sense, but there was something in what she said that didn't. "Why did you agree to it?"

"Oh, no." She shrugged off. "I did not *agree* to it."

"Then it wasn't BDSM. BDSM, or Leather, is safe, sane and *consensual*. Both parties have to agree. It sounds like you were simply abused."

"There was nothing simple about it."

"Now, when you say *gone*, you don't necessarily mean physically."

"No."

That made sense to Jordan. She's seen Morgan withdraw within herself. Now she knew why. "I wondered why you didn't date. Robbie said she didn't know, and I couldn't imagine why. You're so…so… desirable."

Morgan broke out laughing. "Jordan, if I ever get into a relationship again, I want an equal relationship. It mustn't be one-sided. I shouldn't be worshiped. I don't want to have to lead and I don't want to follow, at least not all the time. I know there are places where I have to be in charge, but there are places I'd like to let the other person take control. All in all, I want someone equal to me."

"There'll never be anyone *equal* to you. You're always ahead of everyone." She knew Morgan's mind worked twice as fast as anyone else's.

Morgan laughed. "Now you're talking crap. I'm not always ahead. When we're onstage, you far outshine me."

"Only because you've programmed it that way. Please, Morgan, know that I would never abuse your emotions."

Morgan looked at her lap. "Sure you will. Maybe not intentionally, but sometime, you'll say something without thinking or in the heat of an argument."

"I'll always be careful." Jordan looked into her eyes. "I promise. I'll never humiliate you, wound your ego, embarrass, or debase you in any way. I think you're one of the most intelligent people I've ever met, and I admire your musical ability. Aren't you attracted to me at all?"

Morgan grinned. "Of course I am. I've been hot for you since the first night you sang with us. You had me right from the opening notes. When you made that first octave jump on 'Rainbow,' I almost couldn't finish the song, I was so undone."

That was all Jordan needed to hear. She knew in her heart that Morgan had liked that, but now it was confirmed. That was all the impetus she needed. She leaned over the keyboard and placed her lips on Morgan's. She grabbed hold of her head and didn't let go for quite a while.

Morgan started to pull away, but it seemed as if there was something in this kiss that held her there. Jordan risked putting her tongue into Morgan's mouth. Then Morgan pushed her away, and her eyes seemed to examine Jordan's.

"I can't do this here," Morgan said. Jordan's heart sank before Morgan said, "This keyboard is in the way." She stepped around the keyboard and drew Jordan into her arms. "You're a beautiful woman. I thought that from the first time I talked to you." She pulled Jordan closer and pressed her lips into hers. Her arms closed around her as they continued to kiss.

Jordan pressed her hands into Morgan's back so she couldn't step away. Morgan's slid downward until she was grasping Jordan's ass firmly.

Finally, Morgan said, "Let's go into the bedroom."

Jordan's smile returned.

Morgan took her hand, switched the light off, and led the way to the bedroom. "I don't usually take a woman to bed the first time I kiss her."

"And I'm the exception to your rule?" *Oh, please, please, take me. I can give you anything you want.* She would have done anything at that moment, anything to continue this.

"Jordan, you're the exception to everything."

Morgan led Jordan into the bedroom, relieved that she'd shared her secret with her. She'd wanted her since that first Saturday night. Maybe, if she let herself, this relationship could work. At least it wouldn't have to sit in her stomach for the next twenty years or more. But that exchange of power thing…oh damn. That was it. Suzanne had always had the power in their relationship. *Did I just give it to her? Was I partially at fault or did she take it without me understanding what was happening? Yes, I guess I did relinquish all the power to her without even realizing it. But, did I have a choice?*

But she'd wanted Jordan for weeks. In the bedroom, Morgan turned and unbuttoned Jordan's shirt while she kissed her. She wrapped her arms around Jordan tightly. Jordan started to pull her close, but Morgan planted her lips onto Jordan's neck, her shoulder, and then back to her lips. They started to undress each other without breaking their lip-lock. The mood was a lot more frantic than it had been earlier. As the clothes came off, Morgan stepped back to inspect Jordan's body. Yes, everything was as perfect as she'd imagined. The tits were round and full and hadn't started to sag. The nipples were a dark rose color with darker areolas, and her belly was flat, with just the hint of a six-pack above it. Jordan was even more magnificent than Morgan had envisioned these last few months from her bed every night.

Morgan pulled Jordan onto the bed as she threw the comforter to the floor. She kissed down Jordan's chest and onto her belly, not allowing Jordan to touch her.

"My God," Morgan said softly. "You're even more magnificent than I imagined." Then she took total control and moved up to Jordan's right nipple and licked and sucked while caressing the other. She switched. She couldn't get enough.

"Morgan, I've dreamed of you sucking me for weeks now." Jordan's voice sounded as if she weren't on this earth.

"Sucking you where? Here?" She attacked her left nipple. "Or here?" She switched to the right. "Or down here, farther south?" She slid down, ran her tongue across Jordan's opening, and took her hard, slightly swollen clit into her mouth.

"Oh God, yes. Yes, to all of those…and anywhere else you want."

"I want to suck all of you," Morgan whispered.

"I'm all yours."

Morgan couldn't believe all the feelings and emotions that were running through her. Hadn't she wished for this for the past couple months? She licked into the opening, then up the folds, below it, and all around the clit. "You taste magnificent," she murmured.

"It's for you," Jordan said. She ran her hands through Morgan's hair and across her shoulders. Morgan slipped her fingers into Jordan and curled upward as she pumped in and out and in and out. She caressed Jordan's entire sex with her tongue, up and down, and wherever possible, in and out. She made love to Jordan with more intensity than she'd ever done with anyone.

"Yes. Oh my God, that's it," Jordan yelled as her body stiffened. Morgan rested her fingers on Jordan's G-spot, but didn't stop pushing and rubbing. She pushed and pushed, then pushed and rubbed some more.

Jordan shook violently as the release flowed out of her. Morgan stopped moving to hold her tightly. Jordan lay there as the rush of orgasm drained out. She finally rolled over to Morgan.

"You're magnificent," Morgan said softly.

"You're more than I ever imagined."

"And you are even better than I imagined." Morgan wrapped her arms around her, caressing her. "Think this will impact our music?"

"It can only make it better, more romantic. From now on, every love song will be about you."

"That will make all the music monotonous."

"Not really." Jordan said as she ran her fingers through Morgan's hair. "But I need to ask you a question. The band's name is Stone Cold Perception. You're not stone, are you?"

Morgan raised her eyebrows. "Why would you think that?"

"Robbie said you don't date, and you just stopped me from making love to you. I just wondered."

Morgan grinned. "No, I'm not stone. I'm as soft and wet as the next woman. I stopped you because I couldn't hold myself back from taking you. I've wanted to touch you since that first night."

"Phew. That's a relief. I couldn't hold back from touching you, either. I know we'll still agree on most things but disagree on a few others. We're both pretty determined about what we want from the music. You do all the arrangements, so you're really in charge."

Morgan chuckled. "And you change whatever you want when we're in performance, so it really doesn't matter. I just provide the skeleton. You bring it to life, and that's okay with me because you add so much."

"No, you just brought *me* to life." She stared into Morgan's eyes. "The last time I made love to anyone was the night before the accident, back in California."

"It's been even longer for me. It's been months."

"It feels like years, doesn't it?"

"Yes, years." Morgan leaned forward and kissed Jordan again, gently. She would have to delve into those thoughts. The sex was different, much more two-way. Could this work? *My God, I hope so. This is what I've always wanted.*

"Then let me make sure." Jordan kissed Morgan as her hand started across Morgan's breasts. "Do you like to be touched here?" She ran one finger over a nipple.

"Definitely."

"And here?" She moved to the other one.

"Absolutely, but you're not going to test all of me like that, are you?"

"Not right now," Jordan said as she pressed herself closer to Morgan, rubbing her chest up Morgan's belly. "And not this slowly." She squeezed the first nipple as she kissed up Morgan's neck into her ear. "No, I won't ask. You'll just have to stop me if it's something you don't like." She nibbled her way down to a nipple and took it between her lips, rubbing it with her tongue. "I want all of you, Morgan Sparks. Every little centimeter,"

"Really?" *Can I give it all to her? This is so new, different for me.*

"Really. And don't try to deny me. I always get what I want." She licked her way over to the other nipple and started there.

This was going to be a lengthy and satisfying adventure. Morgan leaned back and let Jordan have her way. This was far better than anything she'd had before. There was no comparison. *Yes, Jordan can do this all she wants.*

CHAPTER NINE

That Wednesday night, Morgan was more communicative, and Robbie seemed to notice it. After the second set, she went over to Jordan. "Our leader seems to have returned," she said.

"Yes. Isn't it wonderful?"

"Did you have anything to do with it?"

"Oh, I hope so." Jordan looked down, feeling a blush start to warm her face. "I got the one-night-stand. Now I'll see if I can get the return engagement."

Robbie's eyes widened. "Think you can?"

"I sure hope so."

"That good, huh?"

"Did you doubt it?"

"Well, she's a little too butch for me, but it sure looks good from the outside."

Jordan smiled and nodded. "Butch or not, it was phenomenal. The best I've had in a long time."

"Even with all your kinky little subs?"

"I enjoyed getting them off, but it was seldom about me. This one was."

"Then go for it. Get what you can. You deserve it."

Jordan smiled.

A week later, she came out on stage and started her first number. Like every Friday, the audience loved her. As she started the second song, a slow love song, she started to meander through the audience.

She'd gotten through two or three lines before she came face-to-face with someone she hadn't expected to be there. The words and the music fled her mind. Her mouth was open, but nothing came out. She heard Morgan pick up the melody after a few bars of her silence, but Jordan just stared at the cute blond woman sitting there in the audience. Before she knew what was happening, she was kneeling in front of the young woman, holding her hand.

"We're gonna take a short break," she heard Morgan announce. "We'll be back in ten."

Jordan then realized everything had stopped. She got to her feet and came right back over to the piano. "I'm sorry, Morgan, I'm sorry I lost it. Lacey is here."

"Really?" That was Lacey? An emotion that felt like jealousy raced through Morgan, but she denied it. She couldn't be jealous. She had no reason. "That's okay. We can pick it up in a minute. Do you want to continue, or do you need the rest of the night off?"

"No, I'll continue. Just let me get some water. My head is still a little frazzled. I wasn't expecting this."

"I'll do one to get the room back into the mood. Then you can continue your three."

"Can we start with 'Unforgettable'?"

Morgan's breath caught. "Is she?"

"Probably for all the wrong reasons."

"Do you need some time with her? I understand if you do."

"Maybe. Let me think about it." She still seemed stunned.

Well, Jordan was being sincere; she wasn't trying to hide her feelings. Morgan smiled warmly at her. "All right. Whatever you need." Then she rearranged her music set, turned to explain the changes to Robbie and Lori, and sat at the piano.

"Sorry for the interruption," she announced. "We had an unexpected guest tonight. It shocked Jordan so much she had to take a break. But now, back again, Jordan Phelps." Her fingers danced across the keys as she led into "Unforgettable."

Jordan sang directly to Lacey. It was like there were no other people in the room. After a few more clips of the lyrics, Jordan began to sing to other audience members. It became a very private love song between her and whoever she was singing to at the moment. She eventually ended up back before Lacey to end the song. The crowd burst into applause. Jordan leaned down and planted a small kiss on Lacey's lips, then turned back to the crowd as Morgan started the next piece.

As the set closed for the night, Morgan thanked everyone and promised to see them tomorrow. Jordan was now sitting with her two friends. She looked up at Morgan and gestured for her to join them. Robbie and Lori also drifted over to the table.

"This is Lacey Sumner and Blaine Jones," Jordan said. "This is Morgan, Robbie, and Lori." They all shook hands.

"How are you feeling?" Morgan asked. "Jordan told us about your accident." She studied the blonde. She looked a little younger, maybe weaker than Morgan had pictured but was still an attractive young woman.

"Well, it doesn't hurt most of the time, but I have to walk with a cane. It threw my balance off."

"Oh, honey." Jordan reached over and hugged her.

"It's a lot less than what you went through," Lacey said.

Morgan glanced at Lori, knowing she didn't know the entire story. They might have to talk later.

"At least I had everyone around me hoping that I'd get better," Lacey said.

"What are you doing here? I thought your mother put me off-limits."

"She doesn't know. Blaine and I have gone camping for a week."

"Is she still keeping you home?"

"As much as she thinks she can, but I've gotten away a few times. Luckily, my right foot works well, so I can still drive."

"That's wonderful," Jordan said.

Morgan looked around as she realized the restaurant was starting to empty out. "Why don't we all go back to my house so we can talk comfortably?"

"Yes. Morgan has a beautiful house," Jordan said.

"As much as I'd like to meet with you guys, my wife's waiting for me at home. Will I see you tomorrow night?" Lori asked.

"We should be here," Blaine said.

"Good. See you then." Lori slipped away to pick up her bass and head out to her car.

"All right," said Morgan. "Let's go. If anyone prefers beer, I'll have to stop on the way home. It's the one alcohol I don't have."

"You do have rum, right?" Blaine asked.

Morgan nodded. "Bacardi: gold or black and Mount Gay."

"I'm good." Blaine said. Her smile rose a hundred percent.

"Do you still have some of that rosé?" Jordan asked.

"Everything except beer," Morgan said as she stood. "I'll head to the house and get things ready."

"Why don't I ride with Blaine and Lacey so they don't get lost? My car is at your house, anyway," Jordan said.

Morgan nodded her agreement.

"I'll stop and get some chips or something to munch on. Anyone have a preference?" Robbie asked. They shook their heads as Morgan and Robbie left.

Jordan turned to Blaine. "Did you drive or fly here?"

"Drive? Only you would be crazy enough to drive all the way across the country," Blaine said. "It would have taken us five days to get here. It might as well have been in a covered wagon."

Lacey gave her a playful push. "Yes, we flew, but if I'd known the traffic in Boston was so insane, I probably wouldn't have come."

"But you probably started with airport traffic. Logan Airport has the worst traffic in the country."

"Tell me about it."

"LA traffic is crowded, but most people stay in line so it doesn't get crazy. Bostonian drivers go wherever they want, whether there's a lane there or not."

The three got into Blaine's rental car. Jordan got into the back seat so Lacey could ride shotgun and not have to try to manipulate her injured legs behind the front seat. "And the roads around the city are so narrow. They're still just wide enough for wagons."

"Yup. Historic old Boston. Okay. Now, which way?"

"Let's sit here for a minute. Tell me what's really happening with you two," Jordan asked, trying for a subtle but demanding tone.

"Nothing between us." Blaine said.

"My new girlfriend thought I needed time with you without her." Lacey grinned, almost apologetically.

"You have a girlfriend?" Jordan asked.

"Yes. We're not living together yet, but it's getting close."

"Good for you, honey. What's her name?" She had always hoped that Lacey would find someone to make her happy. That was what she deserved.

"Tatalia. She's the sister of one of the nurses at the rehab facility."

"I'm glad you found someone."

"What about you?" Blaine asked. "Is there something between you and that piano player? Morgan?"

Was it that obvious? Were she and Morgan throwing love looks at each other? "Yes, but it's just starting."

"You've been here a couple months. Did you have to break her up with someone?" Lacey asked.

"No. Morgan's not a relationship-type person."

"She's a player?"

"No, just the opposite. It's a long story. She'd have to tell it." It wasn't her place to say what had happened to Morgan, even to her closest friend. Besides, just like her story, some things were better left unsaid.

"Damn," Blaine said.

"She doesn't seem like a sub." Lacey added.

"No, she's so completely not Leather."

"Are you going to take her there?"

"Perhaps I will, if and when the time is right. I sort of got out of Leather. I haven't wanted to do anything since I've been here."

"I wonder why," Blaine said sarcastically.

Jordan turned toward the passenger window to hide her expression of guilt and shame. Did it always have to come back to that? *Will I forever be living that nightmare, trampling over what is supposed to be buried memories only to have them invade my new life? I'm trying to make a new start, trying to forgive myself. I'm in love with Morgan, yes, so madly in love.*

"But you'll slip back in if you can?" Lacey asked.

"If Morgan can."

Lacey turned to study her. "You're really hooked, huh?"

Jordan nodded, still staring out the window. "Yes. I'm hooked... big time."

"You'll land her."

"That's my goal."

"I've never known you not to reach your goal when you set your mind to it." Blaine reached for the key in the ignition. "Now, how do we get to her house?"

Jordan looked forward and pointed down the street, out of the parking lot. "Take a right at the lights."

A half hour later, they pulled up in front of Morgan's house and got out of the car, "Nice place," Blaine exclaimed.

"Wait till you see the inside," Robbie said as she answered the door and ushered them into the living room, which ran the entire length of the front of the house. It opened into a dining room on one side. There were stairs and a hall leading into a kitchen on the other side. The living room had a circular couch that sat around a baby grand piano.

"Is anyone up for a drink?" Morgan asked as she emerged from the kitchen with a bucket of ice.

"Rum." Blaine requested.

"With Coke, soda and lemon, pineapple juice, or straight?"

"With Coke and Bacardi Black?"

Morgan nodded. "And you, Lacey?"

"I'll have the same."

Morgan walked to the bar and began mixing their drinks. "I already know what Jordan and Robbie want."

They all sat down to get to know each other. "Blaine plays a mean guitar," Jordan said, "and a sexy twelve-string."

"But you live in California, not Boston," said Morgan.

Jordan stared. Was it more than just an observation, or was Morgan glad Blaine didn't live around here?

"Yes. But there's nothing keeping me there." Blaine glanced at Jordan. "There used to be a great band around there, but it broke up."

"Really?" Jordan was quite surprised.

"Yes, we tried a couple other singers but after you, we were kind of spoiled, so a couple of the guys just gave up."

"Now I really feel bad about fucking up." *Damn. It affected more than me and Lacey. Now I feel twice as bad for ruining everyone else's chance.*

"If it hadn't been you, I think someone else would have broken the band up. I'm not sure half of them were serious about it. They were just excited when they thought we were going to be famous. I don't think they realized how much work and time it would take."

"Well, if you happened to move out here, I'm sure we could find a place for you, but the gig we have now, which we've had for a few years, doesn't pay that much. We all still have day-jobs." Morgan seemed as if she was beginning to warm up to Blaine now that it was obvious there wasn't anything more than friendship between her and Jordan.

"If you ever need anyone, keep me in mind."

"We'll have to stay in touch," Morgan told Blaine.

After everyone left, Jordan helped pick up the house and put the glasses in the dishwasher. Morgan hadn't said much once everyone was gone because she wasn't sure where her head was at. Should she go for it and ask Jordan to stay the night? How was Jordan feeling about her friends being here? She couldn't imagine what Jordan was feeling after all these months.

Morgan finally turned to her. "Would you stay tonight?"

"I thought you'd never ask."

Morgan felt relieved at her answer. At least now she could make sure Jordan was all right and let her talk. She also had to know if what she was doing was a dead end.

They linked hands as they went up to the bedroom. "How did it feel, seeing Lacey?" Morgan asked as she unbuttoned Jordan's dress.

"I'm glad she's out and around. She looks good, but I'm sorry she has to walk with a cane. I didn't know the burns caused that much damage."

"At least that's all it did. She is able to walk"

"I know. She's is seeing someone, too, and she looks happy. She asked about us."

"What did you say?" What was Jordan thinking about them? Had she told Lacey that they were a couple? *Is that what she thinks? Is that what she wants?*

"That we were at the beginning."

"And it isn't going as fast as you want?"

Jordan took Morgan's face in her hands. "I'm just happy its going. I'm not a race car driver."

"That's good," Morgan said as she pushed Jordan down onto the bed and pulled off the rest of her clothes. "I like you staying here," Morgan said. It was a big leap for her to admit that. She felt her heart pound as she realized she was breaking her own rules.

"Every once in a while?"

Morgan paused, embarrassed. "And that bothers you?" What more did she want?

"That's all right." Jordan said, stroking Morgan's face. "I'll take *every once in a while* over *never in a million years*."

"How can you be like that?" She couldn't understand how someone with Jordan's background could step back and let someone else make decisions.

"Because I'm patient, and I really care about you. I don't want anything to push you or make you do something you don't want to do. I remember when I had to do what I didn't want to do, and it wasn't a lot of fun. I want to have fun with you."

"Why?" It still didn't compute that Jordan didn't want to dominate.

"Because I respect your talents and your past and because I want to stick around and see where we can go with this."

"Really?"

"Yes. Really."

Morgan brought her mouth to Jordan's and started a soft, gentle kiss that grew and grew. As Morgan started to nibble down the front of Jordan's body, she explored everything below with her hands.

Jordan's nipples had become so hard that Morgan was afraid they'd break off in her mouth. She inched her way down Jordan's body to see what else was hard. Finally, she came to her clit, which rivaled the hardness on Jordan's chest. She caressed it with her tongue.

"This is what I like the most," she whispered.

"It likes you, too." Jordan replied. Morgan flicked her tongue, and Jordan jumped a little. "It likes you a lot."

Morgan slipped her fingers into Jordan and pressed just slightly.

At that point, Jordan's body seemed so sensitive that the slightest push made her whole body quiver. Morgan was slow and forceful, going in and out as she lapped. She felt Jordan hold her breath. Was she anticipating the climax?

Morgan moved just enough to move everything to a higher plane, and Jordan was undone. Morgan kept moving her fingers until they reached where Jordan seemed to want them. Jordan grabbed her shoulder and held it tightly. Her arms started to tremble. Everything seemed to stiffen, frozen in place. Morgan continued her assault with tongue and fingers until a loud cry of release escaped Jordan's mouth. Her body shook as Morgan gathered her into her arms.

Beads of sweat glistened on Jordan's body. Her eyes were closed as Morgan cradled her in her arms. After a few minutes, her breathing slowed, and Morgan whispered, "Are you all right, baby?"

"I haven't found all the pieces yet," Jordan responded softly. "They all exploded out of here."

"Well, I'd say you're put together better than most I've seen. Of course, I've seen very few in the last fifteen years, so if they modernized anything, I'm not that up on it."

"Nothing's been modernized or upgraded that I know of. Women are still the same as they used to be."

"You're not," Morgan said.

"I'm not?"

"No. I've never met a woman as perfect as you."

Jordan looked up with disbelief.

"I mean it," Morgan said. She was holding herself back from what she really wanted to say. It wasn't the time yet. She didn't want to be trapped before everything had fallen into the right places. That was what she'd done the last time, and it had come back to rip her to shreds. She must not say how she really felt. No. Not yet.

Jordan looked deeply into Morgan's eyes. "Well, then, you're running a close second."

"Nope. Not yet." Morgan leaned down and kissed her again. This time, the kiss lasted long enough for Jordan to remove all of the rest of Morgan's clothes.

"Now that is an ultra-fine specimen. Just look. Symmetrical in every way." Jordan crawled on top. "I'm going to do everything I've been thinking about for the past week."

The next two days, Sunday and Monday, Jordan spent with her friends from California. Morgan had canceled their rehearsal, saying that Jordan's friends were more important. Jordan had been stunned that Morgan stepped aside for her to meet with her friends. Was there no jealousy? She hoped not because Morgan had no reason to be jealous of these two. She so hoped Morgan was beginning to trust her.

"This is a cute little room," Blaine said when Jordan showed them her place.

"Emphasis on little," Jordan added.

"What's it like sharing a house with a man?"

"He's gay. We don't see a lot of each other. He works eight to five. I work four to midnight. What little we see of each other is friendly. Sometimes, when he does the cooking, there are leftovers in the fridge that are super good."

"I'm not sure I could do it," Lacey said.

"Oh, it's all right. I hope I'm not here for long."

"Yes, that big house Morgan has looks much more comfortable."

"Well," said Jordan, "I'm not pushing her." No, it was still too soon to think of moving into Morgan's house. She had just moved into her *life*.

"Why not? I've never known you to hold back when you really wanted something."

"This one's different…and much more worth the wait."

"I hope you won't have to wait too long."

"I won't. I'm beginning to see her pattern. It's just finding the source, which could take a while. There's something in her background that's holding her back from relationships."

"I listened to her playing. Why isn't she doing more?"

"I think that's from the source. She was working in New York, playing with a big name. Then she came back home and stopped playing for a while. She says it's because of all the drugs, but I'm not sure that's true."

"Think there was someone there that she's still in love with?" Lacey asked.

"It's a possibility. I certainly hope not, but that was fifteen years ago. She only started playing again five, maybe six years ago."

"Seems like a waste."

They talked for a few minutes, then Blaine stood. "Well, listen. I want to go explore Old Ironsides. You know I have a thing for sailing ships, and being in Boston, I can't miss this one. Want to come?"

Lacey looked at Jordan. "No, I think Jordan and I have some things to discuss. Let me stay here. You can pick me up on the way back."

"I'm not sure how long it will take."

"Take as long or as short as you want. We'll be here."

"Now, you're sure you don't want to go?" Blaine asked. "This is a historic landmark."

"No, I'll stay here with my historic kink-mark while I can." Lacey grinned at Jordan.

"Kink-mark? Are you saying I'm old?"

"Not at all, just a treasure."

Blaine laughed and headed toward the door. "I'm out of here. See you two later."

Jordan looked at Lacey, concerned. "Well, how are things back home really?"

"I start a new job the week after next, and it pays really well. Tatalia and I should have the money for an apartment by Halloween."

"What's the new job?"

"Bookkeeping, so I can stay off my feet."

"That's great." She was glad Lacey had her own money again and didn't need to rely on her folks. She was also glad that her disability hadn't stopped her.

"But I wanted to make sure you were okay before I moved on," Lacey said. "I can't tell you how sorry I am that my mother did that to you. I can't wait to get out of her house. We don't talk much, and when we do, it's tense."

"Sweetie, your mother will never understand what she did. She'll never acknowledge the devastation she caused."

"I know. I think my father realizes it, but he won't say anything."

Jordan nodded. "That's all right. I think I understand."

"Most of the town has forgotten about you. The new music teacher is doing all right. He's not great, but he's getting something done. I haven't had a chance to go back to the Loft. Tatalia's not Leather."

"It seems we really picked them, didn't we? Does it feel strange having someone who's not Leather? Sometimes, I think it is life telling me to try another route. It's confusing."

"Yes. There must be something there, or we wouldn't stay with them."

"I am so hopelessly in love with Morgan, and it's not the sex... well, not *just* the sex. Is it the music? I don't know. I felt it that first night when Robbie got me to sing. It just felt right."

"You *are* sleeping with her, right?"

"Yes, of course."

"She looks like she'd be good."

"Yes." Jordan held herself back from gushing. After all, she couldn't bring herself to compare the two—out loud—with each other. Being with Lacey brought back memories, both good and bad. They'd had a happy, comfortable life together, but they had never been in love.

"Vanilla is so different from kink," Jordan said.

"Oh, I know. I'm not sure how I feel about it, but it is so very different, I can't describe it."

"I feel the same way, too. Do you ever wonder how we got along with our relationship?"

"All the time. I know the sex of BDSM was thrilling and exciting, but it's a lot different with vanilla," Lacey said. "I think Tat and I are closer, although I'm not sure how."

"I know what you mean, Lacey. I'm head over heels with Morgan, but it's not like we were.

Lacey nodded. "Yes, it's more spontaneous. We don't have to negotiate everything. If it's something we don't want, we just say so. If there's something that turns us on, we just do it."

"Exactly. Morgan and I do things I would never think to negotiate."

"And you find it exciting."

Jordan nodded. "Yes."

"I've found I like surprising Tat. I could never do that with you."

"We weren't really lovers," Jordan said, a bit regretfully. "We were friends and play partners. You were collared to me, and I cared about you. I don't think we were ever in love."

"No. I don't think we were."

"Don't get me wrong, Lacey. I cared a lot about you. I did love you in a way."

"But we weren't *in* love."

Jordan looked at her with a small smile. "No, we weren't."

"But now we're going in different directions."

"Yes."

"Can I be honest with you?"

"Of course."

"I feel bad about what my mother did, and I'm sorry you had to leave. I think about you a lot. But I don't miss you."

Jordan studied her for a moment. "You're a lot smarter than I am. I didn't realize it until I was halfway across the country."

"No, I'm not smarter, I just had a whole lot of time to think about things while I was in the hospital and in the rehab center. You should see all the things you think about if your leg is in traction, and you can't move around."

"I guess, hon. Do you forgive me for putting you there?"

"That was neither of our faults. It was just bad happenings."

"So you still love me?" Jordan asked.

"Yeah. Do you?"

"Yeah." They drew each other into a tight hug.

They sat and talked for three more hours before Blaine eventually returned, starry-eyed because she had seen the USS Constitution, Old Ironsides.

They made plans to go into Boston Common and the Paul Revere House tomorrow just so they could say they'd been there.

CHAPTER TEN

The next week was back to normal. Tuesday through Thursday, Jordan worked her job as hostess, and then on Wednesday and Thursday nights, the band played. Jordan felt her life was beginning to position itself into a routine. With finding out that Lacey didn't hate her or hold hard feelings about what had happened in California, she could focus on starting anew and begin to mend the memories of what had happened to Lacey and how her life was destroyed in California.

Wednesday night, Lacey and Blaine came to hear them again, and Jordan went out to the diner with them afterward. They were going to leave the next morning.

"It's good that you're happy," Lacey said. "I was worried about you."

"So now you know you don't have to be." *Why would she be worried about me? She's the one who was hurt. My life and career were destroyed by her mother, but she will always have the scars to remind her. And she'll always have her mother badgering her for the lifestyle she was involved in. That woman truly hated me and wanted me buried in a prison cell.*

"And you never have to worry about me, either," Lacey echoed in return.

I suppose since she has Tatalia and Blaine, I won't have to worry about her, as long as she can get away from her mother. "Dang, but we're a civilized pair, aren't we?"

"Yes. I came to Boston to break up with you, and now we're best friends again."

"And I hope it stays that way."

"I hope you get what you want from Morgan."

"I'm sure I will. Don't worry." *From the way things have been progressing, Morgan and I are heading down a future with a promising relationship. We complement each other, from our music to our lovemaking. I just have to get her to trust me, to open up and let go of the past. I want to set her free.*

"Are you two going to get all maudlin?" Blaine asked.

"Nope, we're fine with each other."

"And we'll be growing like this forever." *Yes, I'm going to show Morgan what it really means to trust and be loved. No pressure. No control, just natural, pure honest love.*

Thursday, Jordan was a little low, but the clientele at the restaurant was a happy group, and the band played well, as usual. Lacey and Blaine had left for the airport early that morning. The sendoff was bittersweet. Jordan knew that Lacey would be all right, but she still felt she was losing a part of herself. Perhaps it was the fact that she wasn't a practicing Domme at the moment. *Maybe that will change with Morgan. I just have to ease her into it and build back my confidence. After all, it was an accident. I'm not a bad person. I'm a good lover and was a good Mistress.*

"You look a little down," Morgan said during a break.

"Lacey and Blaine left this morning. I miss them already, but I'll probably get over it when I start to sing tomorrow night."

"Did you wish you could go back with Lacey?"

"No, Lacey and I had a good talk, and we closed our relationship. We're both going in different directions now. I already told you, we probably wouldn't have stayed together much longer."

"If you need a little cuddle to make you feel better, you can come over tonight."

Really? Morgan offering to cuddle on a Wednesday night? "Thanks, but no, I'm going home as quickly as the crowd settles down. I need a little time alone. I'll be fine tomorrow, I promise."

Morgan gave her a soft kiss on the lips, then went back to start the next set.

Jordan was astounded. Morgan wanted something in the middle of the week? *What's wrong with this picture?* Was she making strides to loosen up? She wondered where Morgan's head was tonight. Something was changing in her. Maybe she had made a big estate sale today. *Nah, she would have told me.* Maybe she had been thinking about their relationship and wanted to take it further…perhaps she was getting interested in a little bondage. Maybe? Perhaps?

Friday and Saturday, Jordan sang. The only thing amazing that happened Saturday night was that Morgan asked Jordan to go home with her again. She'd asked twice that week, even though Jordan hadn't gone the first time.

"You won't have to go all the way to Cambridge and come back again tomorrow to run some new songs." Cambridge was just across the river and her house not that far beyond.

Jordan smiled. "That sounds fair." Of course Morgan wouldn't ask her to come over just because she wanted to be with her, and have sex. No, that might be too direct and admit that they were having a relationship. *Then again, perhaps she was loosening up because she realizes Lacey isn't a threat and that I'm true to my word. I just don't know. Morgan is so hard to read.*

Morgan greeted Jordan at the front door. "Welcome," she said with a smile. "I'm surprised you came."

"I haven't come yet," Jordan said with a grin. "You haven't even touched me."

Morgan reached out and drew her into a tight hug. "I can rectify that."

"Really?" said Jordan. "Can you rectify this?" She reached down and cupped Morgan's crotch.

"Wow, Ms. Phelps." Morgan gasped, feeling moisture seeping through her panties. "Aren't we getting a little forward?"

"Better than being a little backward, don't cha think?" she patted Morgan on the cheek and finished walking into the house.

As she started to walk past, Morgan grabbed her elbow and pulled her back into her arms. She planted her lips on Jordan's and pressed in hard. She forced Jordan's lips apart and delved in with her tongue. The kiss lasted longer and was deeper than before.

When she finally pulled back, Jordan said with a smile, "Now, who's getting forward?

"Better than backward," Morgan remarked. "Don't cha think?"

They laughed at each other as Morgan once again wrapped her arms around Jordan. "Are you tired?" Morgan asked. "It's been a long day. Should I put you to bed?"

"Put me to bed? No one has put me to bed since I was four years old."

"Maybe that's the problem." Morgan picked her up, put her over a shoulder in a firefighter's carry, and started up the stairs.

"Put me down, silly," Jordan screamed.

"Don't worry. I will." Morgan felt the weight as she carried her up the stairs. *It's a good thing I'm in shape, and she's small-framed. I could be worn out before we ever got started making love.*

Morgan turned into the bedroom and threw Jordan down onto the bed. But before Jordan could react, Morgan was on top of her. She pressed their lips together again. They cuddled into each other as they held each other as tightly as they could. They kissed and kissed.

"Wow, Ms. Sparks," Jordan said as she finally got some air. "That was some kiss."

"Really? I can do better. Of course, it may not be on your mouth."

"Heavens. Where else could it be?"

"Let me get you out of these clothes, and I'll show you." Morgan started to undo Jordan's dress and slid it back over her shoulders. She pushed it down and slid it out from under her. Then she undid her bra and pulled it off.

Jordan reached up and started to unbutton Morgan's shirt. "It's much more fun if we're both dressed exactly alike," she said.

"Exactly."

Jordan nodded as she unbuttoned Morgan's pants and slid down the fly.

"Well, then," Morgan said. She got up and stripped, then went back and took all of Jordan's off her. "Are we in uniform now?" she asked.

"Perfectly." Jordan looked down the full length of Morgan's body. She held her hand out and pulled Morgan's panties off.

Morgan reached down Jordan's body. The skin was so smooth and warm and almost made her hand shake, it felt so fine. She wanted to kiss every square inch, so she bent and started to place little kisses all the way from her waist to her legs. She looked back up into Jordan's eyes and wanted to give her anything she wanted.

That stopped her. No, she couldn't do that. That was what had got her in trouble to begin with. She was giving too much of herself. She'd sworn she'd never give herself away again. But this was a different woman. Jordan wasn't asking; she was giving. And when she did ask, it wasn't an order. It was a simple request.

She felt Jordan's legs slide apart. She looked down into the gorgeous display being given to her. Yes, given to her. There wasn't a hand on the back of her neck forcing her down there, making her do this.

She crawled up to Jordan's face and planted her lips there, her tongue twirling and kneading with Jordan's. Yes, this was what she'd always wanted, a deep passionate kiss. She continued to work slow, long intense kisses across her lips. A kiss that really meant something and she trusted Jordan not to lie to her. This was exactly what she'd wanted. The exact opposite of what she was given all those years ago.

She slipped back down Jordan's body and delved into her warm wet center. She slipped her fingers in and slid them back and forth up the warm slippery flesh.

❖

Jordan moaned as the tension started in her stomach. Morgan's hands felt so incredible, and her lips held the taste of heaven Jordan always wanted. Something in that mouth was making her forget about the thrills of the Leather world. This was everything she got from a play space rolled into one, into one woman, who held her entire happiness in her mouth and hands. And the tension had no comparison. This feeling was building higher than anything she'd ever done to anyone else. It filled her completely as it rose up inside her unlike anything she'd experienced in a dungeon. This was what she'd craved. She felt the edge coming toward her as if she was standing on the side of a cliff with her back to the canyon, ready to be pushed over the edge.

Then the whole world exploded inside her, and she was into the next dimension without ever lifting a finger. She arched off the bed as sounds of wonder escaped her mouth. Morgan held her tightly as she shook violently.

"Shh, baby," Morgan whispered. "It's okay. You're so beautiful. I've got you."

It was several minutes before Jordan finally relaxed onto the bed and into Morgan's arms. She opened her eyes and smiled. "God, you're so good. You took me someplace I have never been before. I have never experienced anything so deep, so passionate, so euphoric."

"God, you're beautiful," Morgan replied.

They smiled at each other as Morgan leaned down to give Jordan a soft kiss on her mouth.

"I'm almost wiped out," Jordan mumbled.

"Almost? Then I have to start again. I was aiming for totally wiped out."

"I misspoke. You reached your goal. Now I'm not sure I can reciprocate, and I really wanted to."

"You don't have to." She kissed Jordan on the forehead. "We have time later."

Jordan reached up and brought Morgan's lips down to hers. She was relishing what had just taken place. How could she have come so far, land a job doing what she loved, and be sharing a bed with such a beautiful woman who could bring her to such intense ecstasy? *Am I falling...falling for her?*

"We should get some sleep," Morgan whispered. "We have a rehearsal in the afternoon. You have to be in top form."

"Do I? I can be on top?"

"Anytime you want." Morgan lay down beside her and wrapped Jordan in her arms. "Now let's get some sleep. Dream of me."

"All the time," Jordan said as they both drifted off.

Jordan began to dream of Morgan as they floated through a starry galaxy, wrapped in each other's arms. She began dreaming of being drawn into another scene. She could feel Morgan caressing her, kissing her as they moved through the luminous colors. Their bodies rolled through the colors, bending and stretching. Warmth was all around them, and yet a gentle breeze cooled them. Their bodies fell deeper and deeper into the abyss as Morgan's lips began to meld to hers. She could feel her emotions, her desires. She knew what she wanted. She reached for her and pulled her close. Their bodies began to melt, twisting and blending together. They were one. There was no comparison to this moment.

CHAPTER ELEVEN

S unday morning, Jordan woke first and rolled over to look at the long naked body beside her.

Oh, what I wouldn't love to do to that body. She pictured how Morgan would look tied across the bed and how it would feel to cause that perfect skin to ripple with pain. Wasn't that what she wanted? Yes, last night had been phenomenal and at times, was better than anything she'd experienced in a BDSM scene, but could she have taken Morgan to that place? Did she reach the point of submission? *Perhaps not because I didn't get to make love to her and bring her to where I went last night.* How could she persuade Morgan that it wasn't what she thought? There weren't any tools around. Did Morgan have any men's neckties? Those could work.

She got out of bed and rummaged through Morgan's closet. She found a necktie and a bathrobe sash. She brought them back to the bed and sat there examining them.

"You're concentrating on something. I can feel it," she heard beside her.

"I want to prove to you that BDSM isn't abusive."

"You do, eh?"

"Yes. Do you trust me?"

Morgan rolled over to face her. "What are you going to do?"

"Whatever you let me. You're in charge."

"How does that work? Doesn't the Mistress just tell the sub what she's going to do?"

"No, a good Domme will negotiate everything first so they both know what might happen, what to expect. I'll suggest some things and explain how they work, and you can say yes or no."

"Then how does it happen when you see the sub frightened and not knowing what's going to happen?"

"It was negotiated: scare me but don't do this or that. You can do X all you want, but just a little of Y and none of Z." She looked into Morgan's eyes. Would she really be interested? Did Morgan really trust her now? They'd only made love a few times, but it had been fantastic every time. Now Morgan might accept something more? "I loved to have needles put under my skin, but when I got too zoned, it would scare me, and I'd have to stop."

"Zoned?"

"It's when you get a little 'out there.' Sort of like being stoned but with none of the smoke or powder to cause it. You're really not aware of what's happening around you. That's when your Mistress better take care of you. She put you out there. She has to bring you back. Sometimes, it just takes a few words or being held or even a drink of water. Sometimes, it takes a lot of love. It's called 'aftercare.' It's like holding your child when she's had a dream, good or bad. Cuddling, soothing, whatever is needed."

"And you think of this every time?"

"If your Mistress is a good Mistress, yes. Definitely."

"Wow. I thought the candles or the whips or the chains just started. Like, get on the bed and spread them."

"Sometimes it does, but it's been negotiated. Like, you can yell at me, but don't dis my mother or my dog," Jordan said.

Morgan shook her head and thought it through. This was nothing like what she had experienced in the past. Was Jordan for real, or was she just trying to persuade her to go back into a lifestyle that had hurt her in so many ways?

"That sounds totally against what I've heard." Morgan said.

"Since that straight book that calls itself BDSM came out, there's a lot of misunderstanding, or maybe it's really like that in the straight community, but I wouldn't know. It's definitely not like that in the LGBTQ, etc. one."

Morgan frowned. She had read the book Jordan spoke of, and it definitely wasn't anything like she had experienced when she had been part of the scene. Her past was so painful and never had been consensual. *So Jordan is saying this is supposed to be a safe, consensual exchange of sexual power? To trust a partner who has total control? But how?* "How can I give total control to you and still be able to stop it if I no longer like it?"

Jordan seemed shocked at how Morgan continued to question her. Like she hadn't expected Morgan to be open about it at all. "Okay, then. First of all, choose a safe word. Any word that you can remember easily, but you wouldn't normally say in a conversation. I have a friend who uses Philadelphia because it's her home and makes her feel safe. I have another friend who uses pecan because she loves pecan pie, and it makes her feel good."

Morgan felt a blush and thought for a moment, then awkwardly said, "Pembroke."

Jordan raised her eyebrows.

"The first time I lived with a woman was on Pembroke Street here in Boston, in the south end."

"You'll have to show me where it is sometime."

Morgan nodded.

"All right, if something feels wrong, you don't want to do it, or it's too much for you, you say Pembroke, and I will stop and release any bonds. No matter where we are in the scene, Pembroke will stop it right there. Your safe word means I *must* release you immediately. No questions asked. Except to ask if you are all right. Is that okay?"

"Yes, it sounds good." Morgan was easing into the rules being set before her. Her heart was pumping harder as she thought about the possible scenes she could be placed into. Could she fully trust Jordan to keep her promise and stop if she used her safe word? Was she letting her move too fast?

Jordan said, "And you need a *slow down* word. It's not a stop word, just a *give me a moment to catch my breath* word. Most people use yellow."

"Okay, yellow sounds good. But can I still spank you afterward?" Morgan wanted to test the waters and see if Jordan was willing to let her play the role of Mistress, too.

Jordan leaned in and kissed her. "You can do anything you want to me afterward. We'll see if you still want to then."

"Let me go make a pot of coffee," Morgan said as she slowly slipped from Jordan's lips. "Then you can tell me all about this negotiation business.

"You're on." Jordan taunted as she drew the necktie between the palms of her hands.

Fifteen minutes later, the coffee was made, and Morgan had buttered toasted English muffins and brought it all up to the bedroom. They sat and drank coffee and ate and talked.

"So it really isn't just the Mistress doing whatever she wants?"

"Well, sometimes it is, but it's all negotiated beforehand. A negotiation can take hours. Usually, we start with a long list of BDSM activities and the sub puts them in three categories. A, things she'll do or accept; B, things she'll think about, but she wants to know more about before she tries them; and C, things she never wants to try under any circumstances. Then there are lists of limits. You've already said that you will not accept emotional abuse. So that's a no-no in list C. That will include no shaming, embarrassment, humiliation, disgrace, or anything like that. I won't even swear at you...unless you want me to." Jordan grinned. "I had on mine: no marks where they'd show because I couldn't go to school with rope marks on my wrists or whip marks that couldn't be covered up with a sleeve or shirt. And don't use the word bitch. My mother called any woman who didn't agree with her a bitch. It became a sore spot when I was young."

Jordan paused to see if Morgan would have a reaction to what she had just said. When Morgan only took another sip of coffee, Jordan continued.

"These lists can go on and on. And these can be anything. I had a friend once that had on her contract that she couldn't be prevented from watching Jeopardy at least once a day. She was that much a fanatic about it. It can go down to household chores if you're living together. Who does the cooking and who does the dishes? When does that change? What can't be mentioned in front of your mother or at work? Anything can be negotiated. And it can come down to details. If you're responsible for doing dishes, then when must they be done, how soon after you finish eating, and what's the penalty if they're not done according to the negotiated rules?"

"Holy cow. This is totally not what I thought it was. Is everything like that?"

"To some extent. If you live separately and your Mistress summons you, how long can you wait before going to her? What's the penalty for showing up late? How many times can you get a penalty before she finally is done with you and releases you from the contract?"

Morgan sat absorbing all of that. She seemed to find it fascinating.

"But since you're new to all this and aren't sure if you want to continue with it, let's start with something simple. Can I make love to you while you're tied to the bed?"

Morgan considered that for several seconds. "Okay, we can start with that."

"With or without a mask?"

"Without. Definitely no mask. I want to watch you do all this." They both broke out into big smiles. Jordan felt her heart begin to race as she realized Morgan was going to allow her to perform *some* bondage on her. She had to make sure everything went smoothly so Morgan felt safe and enjoyed the experience.

"Okay, handcuffs, rope, or something softer or stiffer?"

"You have handcuffs with you?"

"No. I left my handcuffs at the Loft, but if we're negotiating, it might as well cover everything."

"All right, let's try something softer this time."

"Hands only or hands and feet?"

Morgan laughed. "Oh, what the hell, let's do both."

"Is there any sexual act you don't want me to do?"

"Yes. No rimming."

"Anything that sexually turns you on?"

"Will you be naked?"

"That can be a condition."

"Good, I want you naked."

"Anything else?"

"Will you rub your body all over me?"

"I can consider that. And?"

"That's all I can think of…at least right now."

"Tongue work and penetration are okay?" Jordan asked.

"Of course."

"Can I fist you?"

Morgan chuckled. "Sure. *She* used to fist me all the time."

"Any tools?"

"Do we need them?"

"No, not this time," Jordan said.

Morgan agreed.

"Tickling?"

"Uh…"

"Okay, no tickling *this* time."

"Did we just take all the romance out of it?" Morgan asked.

"No honey, I'll still be as romantic as possible."

"All right, whenever you're ready."

"Before or after our practice session? Or do you want to skip it today?"

"Let's say we'll skip it until something goes wrong, and we're left with nothing to do," Morgan said.

"Sounds good to me. I know just what I'm going to do. Let's take a shower first."

"Together?"

"Remember, after the scene starts, there'll be no way you can touch me," Jordan said.

"Oh God. That will be the hardest."

"Maybe."

They got up, selected some ties that would work, and went into the bathroom. Morgan turned the shower on. When she was sure the temperature was right, she made a sweeping gesture. "After you, m'lady."

Jordan stepped under the shower. Morgan got in behind her and started washing her hair. Then she started to lather her shoulders, her arms, back and her breasts. She took extra special care of every aspect of the nipples.

Jordan took some soap and started to wash Morgan's chest and belly. "If we spend too much time in here, the floor will get slippery, and we'll be sliding all over the place."

"And by then, we'll be in cold water."

"Then let's make sure you're spotless," Jordan said. "I will not have a dirty sub."

"Ooo, what I'm going to do to you afterward," Morgan said as she rinsed Jordan.

"That's assuming you're able."

"I'll always be able to take care of your needs," Morgan bragged.

Jordan merely looked at her with a sly smile. They finally got out of the shower, dried off and blew their hair dry. "Now, Ms. Sparks, on the bed and spread those long legs."

"Yes, Mistress," Morgan crawled onto the bed and lay down.

Jordan stood at the foot of the bed as Morgan seductively positioned herself in the center, belly up with her legs spread wide, exposing her womanhood. Just the way in which Morgan was presenting herself made Jordan's heart flutter. She almost stammered and forgot her role.

Jordan moved to the head of the bed and began to tie Morgan's wrist to the bed post. "Is that too tight?" she asked.

Morgan flexed her fists. "Not yet," she said.

"That's, not yet, *Mistress*. You can't be rude to someone who has you tied up."

"Of course not...Mistress."

Jordan walked to the opposite side of the bed and finished the second wrist, then started on the ankles. Soon, she stood back and assessed the whole scene. "Oh, my heart. I didn't think I'd ever see this. Where's my phone? I want a picture of this."

"No! Pembroke on the pictures," Morgan said right away.

"No pictures? How will you remember?"

"I'll probably never forget."

Jordan laughed as she crawled onto the bed. She sat beside Morgan. "Now, let me see. Where should I start?" She slowly and lightly walked her fingers up and down Morgan's body.

"I thought we said no tickling," Morgan said.

"You call this tickling? You really have been away for a few years. Try this."

She ran her nails up and down Morgan's body, lightly at first, and then she came to her belly button. "You have a real innie. How far down does it go?" She poked her tongue down in there and pressed hard. Morgan shifted slightly. "Don't like that?"

"I can feel it all the way down to my crotch."

"Really?" She got up on her knees and leaned over Morgan, took her face between her hands and planted a kiss there. She pressed hard, her tongue going as deep as possible. She could see Morgan's eyes rolling back and closing. She worked her way to the nipples. She ran her teeth over the areola until it was hard and puckered, then flicked the tight nipples back and forth with her tongue. They could have cut glass they were so clenched and sharp. Morgan let out a moan, and her body wrenched within the binds of the ties. *This is where I've wanted to take her. Yes, baby. Go for it. Move to the zone. I will protect you. I will not hurt you. All I want to do is love you and take you there.* She lay her entire body over Morgan's and slid up and down her torso, her tits rubbing back and forth against Morgan's body.

"What I would do to you if my hands were free right now," Morgan whispered in between gasps of pleasured moans.

"But they're not," said Jordan, planting a kiss on Morgan's nose. "And you didn't address me properly." She straddled Morgan and slid her crotch up and down Morgan's body so she could feel the heat and the moisture between her legs. Jordan was very turned on and exceedingly wet. Morgan was no doubt wrenching with the urge to touch her, maybe even contemplating using her safe word in order to do just that.

Jordan mouthed her way down Morgan's sides, nibbling and biting, scraping with her teeth as she went along.

"You wouldn't believe all the things I want to do to counteract these feelings," Morgan mumbled. "Mistress. I want to turn you over and press you into the bed."

Finally, Jordan reached the area between Morgan's legs. "This is where *I* want to be," she said. "Right here." She flicked her tongue over the hardening clit. She breathed on it and flicked it again and again. She slid just one finger into her. "Oh, you are so wet," she said. "Are you turned on?"

"Fuck yes. You know I am," said Morgan, her voice not at all steady. "Damn these ropes. I need to touch you."

"Mistress?"

"Yes, I'm fucking turned on, *Mistress*," she spat.

"Now, now. That's no way to address your Mistress. Are you getting too unstable?"

"Oh, fuck."

Jordan ran her tongue over a nipple. "Such language."

Between the ties and the fact that she was lying on one of her legs, Jordan sensed Morgan was going crazy wanting to move, to touch her. And on top of that, the kiss had caused another problem.

"My nose is itchy. It's driving me crazy," Morgan said, wrinkling it back and forth.

"Well, I can do one of two things. A, I could scratch it for you or B, I could do something to another part of your body so you won't notice it. Hmm." Jordan looked into Morgan's face with a sly grin. "I think B would be much more fun." She slid two fingers into Morgan's pussy and lowered her head so she could suck that little clit into her mouth.

Back and forth she moved, first with the tip of her tongue and then with the flat of it. She worked it and worked it until she felt Morgan's body begin to push into her, then she stopped. "Are you trying to come? I haven't finished yet, and you haven't asked permission. I want to do a whole lot more to you. Are you trying to stop me?"

Morgan seemed in that zone where she was balancing on needles and right on the edge of coming. Her eyes were dilated and her breathing erratic. Slowly, Jordan slipped her fingers out. She let some of the sensations calm down a little. She watched Morgan carefully as her body began to relax. Jordan then placed her hand back on her clit and began bringing Morgan back into the zone. Morgan pulled at the ties as she begged Jordan to release her hands, to release her orgasm. Then Jordan replaced her fingers with her whole fist.

"Oh God," Morgan moaned. Her body bucked up and down as Jordan's fist closed and opened and closed and opened.

"Come, Morgan, come now," Jordan commanded.

Morgan arched off the bed. Her body was trembling, every muscle seemingly twitching with activity. Jordan slowly withdrew her hand then crawled upward so she could put little kisses all over Morgan's face. She gently ran her hand down Morgan's chest, letting her hand settle over one breast until the nipple was flaccid again, Morgan was still breathing heavily and every few seconds muscles would twitch on different parts of her body.

It took Morgan quite a while to recover. Meanwhile, Jordan undid all of the bindings. She crawled next to Morgan and pressed close to her. Morgan's eyes were closed. Jordan was sure she slept for several minutes.

Morgan slowly rolled her head over to look at Jordan. "Hello," she said softly.

"Hello," Jordan said as she reached up to push a lock of Morgan's hair back into place. "How are you?"

"Wow, I'm still coming down."

"Yes, it takes a while. I can do a lot more when you're not fighting me."

"You drove me crazy. My whole body was on fire. I have never been taken that far. It's a place my body's never been. I wanted to touch you so very badly."

"Hmm," Jordan said. "You've never touched me badly before." She gave a cute little turned-up smile.

Morgan reached for her and then realized the bindings were gone. She examined her hands, then pulled Jordan over. "You are a rabid little minx, aren't you?"

"I have my days. I told you, whatever you want me to be."

"And now I can have my day," Morgan said. She pulled Jordan on top of her and pulled her head down into a long hard kiss.

"Ms. Sparks," Jordan said. "If I didn't know better, I'd say you were trying to eat me."

"Of course I am. I can't let you have all the fun."

"Didn't you have fun?"

"Oh, I had something, but I wouldn't actually describe it as fun."

"Oh, dear."

"No. This will be the fun part." She rolled Jordan off her and placed her on her stomach. Then she sat up and started to spank Jordan's rear.

"I thought you were kidding." Jordan gasped as the spanking continued.

Morgan admired the bright red blooming on Jordan's rump. "No, babe, I seldom make threats I don't intend to keep."

Jordan reached back to feel her butt. "Now, I'll remember you all the way home."

Morgan glanced over at the clock. It was 4:15. "Damn, it's that late already?"

"Time flies when you're having fun."

"Stay for dinner?"

"I could do that."

"Do you like Chinese?" Morgan asked.

"Definitely. That, Japanese, or Thai."

"Great, and stay the night again?"

"Stay again?"

"I might need aftercare. Actually, when I'm done with you, you'll need aftercare."

"Oh, no." Jordan sank back in mock horror.

"Oh, yes. Hahaha." She imitated a cartoon villain. "I'll get you, my lovely." She lay Jordan out on the bed and covered her with her body. After a long, deep kiss, she started going up and down Jordan's torso.

CHAPTER TWELVE

The next week, everything went very well, and on Saturday, Morgan invited Jordan back to her house. They made love but didn't try any BDSM. Jordan again stayed Sunday night. It became the normal Saturday night to Monday morning routine.

Finally, one Wednesday, during a break, Morgan went out into the entryway where Jordan was stationed by the hostess desk.

"Hi," she said.

"Hello." Jordan felt cheery. Then she saw a shadow in Morgan's eyes. "You look disturbed. Bad day at the office?"

"Can you take a break for a few minutes?"

"Sure. Let me go tell Paul." What was wrong? Had something happened? She went back into the office to talk to Paul, then came back and drew Morgan into a small side room they used for breaks. "What's wrong?"

"Well, I seem to have a problem."

"What, sweetie? Can I help?" She tried to assess the worried look in Morgan's eyes.

"Yes, you can. I seem to have a hard time sleeping. Monday and last night, I just rolled around and rolled around. It's been happening a lot lately during the weeknights. The last two nights, I had to get up and go make myself a drink. I paced both nights. It wasn't until this morning that I realized the reason."

"Are you sick?"

"Yes. I'm very sick." She paused to look into Jordan's eyes. "I'm sick of sleeping alone. You're going to have to move in to cure me."

Jordan went wild with excitement. Had she heard her right? But... "I don't know," she said. "That almost sounds like we'd be in a relationship."

"Yes. I thought of that, but there's no other cure. I researched it all day."

"Are you sure?"

Morgan nodded. "I'm very sure."

Jordan smiled. "Well, I hate the thought of you being sick, so I guess we could try it...for a while, until you're cured."

"I might never be cured." Morgan pulled her into a deep passionate kiss. They both pulled back and looked into each other's eyes. "Tonight?" Morgan asked.

"I'll leave here before you do and run home to get some clothes for tomorrow. I'll meet you back at your house."

Morgan stopped. "Our house." She dug in her pocket and handed Jordan a key.

"Our house," Jordan confirmed.

Just then, Robbie stuck her head in the door. "Break's over?"

"Okay." Morgan kissed Jordan once more. "See you later." And went back to the piano.

Jordan watched her walk away. That was a big step forward and on a Wednesday? She didn't wait till the weekend? They'd still have to take it slowly. She couldn't trust that this was real. *Give it time.*

That week, Jordan made the move slowly. Morgan moved some of her clothes into the other bedroom to make room for Jordan's. Most of Jordan's clothes that she wore for work made the move, but she still wasn't sure Morgan knew what she was doing.

Back in Cambridge, she cornered Carole one morning before work. "You're not around much," Carole said.

"No. Morgan asked me to move in with her, but I need to take it slowly. I'll be sleeping at her house every night, but I still want to pay rent here. I won't leave you in the lurch. I'm not sure how this is going to go. I'll leave my bed and dresser here, too, so if someone has a guest, they can use it."

"That's very nice of you. I hope it works out with Morgan. She seems nice."

"Thanks. She hasn't lived with anyone for fifteen years so I know she doesn't know what she's getting into."

"Well, hon. Good luck, and if you decide to completely move, let us know."

"And if you find someone that you all want to move in, let *me* know." Carole turned to leave for work.

Jordan gathered an armload of clothes to take to her car. *Wow. I just moved in, and now I'm in between moves again. I hope they leave this little room open for a while until I know Morgan is going to be able to handle having someone living with her full time.*

Saturday night, when they were getting ready to go to the restaurant, Jordan said, "It was nice of you to completely clear out my side of the closet, but I moved some of your things back. You have a lot more clothes than me, so I spread yours out. I noticed you had a couple dresses in there. I've never seen you in a dress. I've never even imagined you in a dress."

Morgan laughed. "I don't wear them. I had to buy them for a realtor's convention a few years ago. I just never threw them out. If you want them, you can have them."

"I'd love to see you in one of them."

"That won't happen. They're awkward."

"Maybe we can use them in a Leather scene sometime." Jordan smirked.

"I thought abuse was on the never list."

"Is awkward an abuse?"

"It is when it's me, babe. Don't ever try to force me to wear a dress. Please?"

Jordan pulled her over to her and took her face between her hands. She knew that Morgan was very sensitive about her appearance and definitely prided herself on her image. "No, I will never do that to you, not in play or in private. Why don't we drive down to the donation store and get rid of them?"

Morgan leaned in and kissed her. "You can go through anything here except the stuff in the other bedroom and cull whatever you think we don't need. Just stay out of my music."

"No problem, honey. No problem at all."

Jordan gathered the dresses and some old shirts that Morgan never wore and on their way to the restaurant that evening, stopped at the donation box and threw them in with a sigh. *Perhaps I should cleanse my house by throwing out some old things in my past. It seems to be helping Morgan move forward and accept and try new things. The other night was incredible, and now, she's asked me to move in with her? Maybe this is the beginning of a new relationship, a new life, a new start. Baby steps, Jordan, baby steps.*

CHAPTER THIRTEEN

Have you ever been tied up?" Morgan asked as they were getting ready for bed that night.

"Sure. A good Mistress never does anything to a submissive that they have never tried themselves. It serves two purposes. The first is to assure safety and the limits during play. The second is to find out what about the act is enjoyable. For instance, the way you were tied the other night, I had complete access to your body, and you had no ability to stop me or prevent me from doing anything I wanted. That is the excitement because I could make you come to the edge of orgasm and then stop and let you squirm, your body aching for me to continue. But I was in control and continued when I was ready. When I saw you were coming down, then I could tease you back into the frenzy, again and again. And yes, it is one of the most fascinating forms of bondage one can experience. The inability to control your own desire and timing."

"Really?"

"Of course."

"Are all Dommes like that?"

"Unfortunately, no, but they should be. How can you know how hard to hit someone with a three-foot quirt unless you've been hit with one so you know how hard is okay or how hard is over the top?"

"So you've had everything done to you?"

"Anything I'd do to someone else, I've had done to me." Jordan thought back to the candling with Lacey. *Except being burned, I've never been burned, nor do I ever want to be or want to ever experience that again.*

"When was the last time someone tied you up?"

Jordan stopped to think. "With ropes? At least thirteen years ago, I think. Maybe fourteen"

"Thirteen years? Were you still in college?"

"I was a sophomore. It was in the fall." Jordan hadn't thought of those days in a long time. Mistress Heather. That bossy Domme. It had only lasted a few months. "I was working at a music store the summer between my freshman and sophomore years at UIUC. I'd met her at a Leather club play party. She came on real strong and had me collared before the school year started."

"Collared? I thought you said that was a very serious commitment, akin to marriage."

"It's also a sign of ownership."

"She owned you? Was that what you wanted?"

"At the time, I wasn't sure what I wanted. I'd gone through my entire freshman year barely dating, and those I did date were all very vanilla. I just spent that year studying, reading, and practicing. I'd been so lonely. I mean, I got great grades, and I progressed a lot in my singing, but that was about all. There was no one important in my life, no one who made me feel special. So when school let out, I had decided not to go home for the summer. I found a job and got a small temporary living space and began searching for something to fill my social life.

"Then I finally found a Leather club in a nearby town, and I was there every chance I got. I was impressed by the scene. There were play activities most nights so I got a feel for the action and what it was like to be a submissive in an open environment. It was when Mistress Heather, one of the major Dommes in the club, showed some interest in me, I grabbed hold of it. I thought she would take me into her life and teach me the ropes, and my sexual fantasies would be answered. She was taller and a little heavier than me, and she had a lot of power.

"She moved me into her apartment, collared me, and basically told me everything to do, where to go, what to think."

"Good heavens. That doesn't sound like you."

"Well, back then, I thought it *was* me. I had grown up with my sister Judy telling me everything to do. But being away from home for that year and having to make all my decisions myself was out of my comfort zone. So when Mistress Heather took over my life, it seemed right. Then my grades started to slip, and all my professors noticed. My mentor took me aside and asked what was wrong. Of course, I couldn't admit the Leather thing, so I said it was my living arrangements. By then, I was in jeopardy of losing my scholarship. I knew I had to break away from her. So I took the collar off and gave it back to her, packed all my stuff, and moved back on campus. That's when I met Robbie."

"She wasn't mad?"

"Well, I explained it all so she'd understand. She wasn't happy, but she didn't fight it."

"Wow. So you weren't a Domme your whole life?"

"No, for the first two and a half years, I was very submissive. Then I decided to take back my life and be in charge of it. I guess that's when I realized I had an inner power side that was just waiting to come out. I enjoyed being submissive, but my mind craved control."

"Which do you prefer?"

"With almost everyone, I choose to be on top. I love to dominate everyone...well, almost everyone. It fills my creative side when I have to think of a new scene to play."

"You said *almost everyone*."

"Yes, there are some women who make me want to fall to my knees and others I want to joust with to see who'll come out on top."

"And me? Do I make you want to fall to your knees?"

"Well," she said with a small smile. "That first night, yes, definitely. I would have done anything you asked. Then I found that you weren't the least bit Leather, so that made me want to test myself against you."

"Really? How?"

"To see if I could break down that ten-foot barrier you'd created around yourself."

Morgan wrapped her arms around her. "And you certainly did that." She planted her lips on Jordan's. It lasted quite a while. "And what would you say if I wanted to tie you to the bed?"

Jordan thought for a moment. "Well." She hadn't been on bottom in years. Although she really didn't mind, her thoughts kept picturing Morgan in her control. *You have to relax and let her play out her fantasies. Let her bring you to the zone. You haven't been there in forever.*

"I let you tie me," Morgan reminded her.

"Then I guess it's only fair."

Morgan pressed her down on the bed. "Now what did we do with those ties?"

"We really don't need them, you know. I've been trained to behave without restraints."

"Really?"

"Yes, you just have to throw me into submission."

"Throw you into submission?"

"Yes, get my mind into that space where you're the boss of me."

"And how do I do that."

"Are you ready for it?"

Morgan nodded. "Are *you*?"

"Yes, please, Mistress. Wrap your hand around my throat and stare into my eyes as if you want me right this moment. Let me feel that you're in charge. Then place me where you want me and tell me not to move."

"That's all? Just like that?"

"Basically, yes, there are a few other things, but you'll find them. Now, my safe word is Camelot."

"Really?"

"Yes, I was in that show when I met my first Mistress."

"I wish I could have seen that."

"I was in high school."

"You were doing Leather in high school?"

"Yes, I know. I wasn't underage, but I shouldn't have been doing any of that. We'll discuss it someday. It's a long story."

"All right. Now, how do I start this?"

"Just give me a moment to get out of my Domme mode, and then I'm yours."

Jordan closed her eyes and breathed deeply for a moment. *You can do this. This is Morgan, no one else. You've wanted to belong to her for weeks. Slow your breathing. Think of being bound, hands to ankles on either side of your body, your ass in the air.* She took several more deep breaths and then looked at Morgan.

"Okay. I'm ready," she said.

Morgan kissed her gently, then reached up and grasped Jordan's throat. She stared into her eyes. "Yes, I want you totally. All of you." she whispered.

Jordan's eyes half closed, and her hands went limp in her lap. Her head fell forward into the hand that was taking ownership of her. She felt her body giving way to compliance, drifting to this sweet realm of tenderness and protection. It was like being wrapped in a cocoon of silky softness, and she had left the room, floating in a headspace far, far away. She was owned from this moment. She relinquished her whole body, mind, and soul to that hand, to Morgan.

"Let's put these up here," Morgan said, stretching Jordan's hands toward the bedposts. "Do not move," she whispered. "You belong to me now, all of you, totally."

"Yes, Mistress," Jordan whispered without realizing she was responding. Yes, she was ready. She'd given herself, all of her, without limitation. This felt right. It felt complete.

She felt Morgan's hand start down the sides of her torso. Her whole body reached out to meet those hands as they burned into her. Little by little, every touch, every finger, and every breath felt like a brand that burned into her soul. Yes, tonight, more than ever, she belonged to Morgan.

Morgan licked around her right areola and then her left one. Jordan strained to get her nipples into Morgan's line of sight. *Yes, take whatever you want*, Jordan said silently.

Morgan's mouth started slowly down Jordan's body until she was right over Jordan's clit. She blew on it, and Jordan's body reacted by starting to curl into a ball. She wanted to reach down and pull Morgan's face into her, but Morgan stopped and looked up at her, and Jordan relaxed back into her previous position. No, she wouldn't fight this at all. She'd given up control. She'd take whatever Morgan wanted to give her, and she'd relinquish whatever Morgan wanted to take.

Morgan sucked the clit into her mouth and massaged it with her tongue. Slowly, her fingers slid inside.

"Oh, yes," Jordan moaned. Her body stretched out toward Morgan, the space between her legs getting wider and wider.

"And that is what I want," Morgan said, letting the words vibrate on Jordan's clit, causing Jordan to shiver. "All of this. Don't come yet. I want even more. I may make you come a hundred times," Morgan commanded. Her hand reached in farther.

"Please," Jordan said.

Morgan reached inside and out until Jordan started to shake. "Yes, let it out," she said, and her hand rubbed and rubbed.

Jordan's body stiffened as her release shuddered through her. She started to relax, but Morgan didn't back away. Instead, she pushed farther in until her entire hand was inside.

"Come on, baby, one more time. I've got you. You can do it." Her tongue worked Jordan's clit as her fist stretched and relaxed and stretched and relaxed. She drove Jordan to ecstasy, stretching her inside and drawing her clit with her tongue. Jordan's body wrenched as she grabbed at the sheets and pillows to keep her hands in the imaginary binds.

Jordan was out of her mind. Every fiber in her body was in spasm; her whole body was about to burst into thousands of tiny pieces, all scattered across the bed. The hand balled within her reached for her soul, then squeezed it into as tight a ball as it could. Jordan was already into another zone where pleasure and pain were so close together that there was no room for anything else.

She felt the tension building and building and building. Morgan pushed and pushed, teased and teased.

"Morgan," Jordan screamed as her entire being erupted.

Morgan withdrew her mouth and hand and reached up to gather Jordan into her arms. She held her tightly as she came, every muscle twitching and jerking.

"Good God," Jordan managed to say.

"Yes, her, too."

Morgan gathered her tightly into her arms and kissed her deeply. They clung to each other as Jordan calmed down and began to relish what she had just experienced. She felt Morgan's warm body next to hers and could smell the sweet smell of after-sex in the air. This was what she had wanted, to give herself completely to Morgan. Morgan had taken her there, and she had taken Morgan. Trust was building. A relationship was happening. Was this her future? She drew in a deep sigh, pulled Morgan's arm around her, and let the night drift away.

CHAPTER FOURTEEN

F all and winter flew by, with beautiful eastern fall foliage giving way to snowy winter days. Everything was going well. The holidays meant new material would have to be added, so Morgan and Jordan worked hard to get the celebratory songs in place.

Spring also went very well. Morgan seemed more relaxed, and the relationship between her and Jordan was nesting in quite nicely. Morgan had said she'd developed a newly found trust in Jordan that she had never had when she was younger. She'd said it was so different now and that Jordan had never once made her feel she couldn't trust her during their bondage play. And the sex, it was so passionate, so fresh and new every time.

The band even added a few new pieces that Morgan or Jordan had written. A few weeks into April, a tall man with curly black hair came up to Jordan after the final set. But when he talked about booking the band, she said Morgan did the management and was right behind him when he went to speak with Morgan,

"I'm Stan Weltz. I was very impressed by your sound tonight. Is this the full size of the group, just the four of you?"

"Usually, yes," Morgan said, "but we do have others that join us from time to time, depending on the venue."

"I'm in charge of getting entertainment for a rather large convention in Chicago the third weekend in August. I've been following Jordan's career for a while."

"People outside California know of me?" Jordan asked. "They know where I am?" Jordan felt panic. Her heart sunk into her stomach. She looked at Morgan, hoping her sorrow showed. She never meant for her past to follow her here, especially through any well-known organizations with conventions. This could cause a collapse of the whole band and the restaurant.

"Yes, Jordan, there are quite a few people who have been looking for you. It took us a while, but someone finally found you on the band's website. There were some who were watching your career even before you were identified as Leather. Your unfortunate experience in California put you on a lot of people's radar. I think there may be a lot of changes falling into place for you very soon."

Jordan took a step back as Morgan talked to him.

"I'd like to hire your group to entertain at the International Leather Consortium convention," he said.

"The International Leather Consortium!" Jordan said.

"Jordan's experience in California should be told to the entire Leather community. What a magnificent talent has been suppressed because of a misunderstanding of our lifestyle."

"Just what do you want us to do?" Morgan asked.

"Would you do a complete concert on that Saturday night and maybe a short teaser at the banquet on Friday evening?"

"We'd have to increase the band to do a concert," Morgan said. "It's not like playing two or three sets at a club. Then there is Jordan. This would be opening up a whole can of worms for her and the band, as well as the restaurant. Few know about her leather lifestyle today, and it's not like the whole community knows her or what happened in California. Not everyone would be as accepting as this Leather association. First and foremost are Jordan's thoughts on this. Then we have to discuss it with the band and others who are close to us. Finally, there will be the details of the performances. Let us talk about it and get back with you."

"Give me a call when you decide what you need, and we'll start the process."

No, this can't be happening. Jordan's breath was catching in her throat. She felt like she should cry or scream, but she didn't know which one.

Leaving Morgan to talk with Stan, she went outside and paced around Morgan's car. This was the worst thing she had heard in over a year. She had tried to stay out of the limelight, but now people wanted her to flaunt it?

Morgan finally came out and unlocked the car. She got into the driver's seat. Jordan got in the other side, and they drove out of the lot.

"So what do you think?" Morgan asked. "Wouldn't that be exciting? An international convention. Weltz says once everyone hears us...or hears you, we'll probably get jobs all around the world. Isn't that wonderful?"

"No," Jordan said softly.

"And he said that once everyone hears your story..." She seemed to realize what Jordan had said. "No?"

"No. I came here to get away from that, not to advertise it."

"But people will get to hear your side. And once they see and hear what was almost lost, everyone will be behind you."

Jordan sat there watching the road go by. She didn't say anything.

"Don't you want to do it?"

"No, I don't want to be reminded. I don't want to live with it again. Don't you see, it will be the Leather community supporting a Domme who wasn't safe and who burned and permanently disabled her submissive. She worked in a school with children while participating in a dark lifestyle, but boy, can she sing! Never mind what she did and who she was. She can sing. You want to take that chance? Having the straight community hear this and not understand, then coming after you like a witch hunt?"

"Honey—"

"No, I won't go through that again. I lost my job and my honor. People were laughing at me. Parents were pulling their kids away from me. My students were making fun of me. I can't go through that again." She looked over at Morgan. "I *won't* go through that again. I should never have let you put me on the website. I knew it was trouble."

There was silence for a few minutes.

"I should have kept going up to Vermont and found a place out in the woods where I could have peace and quiet," Jordan said. "Or maybe during the winter, I could freeze to death."

"Honey, no," Morgan said.

"Honey, yes."

They pulled up the driveway and into the garage. "Let's get a good night's sleep. This will look better in the morning." Morgan held her hand out until Jordan got out of the car, then she pulled Jordan close to her. "Sweetheart, you don't have to do anything you don't want to. I'll call him and tell him we respectfully decline the offer, and I'll take your name off the website.

"The info is already out there. If he found it, there's no telling who else already did, too."

Morgan squeezed her hands as she led her into the house and up to the bedroom. She drew her into a tight hug as they crawled into bed, but Jordan stayed stiff and tense.

The next morning, Morgan woke up alone.

She called for Jordan, but there was no answer. She got up and looked through the house, but Jordan wasn't there. She went out to the garage. Jordan's car was gone. A sudden knot grew in her stomach. *Did I push her too far? Oh, please, don't let this be the beginning of the end.*

She pulled out her phone and called Jordan. There was no answer, so she texted her: *Good morning, honey. Where did you go?*

She waited for an answer while she made a pot of coffee. She made herself breakfast, but she just sat there toying with it and looking through the morning's news. There was still no reply. Had she left for good? Morgan felt tears pooling up in her eyes. Adrenaline started to flow. Where in the hell could Jordan be?

When there had been no answer by two o'clock, Morgan called Robbie.

"Yo, Morg," she answered. "What's up?"

"You haven't heard from Jordan today, have you?"

"No, why should I?"

"Well, I thought she might have come to you. She's missing."

"What?"

"I woke up this morning, and she wasn't here. Her car was gone."

"Damn."

"And I called and texted her but didn't get an answer. I'm becoming frantic. I figured she would at least let me know she's all right."

"Did you two have a fight?"

"No, but she was upset about that guy last night who wanted to hire us to appear at a Leather convention. She said she came here to disappear, but if he could find her, everyone else could, too."

"And you don't know where she'd go?"

"No. Do you? She kept saying she should have continued up into Vermont." Morgan moved to the bar and began pouring herself a short drink.

"Vermont? Well, at least Vermont is a small state. It's not like looking for her in Texas or Alaska."

"Yeah. Big help."

"If we clog her phone with phone calls and messages, she might respond to one of us."

"And she might not. I don't even know if she has her phone with her."

"I'll see if Chelsea will call her friends. Maybe Jordan went back to the Cambridge house."

"Thanks, Rob. I didn't know what else to do."

"Okay. Give me a few minutes." The phone went dead.

Morgan sent a text: *Please honey, let me know you're all right. We don't have to do anything you don't want. Please tell me where you are.*

That one didn't get answered either. *Shit, what's the matter with you, Morgan? Couldn't you just leave it alone? Why didn't you see that she was upset and clearly didn't want to take on this gig? You pressed and pressed her because you don't have a past that can keep haunting you and destroying you. What a fool I've been. I've let her slip away, and I may never get her back.*

"Yes, she stopped at Cambridge early this morning," Robbie reported to Morgan around three o'clock. "She took her pillow and a blanket and asked the quickest way to get to Vermont. Carol told her to take I-90 west to I-91 north."

That's what Morgan had feared. When she heard that, her chest hurt so badly she was afraid she was having a heart attack. Nothing seemed right. She couldn't eat dinner, and she didn't want a drink in case she had to drive someplace tonight and get Jordan. Robbie and Chelsea came over and stayed to keep her company and lend moral support. They left early Monday morning. There still hadn't been a response from Jordan.

Morgan was still perplexed. There was no reason for her to ask the state police for help. Jordan was in her own car with her own money. There was nothing illegal she was running from.

The next morning Morgan sent: *Hope your night was okay. I miss you. I love you. I'll be at work, please call me.*

Later that afternoon, a text came through: *I came to Boston to get away from California. I'm not going back for anything.*

That was all, no info of where she was or how she was. Morgan sat there holding her phone and staring into the few words Jordan had texted. She desperately wanted to know where she was. She wanted to go to her and tell her she didn't have to do the concert, that she didn't have to do anything. All Morgan wanted to do was hold her, love her, and keep her safe. She never meant for any of this to happen. She wanted her Jordan back, back in their home.

That evening, Morgan's phone rang. She looked at it hopefully, but it was Robbie.

"Hi. Any word?"

"Just one sentence." Morgan read it aloud.

"That guy said Chicago, not California."

"I know that, and you know that, but I have no idea what she's thinking."

"Hopefully, it's of coming home."

Tuesday afternoon, as she got ready to leave work, Morgan called the restaurant to see if Jordan had gone to work. Paul answered with,

"No, she's not here. She called and said she had a personal emergency and would call but didn't know when she'd be back."

"Did she say anything about Friday and Saturday?" Morgan had some hope that she would return to the one thing she loved: her music.

"Just that she didn't know."

"Okay. Thanks."

Morgan hung up, put her head down. She wanted to cry, but that wouldn't bring Jordan back. Could she even continue playing without Jordan? Their world was crumbling, and there was not a damn thing she could do about it.

CHAPTER FIFTEEN

It hadn't been a long drive. Halfway across Massachusetts and north into Vermont had only taken a little over two hours. At first, she was just driving, getting away, but as she got farther north, she started to look around. Vermont was gorgeous. It was mid-spring, so the trees were almost fully leafed, and there were so many different shades of green in every direction. She watched the road signs. Woodstock, forty miles, but that wasn't the famous Woodstock. That one was in New York, not Vermont. She passed all the exits for Springfield. Vermont had a Springfield, too? Did every state have a Springfield? Every once in a while, Morgan passed through her thoughts, but Jordan quickly brushed her away as she drove down the highway.

She finally decided to pull off the highway and check out some of the side roads. She passed a small motel and pulled in. It was an older place but still looked clean and well-kept. It seemed to be a "Mom and Pop" outfit. It wasn't a national franchise. She checked the rates and decided to rent a room, at least for tonight. The room was small and quaint but looked better than some of the motels she'd stayed at coming out here from California. She asked the woman in the office where she could buy groceries and liquor and was sent into the next town, a cute little community that looked like a friendly place to live. It was so different from where she grew up in Texas or California or even in Illinois.

She found a little grocery store and bought bread and lunchmeat to make sandwiches and also a bag of chips, a three-liter bottle of cola, and a fifth of bourbon…an unknown label, not the expensive one.

She went back to the motel, brought her groceries, her pillow and blanket, and the few clothes she had with her into the room, placed the *do-not-disturb* sign on the outside doorknob and locked the door behind her.

It was too quiet, so she turned on the small TV and let it run through a sitcom softly. She had neither the interest nor the knowledge to know what was happening on that show, but at least there was someone talking in the background.

What was she doing here? Was she running away yet again? Was that the story of her life?

Damn, Phelps. Why do you always end up in these predicaments? Having to get away from a place that seemed so right to begin with but ended up being so terribly wrong?

Even at home with her family, the boys were okay, and Daddy was wonderful, but Mom and Judy? Had they been the real reason she'd ended up with Amy? Looking for a woman who seemed to be able to take care of her? Who didn't push her aside? She would rather they had ignored her completely than actively let her know how unimportant she was.

Judy was okay, for an older sister. Judy was just three years older but always acted as if she was the boss of the family. She was older, yes, but wiser? Jordan didn't think so. Well, Mom had always put her in charge while she'd looked after the twins: her younger brothers, Alvin and Vernon. Yes, they were a handful, but why was Judy always in charge? She swore that Judy was the reason she got into BDSM. Just so she could be in charge once in a while.

Actually, it had been Amy, Ms. Davis, the music teacher at the high school, who had opened that door for her. Because Jordan had such a great voice, was a senior, and was planning to study music in college, she'd become Ms. Davis's prize student. She'd been the one to follow Ms. Davis like a puppy dog, doing anything Ms. Davis needed done. They had both been extremely happy that Jordan and several members of the high school chorus had been selected for the DFW Metro High School Chorus.

She remembered when she found out they'd be performing in Dallas in a month. Jordan even had a small solo piece. She thought back to that time:

Jordan felt privileged. Amy asked her views about things. She felt safe offering opinions on other things, too.

"Some of the kids are really nervous about this," Jordan said one night.

"Most people don't know how to perform. You don't perform for an audience. People get nervous because of all the people out there, but they shouldn't. You perform just for one person, like one person in your family, your boy or girlfriend, that cute redhead in the fifteenth row. Perform, sing for that one person as if it's the one thing you want to tell them, and the whole audience will feel it."

"Really? That's the secret?" Jordan remembered trying to envision Ms. Davis being that cute teacher in the fifteenth row. How she could and would sing to her and never miss a beat.

"Absolutely. Now, concentrate on that because I expect you to become a premier songstress."

"Thank you." The thought stayed in Jordan's heart day after day. It floated in her brain until the night Ms. Davis kissed her. Amy was only an adjunct-teacher, a student-teacher "practicing" her teaching skills so she could go to another school next year and get a real teaching job. Next year, she'd have a job somewhere else. This year, she was a mere five years older than her charges.

Jordan was in the in-between stage where she hadn't made up her mind yet whether she was straight or lesbian or bisexual. She dated both boys and girls...until that night. She went to Amy's apartment to help collate all the pieces of music that had come from the DFW Metro Program. Amy would teach it to the chorus starting the next day.

"Done," Amy said at last. "Finally, thank you, thank you." She reached over and hugged Jordan, then it almost seemed natural...they kissed.

Jordan hadn't known what to say. She had wanted the kiss to happen, but this was a *teacher*. Jordan was her student. She had dreamed of this, but it was never supposed to happen. It felt so right. She was so confused.

"I'm sorry, Jordan. I shouldn't have done that."

"That's okay. It felt nice. I'm kind of glad you did."

"No. It wasn't right. I'm your teacher. You're my student." She looked into Jordan's face with such a perplexed look. "It was totally wrong. You know you can't tell anybody. I'll lose my job and never be able to get another one. You'll be put into counseling and miss out on going to college next year."

"I won't say anything. I promise." *But why would I miss out on college and be put into counseling. What is wrong with a kiss? Why would she lose her job? Is it that big of a deal?*

Amy turned away, her hand over her mouth.

"It's okay," Jordan said as she tried to turn Amy back to look at her. "I'm really glad you did."

Jordan had been attracted to Amy Davis since the first day of school. Amy stood tall for her five-foot-five, with a very straight back. She always looked in charge. She wasn't heavy, but she looked *substantial*.

"We have to forget that," Amy said.

They continued cleaning up the papers they'd scattered, although there was a certain amount of uneasiness between them. They each started to say something but stopped. They'd both reach for the same pile of music but pulled back. It was becoming rather uncomfortable. Ms. Davis seemed different all of a sudden. It was like she wanted Jordan out of the house, away from her. Jordan kept wondering if she had done something wrong.

Jordan went home that night with her mind turning this way and that. She was completely confused. Amy's kiss had felt so good, had seemed so right. Her insides were teeming with heat and craving. But she was also torn with guilt. How could their kiss jeopardize Amy's job and her future in college? Why would she have to go to counseling? None of this made any sense.

The next day in school was hell for Jordan. She couldn't concentrate on anything and found her thoughts miles away when she was called upon in class.

Two days later, Jordan found herself outside Amy's apartment.

"Hi, Jordan. What's up?" Amy said as she opened the door. "Is something wrong? You probably shouldn't be here."

"I have to talk to you. Can I come in?"

Amy stepped back to give her room to enter, then closed the door behind her.

"I need to talk about the other night," Jordan said outright.

"The other night," Amy said, "shouldn't have happened."

"Why not? It felt right to me. Didn't it to you?"

"Whether it *felt* right or not, it was wrong. I'm your teacher. You're my student. There should be nothing personal between us."

"That's ridiculous. There already is."

"There can't be."

"Then you deny you *wanted* to kiss me?" Jordan wanted Amy to feel the same feelings she felt for her.

"Why would I want to kiss you?"

Jordan unbuttoned her shirt and held it open. She wore no bra. Her nipples were standing erect, with her areolas tightened by the stimulation of her blouse. She wanted Amy to touch them, to kiss them gently like she had kissed her lips the other night.

"Jordan! What are you doing?"

"What does it look like?"

Amy stood staring. Finally, she took the chance and asked "Are you a virgin, Jordan?"

"I've been with both boys and girls," she answered.

"Do you have a preference?"

"Yes. A big preference." Jordan revealed what was on her mind. "I want a person who knows what she's doing."

"*She's* doing?"

"Yes, a female." Then Jordan took the chance. "I'm eighteen. I'm not a baby." She reached out and took Amy's hand and placed it on her breast.

Amy withdrew as if it burned.

They looked into each other's eyes. Jordan leaned in again and kissed her gently on the lips.

They both stared at each other. Amy's lips were pursed in thought. Jordan moved in closer, her mind only focusing on what she wanted to do next. She had Amy next to her bare breasts; she was convincing her it was all right to be with her. Jordan rested her head against Amy's shoulder as she rubbed her skin against her blouse.

Amy pulled Jordan to her and kissed her deeply, passionately. When Jordan moaned and leaned closer, Amy closed her arms around her tightly. The kiss continued and continued. Jordan pressed her body deeper into Amy.

Soon, Amy had slid her down onto the couch and was on top of her. They continued kissing and kissing. In just a short while, Jordan was out of her shirt and jeans. Jordan was sweating, and her clit was pulsating as if it could climax on its own. Amy took it very slow, stopping at each juncture to see if Jordan wanted this or not. When Jordan finally lay there without her clothes, Amy sat back to look at her.

"We shouldn't do this," she whispered.

"You keep saying that. But we are doing it," Jordan replied. "Why shouldn't we?"

"Because you're a student and I'm a teacher."

"You're a student teacher. Doesn't that make us closer?"

Amy lay back down on Jordan as the kissing started again. Jordan took Amy's hand and placed it on her center. Jordan arched into Amy's hand, her buttocks lifting off the couch. She was wet and on the edge of coming and felt that if Amy rubbed her just a couple of times she would explode.

"Are you sure?" Amy asked.

Jordan nodded. "Yes, please. Do me. I want you to."

Amy's hand slowly brushed the hair. Then she slowly rubbed across the wetness that had collected there.

"See?" Jordan asked.

"You are a terrible enticement," Amy said. Her fingers started to rub back and forth.

Jordan's hips pushed up at her, and soon Amy was reaching inside her, taunting her vaginal lips and clit.

"Yes," Jordan moaned. "Please. More."

But Amy withdrew. "I can't. This isn't right."

"I will not wait. If you're not the one, then I'll find someone else," Jordan said with a growl. She tried to reach for her clothes.

"Okay, okay," Amy said as she reached back down and went deeply into Jordan.

"Yes, yes, yes," Jordan moaned. Amy pumped back and forth until Jordan couldn't see anymore. "That's it," Jordan screamed as her body erupted in a hard orgasm.

Amy held her tight until Jordan's breathing returned to normal. She had reached climax with the one she admired most in the whole world.

"Incredible," Jordan whispered. "I knew there was more."

"Oh, Jordan," Amy said, holding her closely.

"That was unlike any I'd ever had before."

"We can't tell anyone about this," Amy warned her. "Not even your sister."

"No, especially not her."

"Go into the bathroom and freshen up so she won't smell what you've been doing."

"And wash you off me?" *Why can't I keep what I just experienced? I dreamed of this and now you want me to wash it all away? Jeez, don't tell, wash it off, what next must I not do?*

"Yes, sweetie. You mustn't go home like this, and you'd better get home before she worries."

"Yes, right. Can I come over tomorrow?"

"Let me think about it. I'll tell you in class. Now go, wash up." Amy pushed her into the bathroom and gave her a towel and washcloth.

So Jordan had gone home that night with the biggest secret of her life. She wanted to tell everyone but knew she couldn't. Amy had made her promise not to tell although she couldn't understand why.

"What's gotten into you?" Judy asked when Jordan came home.

"Nothing, so why are you asking?" *Oh, God. Don't let me give this away.*

"You're acting like you're hiding something."

Damn. Judy could read her like a book. But Judy was the one person she couldn't tell. "We got all the music in for the Metro chorus concert this week, and I really like it." Would Judy buy that? *I have to convince her that the chorus music is what's got me beaming.* "Yeah, Amy has given me some tricks to keep my mind focused as I sing my number, and I think it's going to help."

"You're strange. Getting all excited about some music."

So, she had gotten it past Judy. She felt if she could get past Judy, she could get by anyone.

From then on, Jordan went over to Amy's apartment whenever she had time. Then one time, they went into Amy's bedroom. Jordan had been surprised because there was so much stuff in Amy's room: lots of books and papers and clothes that hadn't been put away.

And handcuffs. Jordan had been intrigued by those, but Amy said she wasn't ready for those. That night, Jordan gave up, and Amy put the handcuffs away, but Jordan didn't forget them. Time after time, she pleaded with Amy to let her try them until finally, Amy handcuffed her to the bed. That was an extra special time; the sex was much more exciting than she had ever had. Several times after, she begged Amy to use the cuffs again.

Amy had started to show her other things: a flogger, a pony whip, a paddle, and a quirt. Amy started slowly and gently. She tried not to leave marks. Jordan would go to school the next day having to sit off to the side because one side of her rear hurt too much, but she was surprised that it was enjoyable, too…because Amy had done it. As the winter progressed into spring, they had to be careful because it was getting to the season to wear clothes that showed much more skin.

That previous fall, Jordan applied to college. She knew the University of North Texas in Denton wasn't far away or terribly expensive for a Texas resident, but Jordan wanted to get way from Texas. She didn't want to stay under her sister's thumb. She asked Amy which music schools far away from Texas she should apply to. Amy suggested several: Boston University where she'd gone, UCLA in California, the University of Illinois at Urbana-Champaign, Oberlin Conservatory in Ohio, and Eastman School of Music in Rochester,

New York. Jordan got up the money to apply to all five. At least one would accept her, she hoped.

Then when Judy had elected to go to the Police Academy, it made sense to Jordan. Judy had grown up acting like a police officer; she'd be a natural. Maybe Jordan should consider something like that, too. At least she wouldn't have to always be ordered around by others, although there would always be someone stationed above her. Her mother kept reminding her that she had to get scholarships because they couldn't afford a big college education for all three of the younger Phelps children, and her brothers would probably choose better professions than a simple *music teacher*. And they'd have families to support. Would she have a family? She hadn't planned on it. Maybe her mother was talking about her siblings. Maybe she didn't care how Jordan supported herself or even if she had enough to support herself.

Of course, if one college did accept her, this would be her opportunity to prove she could become well educated and make it on her own. However, this would also mean moving away from Amy. Was this what she wanted? Or did Amy love her and would come with her? Well, the money was already in for the colleges, she would just have to wait and see what played out.

Chapter Sixteen

Jordan remembered that right after Christmas, there were try-outs for the spring musical. This year, Ms. Amy Davis would direct *Camelot* as their spring musical, and Jordan got the lead. There were rehearsals almost every evening. Playing Queen Guinevere was okay, but Jordan wished she could have played King Arthur or Sir Lancelot. They got to kiss the girls. At least she got to see Amy at every rehearsal, though Jordan had to rush home afterward to complete her homework. Because it was the end of her senior year, she had term papers to complete in two classes, and they required a lot of reading and research. Jordan and Amy tried to find at least once a week where they could be alone together. Her feelings for Amy had been growing stronger. She had been finding her love for bondage through Amy's play. It was hard to keep her concentration on school and the musical.

The spring musical was a huge success, and everyone thought Jordan and Roger Wilks were the perfect Guinevere and Arthur. Jordan didn't enjoy kissing Roger throughout the play, so she kept imagining it was Amy's lips she was kissing.

Two weeks after the show was the senior prom, and of course, Roger asked Jordan to go with him. Because she had been so wrapped up in exams and the musical, she had forgotten all about the prom. Roger really wasn't her first choice in a date, but then again, Amy couldn't be. She didn't want to go alone; hell, it was senior prom, the one event in a lifetime. And everyone had seen the musical, so would have no problem assuming Roger and her were a thing.

"I've got to go find a gown to wear," Jordan groused one day to Amy.

"What do you want?"

"Anything. Mom says to wear the one they bought Judy two years ago, and no one will remember it. They said they'd already put out enough for me to apply to colleges and don't want to spend more money. I don't know why they treat me as if I'm a burden. This is my last year of high school. I'll be moving out of their house, and they'll be rid of me. No more money squandered on their failing child. Maybe I should just stay home or spend prom with you." Jordan fell into Amy's body with tears rolling down her face.

Amy wrapped her arms around her, "Hush now. You deserve all the riches of the world. You have worked hard for this. Now quit your crying and let's see what we can do." Amy brushed the tears from Jordan's cheeks. "Why not wear your Queen Guinevere dress? You are a queen in my book," Amy suggested.

Jordan frowned.

"Let's take a look at it and see what can be done," Amy said. "Bring Judy's dress over, and we'll see if we can combine them."

Jordan rushed home to retrieve the dresses. When she returned, Amy had made a cup of cocoa for the both of them and had gathered her sewing materials onto a table in the living room. Within several hours Amy had taken both dresses, cut and combined each into one that made Jordan feel comfortable. Jordan tried on the dress and stood before a full-length mirror to look at the work her lover had done for her. She imagined Amy dancing with her at the prom. The twinkling lights dancing against the dress and following them all around the room. Why did she have to waste this dress on Roger? Why couldn't she just be bold enough to ask Amy to take her to the prom? It just didn't feel right. The hands that made such a beautiful dress couldn't even dance with her in it.

Roger picked her up that night, and they went out to dinner, then to the prom, and then to a party at Tom's house. Tom was the boy who'd played Lancelot. Actually, it was his sister Coral's party. She was the senior. Tom was a year younger but was very friendly with Jordan, Roger, and a few other seniors in the cast.

The party played well into the night. Music was loud, and most everyone was drinking. Some left early as things got a little rowdy and as the booze begin to dwindle. Jordan had had too much to drink and had last remembered dancing with Elizabeth. The music played in the distance as Jordan stumbled upstairs to pee. People were sitting on the stairs drinking and talking as she passed. When she got to the top, she asked a boy where the "john" was. He pointed down the hall, and she tried to keep on her feet by placing her hands on the wall. Once she got to the door, she turned the knob and went in, stumbling to the toilet. Hanging on to the basin, she pulled her panties down and sat. Suddenly the door flew open. "Shit," she exclaimed as she tried to hide.

Laughingly and gesturing in a Camelot sort-of-way, Roger drunkenly said, too loudly, "Oh, excuse me, my dear Guinevere. Have I interrupted your royal pee?" He laughed and then quickly closed the door.

"Damn him," Jordan said under her breath. She drew tissue from the roll and pulled herself up. After redressing, she washed up and opened the door.

A hand quickly grabbed her and pulled her into a dark room. "Here, dear Guinevere. Have a drink." Roger held some sweet liquid to her mouth and tilted the glass. The liquid found her lips as she drew in the flavored drink. She had already had too much to drink, but this tasted so good, and what the hell, it was a celebration. They drank some more of the drink together.

Jordan realized later that she was suddenly naked in Tommy's bed with Roger, who was also naked. She managed to fight her way out of bed while grabbing Roger's shirt, the closest piece of clothing she could find.

"Stop, Rog. I can't do this." She pulled away as his penis went limp.

"Don't be a bitch, Jord. Of course you can. Everybody else is."

"No, I can't."

"Don't try telling me you're a virgin because I know you're not. Everyone knows you did it with Steve and Justin...and Janice Ripley."

"I've had too much to drink…and…and…" She slipped into the shirt and held it around her. *I can't believe this, and how does he know who I've slept with? Everyone knows? Am I a slut? I've got to get out of here.*

"Why, then, because I'm not Ms. Davis?"

"What?" Oh no. Not Amy. *Everyone knows about Amy? I'm ruined. She's ruined.*

"I've seen the way you look at each other. Is that how you got the part?"

"Good God, no. How can you say that?" Jordan's breathing was tense.

"Because that's the way I got Arthur."

"What? You're lying. She would never sleep with…wait, when did you? No, you are lying, I know her, and she would never." *Or would she? How can I get out of here without anyone knowing?*

"How do you know? Were you with her every single night?"

"No!"

"She's not a bad fuck, is she?"

Jordan wasn't sure what to do or what to believe. She'd had too much to drink, and her mind was littered with all sorts of garbage. It wasn't going away. Her brain was in overload. Back to the first kiss, the handcuffs, the couch, and her body, all so beautiful. *Don't tell, don't tell. Why not tell? You didn't tell, but it got out. What to tell Amy? What to tell Judy and Mom? Do I have to tell?*

She turned and ran out of the house. She was out in the middle of nowhere, a small ranch about twenty miles outside of Fort Worth. She started running down the dirt driveway, but what if Rog and Tom came after her? She heard car engines starting from back at the house, so she dove into the woods beside the road and hid in the tall grass behind a tree until she saw them drive past.

Jordan only had Roger's shirt. What a fool she was. *Why didn't I grab my clothes? I can't go home like this. I'm in no condition to walk the streets in only a shirt and while half-drunk. What am I going to do? I don't even have a phone to call anyone.*

She tried going through the woods but was scratched by bushes and thorns, and her feet were battered by rocks, branches, and who knew what else. She eventually went back onto the dirt road. Lucky or not, a car came back up the drive and turned the corner so she was right in the lights. It pulled up next to her. It was Tom. She didn't know whether to run or scream. So she just stood there and burst into tears.

"Want a ride?" he asked.

She cried even more heavily.

"Let's go get your clothes first. I don't think you want to be seen in only Roger's shirt."

Without saying a word, Jordan got into his car, and he drove back to his house.

"Dress, shoes, purse, and underwear." He counted out on his fingers." Anything else?" he asked her gently.

"Bra, please," she replied with embarrassment.

"Okay." He waved five fingers. "I'll be right out. Wait here."

It only took him a short time to come back out with her gown and other things. She sat there as they began to drive down the dark road. Her body shook at what she had experienced back at the house. Her legs and arms stung from the cuts she'd received in the woods. She wasn't sure Tom wouldn't attack her, too. She didn't want to talk, and he must have sensed it. They drove the thirty minutes to her house in complete silence. "Thank you," was all she said as she ran in, clutching her belongings, hoping to get into her room before her parents saw her.

"So how was the prom?" Judy asked as Jordan came into the bedroom. She stopped and looked Jordan up and down. "Couldn't you have gotten dressed again before you came home, or was that right outside in the car?" She laughed hard then looked down at Jordan's legs. "My God, your legs are all bloody."

Jordan broke into tears. "Roger tried to rape me, and then he called me nasty names when I pushed him off."

"And lost his hard-on, didn't he?" Judy chuckled again.

"I don't want to talk about it." As tears continued to flow down her face, she slipped off Roger's shirt and got into her own bathrobe. She used Roger's shirt to wipe the blood off her legs and dirt off her feet.

"Are you still drunk?"

Jordan nodded. There was a knock on the door. Judy went to it. It was their father. Jordan tried to hide in her robe and faced against the door so her father couldn't see her crying.

"Did your sister just get home?"

"Yes, but as happens at every prom, she's drunk."

He laughed. "Glad you had a good time, Jordsie," he called into the room, barely peaking around the door to wave at her. "Make sure she drinks a lot of water before she goes to sleep," he reminded Judy.

She nodded and closed the door as he went away.

Judy turned back to Jordan, who began to collapse onto her bed. "Okay. Should I arrest him?" She had graduated from the police academy four months earlier. Do you need to go to the hospital? We should have a rape kit done on you and have him prosecuted?"

Jordan sat up and shook her head. "No, nothing happened. School will be over next month, and then I never have to see him again."

"Are you sure? I can, you know."

"No. Leave him alone. We both had too much to drink. They would never believe it was non-consensual. I mean, look at me. I'm drunk. I can't actually say I didn't say yes to him, even though I know I would never." Jordan would really love to punish this guy but not for the rape. She couldn't believe all the horrible things he'd said to her. All those things about sleeping with Amy, they just couldn't be true.

"That's no excuse for what he did. Did he drive you home? I could at least get him for drunk driving."

"No. Tom drove me home."

"You were out at the Parsons' ranch?"

Jordan nodded.

"You were lucky Tom wasn't drinking. Was his sister drunk?"

"I don't know. I only saw her for a little while when the party began."

"Go take a shower, then drink a lot of water and take a couple acetaminophens. You'll feel better, and we can talk about it in the morning."

Jordan sneaked into the bathroom and turned the faucet to hot. That was the hottest and best shower she could remember. The only discomfort she had were the scratches on her legs that burned when the water and soap hit them, but the physical pain was a good counterpoint to the pain in her heart. Had Amy really cheated on her? Could she even call it cheating? Were they in a relationship, or did Amy see it as a student and teacher romance? *Hell, I am a student, and she is a teacher, but I'm also an adult with feelings, and if she has slept with other students, then what am I to her? I gave my heart to her when I was eighteen and vulnerable. Was she fucking the whole school? Damn it, Amy. What have you done to me?*

CHAPTER SEVENTEEN

Jordan walked over to the motel office to get a cup of coffee the next morning. It had been a rough night; she'd dreamed that she was back in Texas, that she was with Amy Davis again. That had been one of the first things she'd done wrong. She never should have kissed Amy, but when she had, she let it go much too far. Let it? No, she had almost forced it. She had wanted Amy or any older woman who could initiate her into that lifestyle. And now, had she made another mistake with Morgan?

"Good morning," the woman in the office said. Her name badge said Tracey. "Come in for a cup of coffee?"

"Definitely."

Tracey poured her a cup and placed it on the counter. "Creamer and sugar's over there," she said, pointing to the end of the counter.

"Where's a really good place to grab a small bite to eat that's not too expensive?" Jordan asked as she doctored her coffee.

Tracey suggested a few places and gave her directions.

"And I guess I'll be staying a couple more days," Jordan said. "Don't worry about changing the sheets or towels, and I'll keep the bathroom clean myself." She took a sip of the hot brew and looked out the window. Her body shivered as she let the heat from the coffee flow down into her stomach. It reminded her of the moment she'd laid eyes on Morgan. She had been running scared, and Morgan brought her into a safe place. But the past was catching up with her and now, and she might have to let Morgan go.

Just then, her phone rang. She looked at the name.

"Leave me alone," she told the phone without answering it. "I'll come back when I'm ready, if I ever am."

"That's telling him," Tracey said. "Let him stew in it for a few days. He'll think twice before he messes with you next time."

Jordan looked at her and laughed. "Thanks. I needed that." The pronoun was wrong, but the sentiment seemed genuine.

"Having problems with him?"

"No. It's not really that. We were offered a job out of state, but it means revisiting the problems I had when I lived in California, and I will definitely not go back there."

"Good for you. Hold your ground. Are you married?"

"No, just living together."

"Better still. Don't give up."

"Thanks, Tracey. I'm trying to hold off."

"Good. Keep it up. Show him who the boss is."

"I will." She toasted Tracey with her coffee and went back to her room. She'd been able to skirt the truth enough that she felt better. At least she had someone who thought they were on her side. That felt better. Now if she could just get those dreams out of her head.

Later, Jordan was a whole lot improved after she'd eaten the chicken sandwich and french fries at a cute little diner. There were ten messages on her phone. All but one was from Morgan. Maybe she should say something. She typed in that she had come to Boston to get away from all her problems in California, and said, "I'm not going back for anything." No, she wouldn't let her mind go back there, either. She was here now, or at least in Vermont. Maybe she should look around while she was here. This was a nice-looking little place. *I wonder if there are any jobs open here. Damn, I had a nice thing going in Boston, two jobs, a place to call home, and Morgan. Where was my head? Why did I let her put me on that damn website? I didn't need the fame. I really wasn't looking for that. All I wanted was to sing and to find someone to love. Now I have to choose again. Hell, I'm going to run out of places to run to.*

She drove around the town and saw beautiful small houses, children playing in a playground, and older kids walking along the street. One older boy had an instrument case hanging from his hand, perhaps a clarinet or oboe. It made her long for her old teaching job. She knew Mrs. Wright would give her a good reference and hopefully not mention why she had left mid-year. Maybe that was what she should do. She missed teaching. She missed her life in California. She missed her life in the Leather community. What she didn't miss was dodging parents and their disrespectful kids.

She drove back to the motel and went into her room. She really hadn't searched for a job. She just took in all the quaintness of the small town and the people within it. It wasn't Boston, and it definitely wasn't California, but she could live here.

It was still midafternoon, so there wasn't anything on the TV she wanted to watch. She sat back on her bed with another glass of Bourbon and cola. Her mind reflected back to the night she'd confronted Amy:

"Roger said some nasty things about you and me last night after the prom." Although they had another day before they had to return to school, Jordan wanted to know if Amy had really fucked Roger. Hell, she wanted to know if she had fucked the whole school. Was she the only one who didn't know?

"Really? Like what?"

"That I had fucked my way into the Queen Guinevere role."

"And do you really think I cast you because I was screwing you?"

"No, but he said that was how he got his role."

"Are you kidding me? You really think I'd put my job on the line for a seventeen-year-old boy?"

"Would you?"

"No. How can you even consider it? Okay, first of all a boy, a young man? I don't even want a full-grown man. I definitely want a woman in my life, in my bed. That's why I have you."

Her words made Jordan feel a little better. "Oh, Amy, I was so upset last night. I had too much to drink, and Roger got me into bed, and then I was naked. I was lucky I got my mind back together when it happened. Then he started saying such nasty things. I was so confused. I didn't know what to think. He had me believing you had been with more than just me and him. I don't know, maybe I heard it wrong. I was so upset."

"He is a typical male, thinking that if something goes wrong, don't blame yourself. Blame the other person. Find something totally outside yourself to blame. It's a boy thing."

Jordan lowered her head. She felt embarrassed at confronting Amy.

"Come here, baby." Amy held her arms out. "Let me hold you and wipe away your fears. I have you now, not some silly little boy."

Amy drew her into a tight hug and kissed her.

"Amy..." Jordan started. She wanted to tell her she loved her, and she never wanted to leave her.

"No, my sweet little sub, you'll spend the next few minutes with your Mistress and forget that little boy. He means nothing to either of us."

"Amy." She sighed.

Amy held her gently while she whispered endearing little things into her ear. "Now, what would you like to try tonight?"

"It's up to you, Ma'am."

"I really want to try some needles, but it will probably take you too long to come down from them, so...how about some candles?"

"Yes, please, Mistress." The thought of going off to college kept slipping into her mind. She would be leaving Amy. But she would still love her.

"Good, come on into the bedroom."

The next few days, between finishing her term papers, studying for her finals, and seeing Amy, Jordan was stretched to her limits. As it turned out, she got accepted to three of the schools, but the University of Illinois in Urbana-Champaign offered her a full scholarship. She was elated, as was her family. She knew this took a weight off her mother and dad, but this left little room for Amy. They would be so far away, and they had never really discussed Amy moving with her.

Finally, graduation day arrived. Jordan's entire family gathered. After the graduation ceremony, her uncles and aunts and all her cousins gathered at the house for a barbecue, supposedly in her honor, but she didn't feel it. Uncle Ed bragged and bragged about his son, Ed Junior, who'd caught a monster catfish that had fed the entire family. It weighted almost thirty-five pounds. He bragged that the fish was so big, it had taken Junior almost an hour to get it into their boat.

Jordan hadn't doubted it. Junior wasn't that bright.

Aunt Edna talked and talked about the sweaters she and her friends were knitting for the entire rest home where Grandmother Katie lived. There were at least seventy-five seniors there, both men and women, and they hoped to have them completed by Labor Day.

No one mentioned the scholarship the Community Music Society had awarded Jordan for her musical contribution to the city. It wasn't big, but two thousand dollars would pay for the books and fees her freshman year.

Her brothers and cousins went down the street to a park and played baseball. Judy and Louisa, the only other older cousin, just sat and gossiped, totally ignoring Jordan. Jordan sat on the porch swing dreaming of being the center of attention for once. She talked in her head. "Oh, hello Jordan, how wonderful you were accepted to the University of Illinois. You are so talented. And that music scholarship, two thousand dollars, wow, that should help you a lot," Jordan exclaimed. She replied to herself, "Why, thank you, head friend, how nice of you to notice." She looked around to make sure she hadn't accidently spoken her thoughts. *Well, I guess that was a sweet pump up of my innermost feelings. I will have to visit that space again sometime.*

By the time everyone quieted down and got ready to leave, Jordan was already in bed sound asleep.

The next week, she went over to Amy's apartment to find her packing. "Are you moving somewhere?" she asked.

"Yes, baby. I got a job down near El Paso, and they want me to start with summer school. I need to be there on the fifth."

"But I thought we'd have part of the summer together," Jordan said with an annoyed tone.

"I'm sorry, baby. This is my new job. I have to go when they want me. You'll be going off to Illinois in a few weeks. You'll be fine."

She continued to place garments into the suitcase while mumbling something about what needed to go now and what could wait.

"I hate this." Jordan spit as she plopped down on the bed, almost spilling the folded clothes that awaited their turn in the case.

"Listen. You are a smart young lady. In four years, you'll be going off to find a job, and you'll have your whole life ahead of you. We knew this was just for the present, that we'd both be in different places next year." She continued moving about the room as if avoiding Jordan's tantrum.

"Yes, but this isn't next year yet."

"That's the way it is with life. You can never predict tomorrow. Look…we still have a week. Let's make the most of it." She stopped and dropped the clothes she was holding, walked to Jordan, and took her hand and drew her up close. She stared into her eyes and planted a long hard kiss on her mouth, and then she removed the suitcase and clothes and pushed Jordan gently back onto the bed. The handcuffs hadn't been packed yet.

When they finally parted a week later, Amy left Jordan with a serious message. "Listen to me closely, my sweet sub. This is important. Do not remain a sub for the rest of your life. You've had your sister telling you what to do and you've had me, but now you're going off on your own, to a new state and a new school. Start over. You're smart and strong, and you can make your own choices. I imagine there is lots of Leather in Illinois. You're a bright young woman. There's no reason you should remain someone's sub. Find your own girl. Be the best. Promise me?"

"But…what do I do?"

"You'll figure it out. You know what you like done to you. Do it to somebody else. Don't let any sub-zero Domme try to top you. You're better than that. You deserve far better than me, even. If you want to be a sub, at least go look for a dynamite Domme. Don't settle for second rate. Take the Supreme Top."

She stared into Amy's eyes. *Is she leaving me for good? Why is she telling me this?* She took a deep breath. *I have to stand on my own two feet. First, my family pretty much abandons me, and now, Amy.*

"Promise me?" Amy asked.

Jordan nodded.

"Look for Leather groups. You can usually find them in big cities or around colleges. Look on the web. Look for Leather bars or clubs and ask around there. Check out the International Leather Consortium and see if they have a chapter near where you are. Go to meetings and watch. With your looks, you'll be one of the Dommes who everyone prays will look at them. You'll get lots of offers to allow someone to serve you. You'll have anyone you wish."

"Everyone except you."

"Yes, baby, everyone except me. But you can let me know how you're doing."

Jordan threw her arms around Amy and hugged her tightly. *I can't believe she's sending me off, just like that.* A few words of encouragement, a few words on how to find people in this lifestyle, but sending her off like a piece of luggage lost in a terminal on the baggage carousel, hopelessly trying to find an owner or someone to own. *I'll just work my way through the summer and head off to Illinois in mid-August. And maybe, just maybe, I'll find out what this lifestyle is all about.*

Jordan awoke to a darkened room. The shades were open, and she could see the car lights passing by. She had a bit of a headache from the drink she had and sleeping with her head half-cocked on the pillow. Grabbing the open bag of chips from the table, she nibbled on a few to get the hunger pangs to go away. Why did she keep dreaming about Amy? What in the world was bringing up those old memories? *Maybe Morgan is twisted in there somewhere. I mean, I did just walk out on her with really no explanation. I know I love her, just as I loved Amy. I can imagine how Morgan is feeling right now. What have I done?*

Saturday night, the band showed up at the restaurant. Jordan hid and watched. They played their usual sets, but Morgan didn't seem into the music. Her fingers didn't seem to want to flow across the keys as fluently as they had when Jordan was singing. She even missed a few notes. After they had played the first two sets and were on break, Jordan walked in.

The whole band froze and stared as Robbie rose from her chair and marched over to Jordan. "Jordie," Robbie said. "Where have you been?" Robbie hugged her tightly.

"Here and there," she said. "I'll talk to you about it after you finish."

Morgan just stood there staring at her. Her eyes gave nothing away. "Do you want to sing?"

Jordan smiled at her. "Whatever you start playing, I'll sing, except the money song."

"All right." And they started the final set for that week. After their final number, Lori packed up, Robbie covered her set, Morgan organized her music, and Jordan went to apologize to Paul. Then, as the employees were finishing up, the four sat at a table to talk. Jordan had gotten them each a drink. She was nervous as she tried to find the words to say. She looked at each of her friends and then began.

"I'm not going to apologize," Jordan started. "It was something I had to do. This California thing has been eating at me for a year, and I had to get past it. I thought I had outrun it until that guy came in last week and said he'd found me on our website. I knew it would eventually happen."

"I've taken your name off," Morgan said.

"You can put it back on. It doesn't matter. I can't hide for the rest of my life. I went to Vermont and looked for a place to hide where I could be anonymous, but it turned out that wasn't what I wanted. I've let other people make decisions for me my entire life, but I will not allow Mrs. Sumner and people in southern California to make decisions for me now. I can't live by running away and being afraid of how someone's going to judge my life, my choices. I'm better than that. I already have what I really want right here in Boston: a good home, a chance to perform, and a good job to pay my bills. Yes, I miss teaching, but that wasn't everything. Here I have someone that I adore, and I hope she still loves me." She took a quick glance toward Morgan. "If people find out about California, then I'll face up to it. I paid for it. I guess I have to own it." She took a deep breath and sat back in her chair, waiting for the reaction of her friends but mostly for the reaction of Morgan.

Lori and Robbie applauded her. "Good for you," Robbie said. "Glad you came back."

Lori nodded. "There are a lot worse things than being Leather. At least you didn't have a kid by one of your eighth-grade students, and you didn't try to sell any of them on the black market. Did you?" She gave Jordan a syrupy smile.

Jordan laughed and shook her head. Leave it to Lori to find something comical in all this. She was relieved that the group was supporting her in her decision. But the one person who meant the most to her hadn't said a word. What was she thinking? Was she angry she left? Didn't she understand why Jordan had to get away? *Please, Morgan, say something.*

"I'd say you had an accident in your own private life, and that's all." Robbie seemed sure of it.

"Thanks."

"Glad you're back," Lori said.

Jordan smiled at her.

"So are we good?" Robbie asked.

"*I* think so." Jordan nodded, still needing an answer from Morgan.

Lori agreed. "Then, I'll see you guy's later, okay?"

"I'll call if we need to meet," said Morgan.

The other two nodded, leaned over to give Jordan a kiss on the cheek, and they left.

Jordan moved closer to Morgan and drew up the courage to ask, "Are we all right?"

Her face changed into a look of seriousness and worry. "You scared the hell out of me. Not only did you leave without telling anyone where you were going, you wouldn't answer my calls or texts. I didn't know if you had been in a car accident or were out on the road dead somewhere after the last text. And then you left me thinking it was my entire fault and that you were leaving me forever. I just couldn't imagine we couldn't work it out. You know I will always protect you. No matter what, I will always be here for you. I would never run out on you. And you ask if we are all right? What do you think, Jordan Phelps?" Morgan's face eased into a slight smile. "I may have to spank you."

Jordan broke into laughter. "No way, Jose, I've done enough self-flagellation in the past week to cover the next three decades." She felt red, knowing she was going to get a submissive beating when she got home.

"Damn, and you didn't leave any for me?" Morgan seemed a bit angry but glad to see Jordan safe and back where she belonged.

"We'll think of something."

"Then, let's go home," Morgan said.

"You still want me?"

"I'm not sure why, but yes. I still want you, even though you drove me nuts this week. I was going out of my mind; I was so worried about you."

Jordan knew she was still upset, and it would take a while for her to calm down. She remembered how she'd felt when Amy left. It took months for her to get past the attraction and emotional draw she had for her. But this was different. She had come back, and Morgan wanted her back, even though she was angry at her for leaving. Jordan needed to show her that she just got scared and panic set in. She had to run. No one had ever loved her and protected her. It was a trust thing. The trust with Morgan was new, and she was going to have to believe in it.

"I worried about you, too, but I had to run. I had to get California out of my mind."

Morgan nodded as she reached for and took Jordan's hand. "Robbie reminded me that Vermont was one of the smaller states if we had to go look for you. There are only five states smaller."

"You really thought that out?"

"Robbie did." Morgan looked her squarely in the eyes. "You've been away for a long time, and it seems I'm having a relapse of my sleeping problems."

"Oh, honey, I'm so sorry I didn't explain why I left. I know now I should have called and told you I needed some time. But then, I really didn't know if that was what I needed at the time. I was so upset and confused. I felt my former life was haunting me and was tearing up everything I had worked so hard to build. But you're right. It was wrong of me to not talk to you and at least keep you abreast of my plans. I never meant to hurt you or to cause you to have sleepless nights. It's been a long and stressful week. We should go right home and get you some sleep."

Morgan kissed Jordan gently on the lips and led her out to their cars, hand in hand.

Chapter Eighteen

On Monday evening, the four met for dinner at Morgan and Jordan's house to discuss the convention.

Morgan started the discussion after they'd eaten. "I'm going in two directions on this. One, it will be a wonderful experience for all of us and a chance to pick up some good change, but...we're leaning on Jordan's unfortunate experience in California. They'll make that the pinpoint of us being there. They're going to do a write up on Jordan's story, what happened in California and how she got here and revived her life."

Jordan looked around the room, knowing that each one of the band members would be exposed to what happened and be considered a part of it even though they were never in California. Participants by association, as people called it. *You don't necessarily have to do the crime, just being an associate of the person can make you just as guilty. This could wreck their lives, too. What are we getting into?*

"It will be a whole gaggle of perverts all in one place," Jordan explained. "Although, everyone plays at being safe, sane, and consensual, and none of them would ever do anything without everyone agreeing to it, in case you're worried."

Lori was chewing on her lip. "I guess I need to tell you that Mel and I are Leather, too. That's how we met. She's my wife and Mistress."

"Well," Jordan said. "Why didn't you tell me?"

Lori shrugged with a small smile on her face. "We haven't been out with it since we got married."

"Do you do that stuff at home?" Robbie asked.

Lori nodded with an enormous smile. "That's why I have to do whatever she tells me."

"Good for you."

"So if we did this convention, she'd let you go?"

"She'd come with us. We go to that convention every year."

"Did I ever see you at one?" Jordan asked. "I went almost every year."

"Well, I always kept a very low profile."

"I thought you looked a little familiar, but I couldn't imagine where I'd seen you."

The others all relaxed back with a grin.

"So I guess for me, this all comes down to Jordan. How do you feel about this? Do you want to do it?" Morgan asked.

"I came here to get away from California, but it looks like it'll follow me for the rest of my life, so I'm thinking, why not turn it around and make something positive happen out of it?"

"Your name and story will be plastered on all the advertising... all over the world."

"What's the saying? When life gives you lemons, make lemonade?" Lori offered.

Jordan said, "Maybe it'll help someone else from having to go through this." The others nodded.

"I think your voice is what's going to sell this, not your sob story. Once they hear you sing, everyone will see what a bigot almost took off the market. You'll probably get more jobs or even recording offers because of it."

"And if you fly without us, that will be okay, too. Robbie and I are lounge musicians. We don't expect our lives to turn vinyl," Lori said. "I'd be happy just to say, I used to play behind her when..."

Jordan and Morgan shook their heads. "If we go anywhere, we go together."

"So is it voted that we do this?" Morgan asked.

Jordan waited in anticipation for the others to answer.

"Definitely," the other three said.

"Now, do we want to add any others?"

"How about using Blaine on guitar? She's very good," Jordan said.

"And let's get Janis on sax?" Lori asked. "She's played with us before."

"We've got three months to put together a full concert. Is that enough time?" Morgan reminded them.

"Blaine already knows my material, and she picks up arrangements really quickly," Jordan said.

"And Janis knows our stuff."

Janis with her tenor sax had sat in with them on several occasions and added more when they did weddings or parties. Jordan liked the idea of adding Janis to the group and she knew Blaine well enough that she wouldn't have to audition. "Can we rehearse every Saturday during the day?"

They all agreed.

"I'll call Blaine and see when she can get here," Jordan said.

"I'll ask Janis," Lori said.

Morgan smiled. "I'll call Stan."

"What am I gonna do?" Robbie asked as if feeling left out of a job.

"Why don't you go through our music and see what might be good for the concert?"

"Four jobs, four women. We're on our way."

Jordan called Blaine. It had been a couple weeks since they had talked, and she wasn't sure Blaine would go for this. It wasn't but a few minutes into the conversation that Jordan had her hooked. She told her what the convention was all about, how they were featuring the band and would be telling her story to convince people that this was an accident and that Leather was safe, sane and consensual.

"Now, where you live is your choice. You can stay here. We have a guest room, and one of us will be around to drive you to where you need to go. In addition to that, I never gave up that little room in Cambridge, but you'll need a car of your own to get around."

"Let me get there to begin with. I can always pick up a cheap older car, and then I can live anywhere. Can I start at your house?"

"Of course you can. That's what we had planned. That way, if this thing doesn't work out, you haven't tied yourself down to signing a lease for an apartment."

"Should I bring all my guitars and amps?"

"It will cost a fortune to get them here. It might be cheaper to buy new ones. Just bring your twelve-string, since that's your primary ax and buy the amp and electric here. You can always resell them later."

"That's a good idea. I'll check the cost first, though."

"Morgan says that if you need extra money for any of that, she can help you. We'll discuss the terms when you get here. Just get here as soon as you can, okay?"

"Definitely. Is there anything of yours that you left with me that you need now?"

"Yes. There's a jewelry box there that I could use."

"Okay. I'll bring it. This is very exciting."

"See you, soon, hon."

"Yes, soon."

Jordan then listened in on Lori's call with Janis on speakerphone. "Yes. It's a big deal," Lori said. "I guess we'll each get six or seven hundred apiece, plus we go to Chicago for the weekend, all expenses paid. But let me explain what we're playing for." She explained Jordan's situation and the whole reason they'd been offered the gig.

"Is everyone in the band Leather?" Janis asked.

"No, of course not. Just Jordan and me, as far as I know, but Blaine is Jordan's friend from California, so she might be."

"Well, I'm not biased, but I'm not Leather, as long as that's okay with everyone."

"Of course, Jan. Have I ever held it against you?"

"Well, no. And I've never held it against you, either."

"Then we're okay with each other. This band is about the music, not the sex…well…at least to everyone except Jordan and Morgan." Lori and Jordan laughed.

"Yes. I can't believe Morgan has a girlfriend. I thought she'd stay single forever."

"They say there's someone for everyone."

Stan returned Morgan's call. "So has everyone agreed to play?" he asked.

"So far. There will be six of us, with all our equipment."

"Will three rooms be enough?"

"Three rooms will be fine, but we don't all sleep together. Actually, Lori will be there with her wife, so that's one of the six. One room with a queen bed is good, but at least one of the others should have two beds."

"You'll play Friday and Saturday nights. Will you need rooms for Thursday and Sunday, too?"

"We haven't really thought of all that yet. Give me time to talk to the others."

"All right, Morgan, I'll also need names of everyone in the band for the program and a small bio, no more than fifty words. We'll also need a full advertising photo of the entire band. I'll need that by the end of this month for all the advertising. Also, we'll want to put a solo photo of Jordan on the front cover. I'll need to talk to her about potentially giving a session about her experiences. Do you have her number?"

Morgan gave him Jordan's number. She felt a little caught in the middle as she did. Almost as if she was giving away some secret. She knew Jordan was going to tell her story, but she really didn't want any part of it, even giving Stan her number.

"All right. Tell her I'll contact her tomorrow during the day."

"I will," she said abruptly as the thought of telling Jordan made her feel even worse. "Is there anything else?"

"Not that I can think of right now. Get me that info on the band members, and I'll be in touch."

And the plans were in motion.

A week and a half later, Blaine arrived at Logan Airport. Jordan met her there. They embraced each other in a long hug and kissed briefly on the lips.

Jordan turned to see the luggage on the floor. "Is this all you brought?" she said as Blaine loaded two large suitcases and her twelve-string onto a luggage cart.

"I figured I'd buy an electric guitar and amp here. The cost to get them here was more than they were worth."

"Okay, that's smart, then. Let's get you to the house, and then we can go buy new ones." Jordan drove up to the loading area, and Blaine piled all her stuff into the car. Then they started home to Brookline.

That evening, when Morgan came in from work, Blaine was testing out the sound of an electric guitar. "I hear that Blaine is here," Morgan said with a smile.

"We stopped at Mr. Guitar on the way here just to look around. But she got a good deal on an amp and guitar, so she bought them. She's in her room."

"I should go up and say hi."

"Dinner's almost ready." Monday was one of the few days they were both free for a meal together. Jordan loved to cook. Morgan loved to call out to have something delivered, but she wouldn't have to tonight. She looked exhausted and hungry. "Smells like Italian," Morgan said as she sniffed and then hung her jacket in the hall closet.

"Yes, it is. Spaghetti with sausage, salad, and garlic bread."

"Did I hear Italian?" Blaine jokingly stated as she came down the stairs.

"Hi, Blaine." Morgan said as she walked over to meet her at the bottom.

"Now both of you come and sit down, it's time for dinner," Jordan said.

Blaine shook Morgan's hand, and they both walked to the dining table where Jordan had placed the table settings. She began serving dinner and broke open a bottle of rosé to celebrate the arrival of Blaine. They talked well into the night about the upcoming convention.

CHAPTER NINETEEN

The band started rehearsing together that Saturday. They all seemed to get along and enjoyed playing together fairly well. Janis knew the original three and had played at several parties with them. Blaine had played with Jordan's band in California and knew all her material. They started by just the four of them playing several of the songs Morgan had written so Blaine and Janis could hear them. Then, they added the two new musicians in places Blaine and Janis felt was right for them to play. By the end of the rehearsal, there were three pieces that seemed to come together nicely.

Morgan liked the way things were coming together. The sound was pure and natural, and each player complimented the others. It was as if they had been playing together for years. Not one person tried to out-play the others so the band had its blended sound.

"Wow," Janis said as they were packing up their instruments. "I didn't know your work had words to it."

"I usually start with the words, but I'm a melody writer more than words, so they work either way," Morgan said. "The words are an inspiration. Sometimes I don't get them finished right to the end. I'm correcting that since we got a singer for the group."

"That's great. I can't wait to hear the words to some of your others."

It was so strange how different Morgan had been working lately. *I haven't been writing music through melody but through lyrics. In fact, I can't write without lyrics first now. They're Jordan's lyrics.*

They're words about her, what I feel about her, what she does to me. She has changed my style, my method of writing. My God, I never realized how much she has changed me.

They rehearsed every Saturday afternoon. Morgan, Blaine, and Jordan each introduced new songs they were writing. Soon, they had almost an hour's worth of music.

In early June, they had a professional photographer do several promotional pictures. They were all excited about the results that were sent to Stan. The entire concert was planned and all the music finalized. There were only two pieces they hadn't written themselves.

At the end of June, they felt they were ready. They had a full hour's worth of material featuring both Blaine's guitar and Janis' sax, with Morgan, Blaine, and Lori doing backup vocals for Jordan. Two new songs Morgan had written were added, and they all liked them a lot. She hadn't expected all of her music would be accepted by the band. They were quite different from what she had written. Of course, they were about Jordan, but no one knew that. But they hinted at the world of Leather and her secret world of bondage. It was just a play on words, but anyone in the scene might get it. Maybe they all got it. Maybe that was why they liked it.

At the beginning of July, the whole world received info about the convention with a list of classes and demonstrations. On the front page was a photo of the band and a closeup of Jordan. Inside, there was information about the band advertising the concert they would be playing. There was also an article about Jordan and her dilemma that told of everything she'd lost. It ended with:

"Luckily, she landed in Boston where a friend asked her to join their band. Today, she is the lead singer for Stone Cold Perception, one of the rising music groups from that area."

"Don't let members of our community be persecuted for being who we were born to be. Bring a Stone Cold Perception to our Leather lifestyle."

Shortly after the announcement went out, Morgan went in to check the band's website. She knew that Jordan needed to be protected from any adverse reaction or comments coming from anyone who was against their lifestyle or who might be hellbent on destroying her life. She needed to weed out those negative comments before Jordan saw them and let Jordan know that Morgan would be there for her through all of this, even if Jordan said she was all right.

The site was overloaded with messages for the band, some sent directly to the band's website, others forwarded from the ILC site. They were all basically for Jordan. But there was one for Morgan. She glanced at it, and then forwarded it to her own part of the site. She'd think about it later and called Jordan in to look at her messages.

While Jordan read, Morgan pulled up the letter addressed to her on her phone. She read it several times, trying to read into what wasn't written there. There had to be some alternate message. It was from Suzanne, who seldom said things directly. Morgan couldn't imagine anything that woman could want from her, and there was nothing Morgan wanted from her, either.

"Oh, heavens," Jordan said. "Now the whole world knows where I am."

"But look at these," Morgan said, looking up from her phone. "Most are supportive. People are on your side."

"Wow." Jordan couldn't believe all that was in there. Did people really support her? Could it be that they understood it was all an accident? Did she just let a few people run her out of California and ruin her life there? *This can't be real.*

Jordan was getting emails and messages, some from old friends who were happy she'd settled in a place that was supporting her. Others were letters of support from strangers who expressed outrage that she had been treated so badly. One especially surprised her.

"I never imagined reading something like this about you," it read. "I'm still behind you all the way. I may even go to the convention just to hear you sing again. Save a few minutes for me? Breakfast or lunch? Love, Amy."

"That was my first Mistress," Jordan explained to Morgan. "I haven't seen her in years. I was still in high school at the time." *Oh my God, I thought I would never hear from her again. I have wondered what happened to her. I wonder if she ever thinks about me?*

"That early? Weren't you underage? You began to tell me about her but said you'd explain later."

Jordan nodded. "She was my high school music teacher."

"No. That wasn't right."

Jordan went on to explain what had happened between them. "We broke some rules, but if it hadn't been for her, I'd have never gotten into Leather. Luckily, I turned eighteen when we first started, so we had several legal months together. If she hadn't gotten me into that, I'd still be teaching in Southern California. I'd never have come to Boston. The only rule we ever broke was her being a teacher and me a student. If they had caught us, she would have lost her job. So we kept it a secret. It was wrong, but I was in love and headstrong. Nothing was going to keep me from her. I had made the decision, and I was the one who pressed the relationship to go on."

"Then, I'm glad she seduced you. I should thank her. Did she bring you out?"

"Into Leather, yes, but I was already into girls. Actually, I dated both before then. She gave me the experience to see what a woman could really do."

"I'm glad you had such a good mentor." Morgan chuckled.

Jordan gave her a gentle kiss and went back to scanning all the messages. She read the ones from people she knew; she'd read them again later and respond to them, but for now, she just scanned them. There were over a hundred.

There were even a couple who said she was using her misfortune to gain fame she hadn't earned or who chided her for her negative involvement in the Leather community. Jordan felt a twinge of sadness and guilt reading those comments. She had enough empathy that she didn't want anyone to hate her for who she was, and she surely wasn't using what happened to gain fame. She could earn that on her own. She was only doing this to clear up some of the misunderstanding about the lifestyle. She quickly clicked on the next message and shook her head to brush the words out of her mind.

"Hang on to the good ones so you'll have something to look back on when you're feeling low. Trash the bad ones. They don't even deserve the storage space they're taking up right now," Morgan told her.

"Some were so mean." Jordan moaned as she buried her head in Morgan's shoulder.

"They don't know you and don't care to learn. Others are jealous of you, of your support, and your talent. That's the big thing these days: if you can't beat it, cut it down. If it scares you, destroy it."

"I know, Morg. It's just coming all at once." Jordan began to realize this might be harder than she thought. The messages just might be the start of what she might have to face. *What happens if there is trouble at the convention?*

"And it will keep coming as long as there are those unintelligent wankers out there. If you let them get to you, they win. We don't want that, do we?" She held Jordan tightly. "People have their own opinions about things. Not everyone can agree on everything. Some like it hot, and some like it cold. But there are some that like it warm. And those that like it warm will never understand those that like it hot or cold. For them, warm gets you a little of both, something to wash your face with and a cool drink when the water cools down. It's the same with just about everything; religion, politics, money, where you live, who you marry, everything. There will always be something someone doesn't like. It's called freedom or freedom to choose. It's when that someone takes it too far and steps over your right to live your life how you choose that it becomes a problem."

Jordan had no response. But that night, she awoke to find Morgan crying in her sleep.

"It's all right, sweetie," she whispered as she drew the sleeping Morgan into her arms. Morgan thrashed for another minute and then woke. She pushed out of Jordan's arms and rolled over to the far side of the big bed. Jordan sat straight up, not knowing what to think. Was Morgan living out a nightmare?

"Are you all right?" Jordan asked.

Morgan was looking around the room as if trying to decide where she was. Finally, she focused on Jordan's face.

"You were having a nightmare. Are you all right now?"

Morgan's eyes were still wandering around the room.

"Morgan?"

"I'm okay," she finally whispered.

"Come back over here," Jordan said. "Let me hold you while we go back to sleep."

Morgan nodded and rolled back over to Jordan.

Jordan wrapped her arms tightly around Morgan, but it didn't feel right. Morgan was tense...too tense. Jordan at last fell back asleep.

That happened again two nights later.

The fourth morning, Morgan got up, showered and left for work without saying a word. Like the night before, her sleep had been fitful. Jordan didn't try to question her but only held her in her arms.

The next night, Morgan began thrashing around and finally she cried out, "No!" then rolled away from Jordan, still asleep. Jordan was beginning to feel like she was losing her. Night after night, she would thrash about, crying in her sleep, and now moving away from her in bed? *What the hell is going on? How can I reach her?*

That week, Morgan said very little to Jordan, Lori or Robbie. They played at the restaurant, but Morgan's playing seemed angrier than usual. They finished on Thursday night, and Morgan went home before anyone could talk with her. Luckily, Jordan had her own car.

Morgan even acted strangely on Friday and Saturday nights when Jordan sang. The music was rougher and the beat faster, as if she wanted to get the set over with. There was no feeling to the music, no collaboration with the instruments. It was like the sound was dead.

Finally, Robbie pulled Jordan aside. "What's up with Morgan? Are you two fighting?"

Jordan shook her head. "I don't know what's wrong. She's been having nightmares, but she won't talk to me about them. In fact, she's not talking to me at all. She's shut me out completely. She gets up, showers, and goes to work without a word, and when I come home at night, she's already asleep. She's been like this all week."

"Let me see what I can do," Robbie said, softly. "Something's not right."

Saturday night, after the final set, Robbie stopped Morgan before she could leave. Jordan stood back, eavesdropping on the interaction

"Hey, buddy. What's up?" Robbie said.

"What do you mean?" Morgan said in a matter-of-fact tone.

"You're not talking to anyone, and you're playing a lot differently."

"I have to talk to everyone?" Morgan growled.

"Not everyone, but we'd like to know what's happening."

"There's nothing happening."

"You're not playing like you used to. Your playing is too angry."

"Then maybe you should get a new piano player." Morgan looked over at Jordan. "Get a ride from someone and don't wait up for me." She turned and stalked off.

"What the fuck?" Robbie said to Jordan.

Jordan shook her head. "You see, this is what I've been going through for the past week. In fact, it's getting worse. I don't know what is going on and don't know what to do. Something is bothering her, and it's really bad because it's causing nightmares."

"She's been like this before. I don't know about nightmares, but she's been angry and hasn't talked to anyone for days, and she's always gotten over it. She'll get over it soon, I bet. It's just one of those phases Morgan goes through. We've seen it before. Maybe it's PMS or menopause. But whatever it is, I'm sure she'll work it out," Robbie stated as she grabbed her things and headed for the door. "Don't you worry your little head none, she'll work it out."

That night, Morgan didn't come home. She didn't appear on Sunday, either. On Monday morning, Jordan called her office but was told that Morgan had taken the week off. She called Robbie.

"And that's all they knew?" Robbie asked.

"Yes, her secretary said she'd called in and said she had a lot of family things to take care of and was taking the week off."

"That's not like Morgan. That's one of the things I love about her, she's always so easy to talk to and seems to be open about everything...except that every-now-and-then thing. It's never lasted this long, nor has it been this intense. I really thought she would have worked it out by now," Robbie said.

Later that day, Jordan was going through the website to find an address from an old friend she wanted to contact. Just to see what else was on the site, she brought up a different page and saw a note to Morgan from someone she didn't know.

Jordan hesitated. She wasn't a person to invade someone's privacy, but this might explain Morgan's behavior. She opened it. The return address was Suzanne Rhapsody in Chicago. Suzanne Rhapsody? *The* Suzanne Rhapsody? The Suzanne Rhapsody who wowed audiences across the globe with her superb interpretations of popular music? Suzanne Rhapsody, the "Goddess of Popular Music?" The Suzanne Rhapsody that everyone was hoping would come out of retirement and record just one more album?

The note read:

Morgan,

Someone brought it to my attention that your band is performing in Chicago at the ILC convention. Good for you. I often wondered where you went when you ran out on me fifteen years ago. But you shouldn't have run away and hid. I could have found you lots of work. Perhaps time has changed us both?

I am also living in Chicago now and would love to spend a few moments with you while you're here. Call me?

Suzanne

Jordan called Robbie. "Do you have any Suzanne Rhapsody albums?" she asked.

"Are you kidding? I have them all, well, most. I never got the last one, but it's on my *want* list."

"Would you look on one from about fifteen or sixteen years ago and tell me who the piano player was?"

"Sure. Be back in a few." Five minutes later, she was back. "Are you fucking kidding me? How come I never saw that? That's who she played with?"

Jordan sighed. "It seems so."

"So she's run off 'cause now we're not good enough for her?" Robbie asked.

"I don't think that's the case. I mean, well, there seems to be some unfinished business between them. I just found a note Suzanne had written to her last week. It may have contributed to her mood."

"What did it say?"

Jordan frowned to herself. She shouldn't have mentioned it. "She wants Morgan to call her."

"Do you think she did? Maybe she asked Morgan to accompany her again."

"I don't think so, but something happened. Morgan had nightmares right after that, and that's when her mood changed."

"Maybe Morgan went to New York to see her," Robbie said.

"No, Suzanne's not in New York anymore."

"Where is she now?"

"Chicago."

"Oh, hell," Robbie said.

"Yes. That may be part of the problem. Well, let me think this through. Maybe I can figure something out."

"I hope you can. This is such a surprise. I never imagined something like that."

"I know, it surprised me, too," Jordan said.

"Well, I'll see you soon. Call me if she comes back."

Suzanne Rhapsody was the woman who had hired Morgan in New York and took her on tour, Jordan was sure of it now. Was she also the one who had emotionally abused her all those years ago? That explained a lot.

Now I have to find out where Morgan is. I need to find her before she makes a mistake and slips back into a volatile relationship. I don't care if it is with Ms. I-Am-Known-to-All. She's not taking my Morgan under her spell again.

It was Saturday night when Morgan went to the restaurant. The others weren't there. There was a sign in the lobby that said: "Sorry, Musicians are on vacation this week."

Morgan walked in and sat at the piano. She started playing some music that the band did and some oldies and some she was composing right there. She didn't acknowledge the people listening. She didn't even respond to the smattering of applause she got from time to time. She just watched her fingers flow across the ivory keys, making sound.

When Paul saw her, he hurried out, no doubt to phone Jordan.

A half hour later, Jordan walked in and approached the stage. Morgan was continuing to play. Jordan stood there watching her. Morgan stroked the keys gently and with tenderness.

When Morgan started a song they had been using, Jordan started singing. Morgan stopped. She reached down and grabbed the piano bench tightly on either side of her.

Jordan walked up beside her. "Hello," she said softly.

"Hi."

"Glad to see you're all right."

Morgan nodded. There was silence.

"Can we talk?" Jordan asked.

Morgan nodded, again.

"Not here. I'll see if we can use Paul's office."

She left but came right back. Morgan hadn't moved but looked up. When Jordan nodded, Morgan got up and followed her into the office. They stood there. Morgan hadn't looked into Jordan's eyes yet. She knew she had just put Jordan through what Jordan had done to her several months ago. She had felt the pain Jordan had felt, the anger and worry.

"Where were you?" Jordan asked. They both stood, neither moving.

"I drove up to Ogunquit, Maine and got a hotel room. I've been walking on the beach."

"And not eating. Your face is thinner."

"No, I haven't eaten."

"And that's a new shirt."

"I needed something clean."

There was silence for a few moments.

"I found the message from Suzanne Rhapsody. It was still on the band's website," Jordan said.

"Did you read it?"

Jordan nodded. "Did you call her?"

"No."

"She was the one who abused you," Jordan stated.

Morgan whispered, "Yes."

"The great Suzanne Rhapsody?" Jordan said with a sarcastic tone.

Again, a nod. "Suzie Scruggs. She changed it. Too ethnic."

"Do you want to talk about it?"

"I want a drink."

"I'll get them."

Morgan was standing at the window when Jordan returned. She took the drink from Jordan and paused. Jordan sat on the chair in front of Paul's desk and waited.

Morgan took a sip of her scotch. "I...I had to decide what to do. I've changed since I was with Suzanne. I imagine she has, too, but it drove it all back into me. I was suddenly right there where I had been." She took another sip and hesitated, looking out the window into the dark beyond the parking lot. She closed her eyes and began.

"I was a lot more butch in those days. I was twenty-two, and my hair was longer, but you'd never catch me in a dress or anything even a bit girly. Nothing other than a T-shirt and jeans with sneakers or boots ever touched my skin. It was spring break of my senior year at Berklee, so my friend Clare and I decided to go to New York for the week. We had a great time roaming around the village, both east and west and all over the good spots: Chinatown, SoHo, Tribeca, farther uptown. You name it, we went there. We ended up at a party in Greenwich Village. There were all sorts of people there, rich and poor, black and brown, mostly. I think Clare and I were the only white girls there. There were people there who were famous. My God. We were very impressed but trying to keep it cool. We roamed around, listening to the conversations, trying to be flies on the wall.

"We came up to this one group. The woman there was complaining she'd have to fire her piano player. It was the great Suzanne Rhapsody. She was shorter than I'd imagined but just as beautiful and majestic as I'd thought she'd be. She oozed power. She was concerned that she'd have to find another pianist, but it was getting too close to her next tour, and she was worried. Her pianist was hitting the bottle much too heavily. She didn't trust taking him on tour.

"Clare burst out that I played piano.

"Suzanne looked me up and down and asked, 'How well?' I shrugged in embarrassment and said I'd been playing for over fifteen years, and that I was going to Berklee, in Boston. She invited me to audition.

"I was in shock. The great Suzanne Rhapsody wanted me to audition for her? Clare said she wouldn't wait up, and I followed Suzanne out of the building. It wasn't a long walk. She had an apartment on the ground floor of a big townhouse just a block or so from West Fourth Street. It was superbly furnished, and there was a six-foot grand.

"Can you believe it, Jordan, a six-foot grand? It was mirror polished, and the keys were pure ivory and ebony and shone as if they had never been played. The bench was mahogany and leather. It had a luscious soft skin feel to it. I felt like I was onstage, and I was shaking like a leaf.

"She named one of her latest, and I played while she sang. She only corrected one small thing and said, 'Not bad, stud,' and we went on with a couple more of her songs. She offered me the job, said she'd check me out with the rest of the band, that I was young enough to be trained well. She laughed and said, 'Let's have a little Moll and try those again.'

"I thought, Moll, as in *Molly*? I wasn't sure what she was referring to, but then she took a jar from her bookcase and held a small spoon to her nose and said, 'Let's see how good you can get.'

"I had never tried hard drugs, but I was so enthralled by being there that I inhaled what she spooned out without thinking. Damn, it hit me hard. My heart was racing, and my breathing was off the charts, too. I'd never felt that good. I could have sprinted around the world at that moment. I was on fire. I sat back down at the piano and played whatever she wanted to sing. At one point, she went into her bathroom and came back wearing a robe. We must have played until three o'clock in the morning.

"Then she was standing beside me at the piano. I looked up at her. There was a strange look on her face. 'Are you good at other things, stud?' she asked.

"I'm not sure I answered, but she leaned down and kissed me. Wow! I kissed her back.

"'Come with me,' she said softly. She turned the light out and took my hand to lead me into her bedroom. She unbuttoned my shirt and unzipped my fly and ran her hand down my chest. I didn't wear a bra in those days. She squeezed a nipple, and I closed my eyes. She told me to take my clothes off and get in bed.

"I took my shirt, jeans, and my boots and socks off, and she said, 'All of it, stud, I want all of you. You're not getting out of this that easily.' She grabbed the elastic on my panties and pulled them down. I finished taking them off, and she pulled me onto the bed. I really didn't know what was happening. It had gone from an audition to drugs to the bedroom in all but what felt like a few minutes. I knew it was the drugs that were altering time, but I couldn't seem to control my actions. I didn't want to have sex, but I couldn't say no. It was just happening and I wasn't in control.

"And wow, my God. She was all over me. Her hand was inside me before I knew what was happening. And I mean her whole hand, not just her fingers. Then her other hand was all over my body, grabbing and pulling on my nipples. She explored everywhere, never asking me what I wanted or if I approved. I'd never had this done to me before. I was hot and excited, yet confused and questioning what was happening. I thought I was going to explode. When I finally came, I thought there was an atomic bomb inside me. She slipped her hand out and held me close and said, 'Not bad, eh?' It wasn't bad at all. In fact, I was ecstatic.

"Then she said, 'Now, why don't you make Mama happy?' She lay back and opened her robe. She was naked beneath it. I leaned forward to kiss her, but she pushed me back and told me to use my mouth somewhere else and pushed my head to her crotch.

"I was in awe. Sure, I'd eaten someone out before, but those were basically my classmates, just as innocent or inexperienced as me. But this was Suzanne Rhapsody. *The* Suzanne Rhapsody. I couldn't imagine where she'd been, what she'd experienced, or who she'd fucked, and she was probably twice my age. Why did she want me? Was this a once-in-a-lifetime thing? I dove in. I'm not sure how many times she came, but I think I came up an hour later."

Morgan walked over to the other chair. She finished her drink.

"Well, was she a good fuck or just a good *old* fuck?" Jordan said half-jokingly. "It sounds like a horrible experience for a young girl, even if it was with a famous old hag."

Morgan continued without answering. "We met with her drummer and bass player the next day, who both liked me. We didn't mention that we had made love, but they knew. She couldn't keep her hands off me that day. We left on a tour around Europe and Northern Africa two weeks later. It was incredible. Paris, Rome, Milan, Casablanca, Marrakesh, Cairo, Barcelona, Madrid. We were gone for three months, performing to sold-out houses, and I fell madly in love. The reviews were outstanding, the travel was magnificent, and the sex was totally unbelievable.

"The abuse started two months or so after we came back. At first, she'd swear at me when we were rehearsing, asking what the fuck was I trying to play? 'Don't rewrite the damn thing now.' I thought she was just upset that we couldn't get the songs quite the way she wanted it. She seemed to be having trouble with a few of the new songs she wanted to add to the next album.

"I'd apologize that I couldn't do something right, and she'd be all sarcastic with, 'Of course you couldn't. Why would you start now?'

"I was composing now and arranging what others had written for her. She was never happy. Sure, we'd go to bed, and she'd ravish me or have me do her, but there wasn't any love like there used to be. We used to lie in each other's arms for hours afterward. Now it was merely slam-bam-thank-you-ma'am, then get up or roll over. I wanted out. I couldn't take the abuse any longer. She was destroying my self-worth and my ability to play. In fact, I didn't have the desire to play any longer. Somehow, she had taken that from me, too.

"I was going insane. According to her, I couldn't do anything right. Nothing. She even slapped me once when I challenged the way she'd sang something. That went on for six or seven months, maybe even longer. I was having trouble concentrating on my arrangements. She said I wasn't doing anything around the apartment and that I was just sitting at the piano scribbling. Maybe I was. I really couldn't tell anymore. My thoughts weren't my own. Everything spoken was coming from her. Everything I heard was her voice. I didn't even have my own thoughts anymore. Once, she said, 'You could at least do the dishes once in a while. You ate the fuck enough.' I began to doubt what I was doing. She had gotten me hooked on meth, and I was using more and more of it, even though I knew it would ruin my body. I started to shake. I couldn't get warm. My life was escalating out of control.

"We recorded an album. She seemed happy with it. Everyone was. Everyone thought we'd sit back and relax for a few days, but not her. She wanted more new songs right away. Now we had to start the next album. Then, one afternoon, after she had railed and railed at me all morning, I walked out. I walked all over Manhattan. Just walking and walking. I'm not even sure I was thinking. I walked all day and all night. I was lucky I didn't get mugged. I guess the angry look on my face made me seem tougher. No one wanted to tangle with me. I was so done. I hated her. I hated this place. I was sick of everything and everyone. I wanted my life back, and I was going to get it. Come hell or high water, I would kick the drugs and take back my life.

"When I got back to the apartment the next morning, she wasn't there. I grabbed my clothes and stuffed them in a shopping bag. I left her a note, just eight words: *I'm sorry. Thank you. It's been fun, Morgan.* Then I took the first train back to Boston."

"My God, Morgan." Jordan sat there with her mouth half-open. "This woman was a torturer, a pure sadistic bitch."

"By then, my friends had all graduated and gone off to do their own thing. I stayed with my grandmother in Lexington until I found a small one-room place. I never wanted to play piano again. I was fed up with it. I was just done, completed, over with it. I worked at 7-Eleven, at a bottle factory, as a waitress, whatever work I could find. Then I fell into the real estate business. I even took a few courses so I'd know what I was doing."

"And now?"

"I'm still not sure what I'm doing all the time, but I do know how this band started. I met Lori when she and Mel were looking for a house. She said she played bass and wanted a second or third bedroom as a practice space. I asked her if she played anywhere. She said no, but she had a friend who wanted to start a band, but they couldn't find a keyboard or guitar player. I said I used to play piano and I suppose I could try it again. And here we are."

Jordan was crying a little. "What a nightmare. I had no right to feel sorry for myself."

Morgan started pacing. "I'm sorry I was such a brat this week. I slipped back into that space where I was totally inept. Just seeing her name on that email brought it all back to me, especially when Robbie said my playing was angry. Every time I looked at you, I saw her. I probably should have called my old therapist right that minute."

"You saw her when you looked at me?" Jordan asked. "What in the world would make you see her in me? We don't have the same build. And I'm not nearly as old as she is."

"You sound like her, and you perform like her. It threw me for a while."

Jordan looked like she wasn't sure how to respond. "Do you want to see Suzanne again?"

"I'm not sure. Maybe I'm scared. I mean, she's a lot older. I think she was almost fifty then, which would make her mid-sixties, now. I'm almost afraid to see her again."

"She's retired now."

"Yes, I know."

"Sixty-five is really still young these days. Do you think there's something wrong with her?"

"I have no idea. It may just be too many drugs."

"I'm glad you don't do them anymore."

"And I won't again, thanks to you."

Jordan frowned as if unsure where this was going. "I don't want to lose you."

"I had you confused. That's why I didn't react to you for so many months. You sound a lot like her. You perform the way she does. I wasn't sure it wasn't her in another body."

"You're kidding me."

Morgan shook her head. "You opened up a lot of memories. It took me quite a while to decide you really were you. There is one major thing that differentiates you from her, though."

"And what is that?"

"You kiss differently. She would never allow me to really kiss her, especially on her mouth and more especially not with my tongue."

"You can kiss me any *way*, any*where* you want." Jordan stood and walked over. "A hug, first?" she asked, her arms ready.

When Morgan nodded, they stepped together and held each other tightly. Then Jordan reached up and kissed her.

"I'm sorry you had to go through that," Jordan said. "I'm sorry we both are going through it right now. We have to work this out. You have to come out of this and realize I am nothing like that woman and never will be."

"I guess you and I have each had our share of good times and bad." She looked into those beautiful chocolate brown eyes and saw the compassion there. She knew it was Jordan looking back at her.

"Want to go home?" Jordan asked.

"You still want me?" Morgan couldn't believe it.

"More than ever."

Morgan grasped her hand and brought it to her lips. *Yes, home, with a capital H.*

CHAPTER TWENTY

That final two weeks were crazy. They played at the restaurant but announced that they were taking a week off because they were going to Chicago to play a concert. Everyone wanted to know about it, but Jordan had asked that they not reveal all the circumstances, so they just said they had been hired to entertain at a convention. Jordan said she'd be back to hostess on the following Tuesday. She didn't want a big fuss at the restaurant due to the fact that most of the patrons were straight or vanilla, and she didn't want to put Paul's business in jeopardy.

They had talked about what they'd wear: similar clothes but in different colors, all alike or each totally different? They decided they'd all dress as they felt comfortable, as long as it was a bright color, at least on top.

Although the ILC had booked three rooms for the six of them, Lori said she was getting her own room because Mel would be coming with her. They were going to stay another few days and make it a vacation.

Besides their luggage; Robbie's drums; Morgan's electric keyboard, stand, and bench; Lori's electric bass and string bass; Blaine's two guitars; and Janis's sax, there were also three amplifiers, microphones, and stands along with miles of cords. There was no way they could check that much on a plane. Morgan paid for a truck rental, and Blaine and Janis would leave Tuesday afternoon and drive to Chicago. The others would fly there early on Friday morning.

When Blaine and Janis arrived Thursday evening, they would check into one of the two bedrooms and unload all the equipment into a secure storage room the hotel provided. The airport shuttle dropped the others off in front of the hotel just before ten a.m. Friday morning. They each had their carry-on luggage, which contained a few emergency things and makeup. Robbie had balked at the thought of makeup, but when shown how washed out she'd appear under stage lights, she gave in. Janis promised to do her makeup before the shows.

They walked into the hotel to register Mel and Lori's and Morgan and Jordan's rooms. They were told that Blaine had already registered the others. Melanie had booked a queen room "close to the others in the band" for her and Lori.

Blaine and Janis were waiting in the lobby for everyone to be registered as someone walked up behind Jordan.

"Well, Mistress Jordan, I see you landed on your feet." It was Harry from Furies Loft.

"Harry," she said. They gave each other big hugs. Jordan was so surprised to see him there. Knowing that he was there to support her made all the difference in how she would perform. He had been such a big support when the fire had happened. She had felt so bad about what had happened to the Loft but knew he held no hard feelings against her.

Jack came up behind him. "How's it going, Jack?" Jordan asked.

"Kind of slow without you, Mistress Jordan."

"Oh, by the way, don't let it get around here, but you don't have to call me *Mistress*."

They looked at her, their eyes wide. "Did you flip?"

"Not exactly." She reached over to take Morgan's hand where Morgan was talking to Robbie. She pulled her over. "This is Morgan, my partner. She's not quite Leather." They all shook hands.

"You've given up Leather?" Harry asked.

"No," Jordan said. "We try a little from time to time, but Morgan is taking it slowly. She's not a masochist, and it takes quite a bit to get her into submission."

Morgan lowered her eyes a bit as if to appease Jordan to her friends. "She can go out and play from time to time if she wants.

I won't deny her hobbies, and there's a Leather club very close to home. We have an understanding."

"Really? That's fantastic."

"She promised to go out with me every now and then," Jordan said. "Maybe she'll see the enticement one of these days. You can never tell what's going to happen, can you?"

Harry and Jack both agreed.

"Are there any other old Californian friends here?" Jordan asked. She hoped there was no one from the school or anyone who was involved in her arrest.

"Roy and Jim are around someplace, and I think Joan and Patricia are coming, too. There were several who wanted to see you, but I haven't heard if they were coming or not," Jack said.

"Do we have time to meet for lunch?" Harry asked. "We should talk before the banquet tonight. I get to introduce you."

"Really? Then lunch would be great. Let us get settled into our room and make sure everything is set."

They made plans and went to finish their convention registration.

"Morgan," Jordan heard from across the lobby. She looked across the hall to see Stan. "Welcome to the convention." He had a pile of folders and papers under his arm. "I thought I'd save all of you from standing in line to get your registration material. Are you all here?"

Morgan looked at the small group. "Six in the band, plus one."

"Yes. I have one here that says, Melanie Richards-Brand. Married to the Band."

Melanie laughed. "I guess that says it all."

"With your nametags, you can attend anything that's happening here this weekend. I hope you'll get to eat at least part of the banquet tonight. You also might find a few interesting sessions listed." He looked around as he handed nametags and program folders to each person.

The nametags had their names with "Entertainer" under it, except for two. Jordan's nametag read *Mistress Jordan Phelps, Entertainer.* Morgan's read *Morgan Sparks, Entertainment Domme.* Everyone laughed at that one.

"Where did you get the idea for that?" Jordan asked, pointing at Morgan's nametag.

"I could tell she was in charge every time I spoke to her, so it seemed natural."

Jordan leaned forward and kissed Morgan.

"Are any of you members of ILC?" he asked.

Jordan, Blaine, Lori, and Mel raised their hands. Morgan looked at Jordan. Jordan gave them all a thumbs-up and then turned around and saw Morgan hadn't raised her hand. She grabbed Morgan's wrist and held her hand up.

"Oh, right," Morgan said.

"I thought you were a Domme," Stan said.

"She is...when she wants to be," Jordan clarified.

Stan handed them ILC membership cards on chains to wear around their neck. That would get them into special rooms and sessions that said "Members Only"

"What time should we set up our instruments in the banquet room?" Morgan asked.

"We're opening the doors for the diners to walk in at five. The silent auction will start then, too. Dinner is at seven. They'll announce the auction winners at about eight thirty, then the two speakers will start. Oh, by the way, I'm sure I asked but just wanted to check, your songs are all copyrighted? We're recording the whole concert."

"Yes, they're all okay."

"Good. I'm glad you agreed to let us record it. We want to sell the recording as a remembrance of this conference. It could bring in quite a bit for our charities. You, of course, will get two dozen copies for your own archives. Jason will also discuss tomorrow's schedule with you."

"That sounds fine with us," Morgan said, looking at Jordan, who nodded.

"You've got a good four hours right now to settle in, talk to old friends, get some lunch."

"All right, that sounds really good," Morgan said. She looked at the others. "Why don't we meet in our room at three? No. What room is all our equipment in?"

"It's all in a storage room behind the banquet hall."

"Okay, there, then."

The others nodded, and they all headed for the elevators.

"By the way," Stan stopped Jordan before she left with the others. "I hope you don't mind, but I scheduled your talk with Harry Lynch and Jack Downy for tomorrow at eleven, just before lunch. I figured you'd want the afternoon free before the concert."

"Thanks Stan. I'm a little nervous about it. I haven't talked to anyone except my band mates since I left California."

"Remember, you'll have Harry and Jack with you."

"Yes, they've always been there."

Jordan and Morgan met Harry and Jack at the restaurant downstairs in the hotel a little after noon.

"Exactly where are you now?" Harry asked Jordan.

"We're in Brookline, which is a historic upgrade neighborhood to the southwest of Boston. It's very nice there. Morgan has a gorgeous house."

"I work in real estate," she said.

"For now." Jordan added. "How's the Loft doing?"

"You wouldn't believe how many curious newcomers we had after you left. Everyone wanted to see where the whole 'Kinky Bitch' scene happened...even vanillas. And we had kids hanging out on the street looking at all the folk who came in. I think they may have been some of your old students."

Jordan put her head down. "Sorry about that. I really never meant for any of this to happen. It was a total accident. I mean, I know that it was my entire fault, but I didn't do it on purpose. And I never meant to hurt anyone or anything. Hell, I especially didn't want to get arrested, lose my job, and have to move clear across the damn country."

"The police had to patrol past there every hour or two. And we've closed off the upstairs. Only people who have met the right criteria can get a key to go up there, no tourists. You have to have a known member sign for you."

"And don't feel bad about it. Those first few months, we sold double our usual drinks," Jack added. "We really cleaned up with our ten-dollar registration fee to get in the first time, there were so many first-timers. I can't tell you how much that brought in during the next few months."

"Glad I helped, then," Jordan said.

"Have you spoken to Lacey since you left?"

"She came to Boston and into the club where we're playing a few months ago. I didn't know she was going to be there, and it totally threw me off my music. I couldn't remember words or anything."

"I had to take over the entire song. She just stopped midsentence," Morgan said as she grinned.

"Lacey came over to where I was living, and we had a chance to talk. Has she been into the Loft?"

"No. We haven't seen her."

"She walks with a cane now, but other than that, she's doing well. She has a new lover, and she totally moved out on her mother."

"Good for her. I hope she's happy. Can I use her name in my speech? It would be hard to keep referring to her as *the sub*."

"I don't see why using her first name would not be okay, just not her last."

Harry nodded. "Now, what about you, how did you get into this band? I have to give the audience a bit of background, besides the fact that you're a well-known pervert in California."

Jordan chuckled, almost to herself. "It was serendipity. I had decided I needed to get as far away as I could, so I was headed for Vermont or even Maine to live out in the woods and chill out. I stopped in Boston to visit an old college buddy, and she asked me to sing one number with them."

"Was that you?" Harry asked Morgan.

"No, that was Robbie, our drummer. But when I heard her voice, I knew we had a keeper."

"And you moved her right in?"

"Into the band, yes. Into my house, no. That took a few more months."

"No, Morgan fought our attraction for almost six months. I almost had to attack her to get her to give in."

"Almost?" Morgan asked.

"Okay, so I attacked her."

"How could you hold out for six months?" Jack asked. "Almost everyone I know would give a limb to get next to Mistress Jordan."

Morgan took a deep breath. "I had a bad experience in my last relationship, so I wasn't looking for another one."

Harry and Jack seemed to accept that. "All right, now tell me about the rest in the band. I can't just talk about you two. Someone would get jealous. Are you going to keep the band together after this concert?"

"I'd love to because there's certainly energy between us, but I'm not sure where we'd play, and one player is not from our area, so I don't know if she'll stay."

"Are you all single? Are you all fair game if someone sees something they like?"

"All except for Lori, the bass player. She's married, and her wife-slash-Mistress came here with us."

"I see. I'd better warn everyone." He jotted that down in his notebook where he'd been making notes.

The night had started when the doors were opened. The silent auction was underway as the band set up and tuned. People looked for their seating. The auction closed as the meal started.

Once everyone had eaten, first the winning bids were announced, and then the first speaker spoke about the future of their community. Finally, Harry was introduced. Jordan took a hard swallow as she looked around the room at all the faces that had come to hear the story. She was suddenly panicky and wanted to run, the same feeling she felt when she ran to Vermont. It took all her will power to stay in her chair.

Morgan reached for her hand and grasped it tightly. She leaned close to her cheek and whispered, "It will be all right." Jordan tried to relax as Harry began.

"I run a Leather bar in Southern California, and I think you all might have heard what happened there last year. I'll recap to remind you and set the record straight.

"Mistress Jordan and her sub, Lacey, were doing a wax scene in one of the private rooms on the second floor of our building. They were both very well-known and careful players, so no one thought twice about it. Those who see Mistress Jordan's wax artwork are always impressed. Suddenly, I heard someone yelling, 'Fire,' so I raced upstairs and saw smoke billowing out of the room they were using. The entire bed was on fire, and both women were choking from the smoke. Lacey's feet were still tied to the bed..."

Jordan sat as tall as she could in her chair, trying to make herself look impervious to the story being told about her. She wanted this to end and to move on to the performance. The retelling of the story brought back so many painful memories. Was she doing the right thing letting it be told? She looked around the room for any sign of disapproval. It seemed that everyone was engrossed in Harry's tale. She listened as he revisited his own place of business and the damage that had been done by the fire. She remembered how quickly he had reacted and how he had tried to smother the flames. Her thoughts were taking her back to that day. She could clearly see him lifting Lacey off the bed, taking her outside, and placing her naked body on the ground. The screams from Lacey as she lay there smoldering. She was being taunted by the children. It played over and over in her head.

She was abruptly pulled from her nightmare as the audience chattered and clapped. She focused on Harry, who was finishing the story.

"Many people have been searching for her for the past year. So when Stan Weltz found Jordan on the internet, on the band's website, he went to Boston and saw them perform. He brought them here for this weekend so you could hear and see what one woman's hatred and excuse *my* bias, *stupidity* almost destroyed.

"They're going to be playing just three songs for you tonight, just to entice you to go to their concert tomorrow. These six women are really something, and four of them are Leather. *But* I've been asked to tell you that Lori Richards-Brand, the bass player, is married and her wife-*Mistress* is here. So if you see anything you like, don't even think of Lori. She's totally off-limits."

There was laughter around the room.

"All the others, Leather or not, are technically single, although Robbie Nelson, the drummer, does have a live-in lover, and Jordan

Phelps and Morgan Sparks, on keyboard, live together, Blaine Jones, on guitar, and Janis Lynkowski, on sax, are completely single and unencumbered."

The audience broke into laughter.

"Ladies and gentlemen, please enjoy Stone…Cold…Perception!"

He stepped down. The band had gotten into position as Harry wound down. Someone in the audience yelled out, "Go, Mistress Jordan!" as the cheers continued. The band members chuckled, and Jordan cracked a little smile. She turned to Morgan and nodded. She was ready to begin. Morgan counted off and the intro started. Jordan took a breath and bellowed out the first note.

Chapter Twenty-one

The audience went wild when they heard the band. They were inundated with applause, and as they started to pack up, they were deluged by people wanting to compliment them and requests to talk about the unfairness of Jordan's experiences. Jordan said over and over that she'd explain everything tomorrow at a session just before lunch. She hugged a few people she knew from Southern California. Then she turned to look into eyes that were extremely familiar. Her stomach tightened as she heard the sound of that familiar voice.

"Mistress Jordan Phelps. God, you sound good," Amy said. She pulled Jordan into a tight hug.

"Thank you. How are you?" She took a step back but held on to Amy's shoulders.

"I'm the same as I was back then, except a little more experienced, a few pounds heavier, and a decade and a half older. Can you believe I'm almost forty?"

"Still seducing your favorite students?"

Amy laughed. "No, baby, you were the only one."

"Then I feel special."

"Do you have time for breakfast or lunch tomorrow?"

"Of course. Lunch?" Jordan really wanted to have Morgan with her if she went to lunch with Amy. She definitely didn't want Morgan to think she had rekindled feelings.

"Do you have someone here that we need to include?"

"I'm living with Morgan, the pianist in the band."

Amy's eyes got wide. "She doesn't look like a sub."

"No, we have a vanilla relationship."

"I would never have guessed that."

"I'll explain it to you tomorrow." She felt Morgan beside her and introduced them.

"Fabulous sound," Amy said as they shook hands.

"Thanks. It all revolves around Jordan."

"I saw that. It usually did."

"Well, I'll see you tomorrow at lunch," Jordan said, stepping back to Morgan.

"Yes. Nice to meet you, Morgan." She smiled at Jordan, then back to Morgan. "And you'll be joining us?"

"Well," Morgan hedged, "we'll see." Morgan looked at Jordan.

"I hope you do," Amy said and walked away.

"Who was that?" Morgan asked.

"My high school music teacher."

Morgan looked surprised. "That was your first Mistress? She doesn't look like what I imagined."

"We've all gotten older, her more than us, I think, and she's gained a bit, too."

Morgan nodded. "We should get some sleep. Tomorrow will be a busy day."

It was a good thought, but there were still more and more people who wanted to have a word with them. Jordan and Morgan didn't get back to their room until very early in the morning.

After a couple of hours sleep, Morgan and Jordan rushed a shower and quickly dressed for the early Saturday morning after-care session. Jordan had been asked by the original speaker to add her views about the safety and cleanup of wax play. After that session, they met Harry and Jack for the session about Jordan's experience. The crowd for that one completely filled the large room.

Harry started the session and briefly explained what had happened. Then Jordan took over, explaining about her arrest, the session with Principal Wright, and what had happened after that. She felt like she was being put through the wringer over and over again. It was stressing her out, and she just wanted to go. She was tired of telling the story and really wanted to spend some time with Morgan in the hotel room. But there were all sorts of questions. Everyone vied to be the next in line to ask something. At one point, well into the hour, someone wanted to delve into what it had felt like to have to face her students.

Jordan broke into tears. It was too hard for her to explain. Morgan took Jordan into her arms and held her until her tears subsided. Harry took over for the moment.

They were then asked about their relationship. Morgan merely said, "We're both Dommes, and we live together. We have a very intense, although vanilla, life."

Jordan nodded. Having stopped the tears, she thanked everyone for coming but said she'd told them everything and wanted to let it rest. She had completed everything.

The crowd wanted more but seemed to respect Jordan's position and left her and Morgan alone. Several followed Harry to the luncheon and continued asking him questions. Jordan was glad this part was over. She needed a break or she was going to break.

Amy came up to Jordan after the session closed. "You're much stronger than I ever imagined," she said.

"Not really. I just had no other choice."

"Are you still up for lunch?"

"I guess so, but let's find some place outside of the hotel. I'm a little over this place after this last session."

Amy nodded. "I'll check with the concierge. Meet you in the lobby." She walked away.

"Are you coming with us?" Jordan asked Morgan. Jordan really wanted to go back to the room and be alone with Morgan, resting in her arms. She was exhausted, both mentally and physically. She needed some sleep and to be held. But since she had made this commitment with Amy, she hoped Morgan would accompany her.

"No. I'll stay here. I imagine you have a lot to catch up on. I'll be in our room. I *have* to catch up on some sleep."

"You can sleep without me?" Jordan said, faking disappointment.

"Not well, but I know you'll be back."

"It shouldn't be that long," Jordan said with little enthusiasm. Morgan just wasn't getting her cues, but they'd discuss it later.

"Take whatever time you need." Morgan kissed her gently and turned to go back to the room.

Jordan met Amy in the lobby. "The concierge says there's a nice sandwich place just around the corner. He said we can walk there," Amy said.

"Then let's go."

"Where's Morgan? Isn't she coming?"

"No, she said she had to get more sleep, and you and I have other things to catch up on."

"Oh, all right."

They walked outside and down the block. "Where are you teaching now?" Jordan asked.

"I'm not. I'm working for a music publisher."

"That's not too much of a change."

"No. I realized that after you, I was unfit for a teaching position. I lasted three years in El Paso before I started to go crazy."

Jordan wondered if, even though Amy had a deep passion for sex, she didn't want to risk putting any other student in the same position as Jordan. She seemed to resent herself for ever falling for Jordan while she was her student.

"Too many hot sopranos?" Jordan smiled.

"Something like that, but none of them compared to you...and look at you now. You are one hot songstress. You'll propel them out of the auditorium tonight."

Jordan looked at Amy and tried to see if the old flaming sparks were there. She looked into her eyes, but the crow's feet definitely made her look older and less desirable. She looked at her hands, and those too were older and showed signs of aging. They weren't the strong Mistress hands that used to take control of her and tie her up. Amy had also let herself go to some degree. Mistresses never did that. They are always in control of everything, including their bodies.

"Well, that's a little exaggeration," Jordan said. "We'll do okay. If it wasn't for my getting arrested in California, we wouldn't even have an audience."

"Until they hear you. I'll tell you, y'all had me wet last night… all of you. And I'm sure I wasn't the only one. Do you write your own music?"

"Some of it. Morgan does the most, but we've all contributed something, all except Robbie and Janis, but you never know, do you?" Jordan was taken aback by her own comment. She had no desire for her music to turn Amy on. She didn't want to even think about it. She sang for Morgan. Everything she did was for Morgan now.

"Which ones did you write?"

"The blossom song we did last night, and there's a new love song we're doing tonight for the first time called 'Just.' I'm going to surprise Morgan with it. She doesn't know we're doing it. Blaine and I started writing it when we were in California, but we finished it just a few weeks ago and then taught it to Lori and Janis."

"How does Morgan not know? Doesn't she accompany everything?"

"Well, yes, usually. But this one uses a twelve-string. I think it's really pretty the way Blaine plays it."

"I bet it is. If you have anything new, send it to me, and I'll see if it can be published. There's a lot of money in it if someone picks it up and makes a chorus arrangement that can be sold to schools, etc."

Jordan remembered when she was picking stuff out for her choruses. "I had to do a lot of the arranging myself if we wanted a new piece. I remember my arrangements were very high-school designed. They wouldn't have worked with the band now. That's pretty much why I left them behind for the new teacher." *What I write today is for Morgan and the band, but mostly for Morgan. They are very personal, love letters to her. I don't know if I would want to publish those.*

"Send me those, too. You never know what can be published. And not just the SATB things. Women's choirs and men's choruses are always looking for things. I've been handling requests from handbell choirs for arrangements, too."

"I left most of my work in California." She was trying to put Amy off for a little while.

"Can you get it back? You may be losing a lot of money."

"I'll have to contact the school. The principal there is still friendly. She hated to see me go." *Yes, I could probably contact her and get copies of everything, but there were so many music arrangements, and it would take them so much time to copy and mail them. It's my music, and I would have to go retrieve it, and I don't want to.*

"I can imagine. You had a chorus?" Amy asked.

"Two. One high school, one middle school."

"And you had to abandon them."

"Yes, the backlash from the parents was so bad I had to resign. You heard the story Harry told." *Why is she asking me to repeat it? I'm so tired and burned out. I just want to eat and go back to the hotel room.* "The kids all thought it was funny that their music teacher was caught being a pervert. I was the Kinky Bitch," she said with a quick sarcastic tone.

"Jordan!"

"That's the way it was. It's over now. And if it hadn't happened, I'd never be here. I wouldn't have met Morgan."

"You love her?"

Jordan looked her in the eye. She wanted to be very clear on what she was about to say to her. "Yes. I'm going to ask her to marry me."

"Wow, all right, is she going to say yes?"

"My God, I hope so."

"Then...congratulations." They reached the sandwich shop and choose a booth near the street window, read through the menu, and ordered. "Now, what about you?" Jordan asked.

"I have a very vanilla lover, too, who doesn't want to commit to a live-in or exclusive relationship. We see each other two or three times a month, but that's okay with me. I go out to play parties, and I date on the side."

"Well, I hope you find *the one* very soon."

"Actually, Jordan, after you, there may never be *the one*."

"Don't say that, Amy. There'll be someone. There always is. You know, after you left, I thought that, too. I went through my whole freshman year without anyone. I mean, I dated from time to time, but no one seemed right. Then I followed your advice and went to Leather club meetings. I got picked up by one of the major Dommes there and was collared to her for almost six months."

Their food was delivered. "Collared?" Amy asked.

"Yes, as in *owned*. She took over every aspect of my life. But I almost flunked out of school, so I had to return the collar and move out. It changed me. I learned a lot about being a Domme by watching."

"You left, just like that?"

"Well, I told her about school. She wasn't very happy with me, but what was she going to do?"

"I'm sorry that happened to you."

"Me, too, but it showed me that I had to be in charge of my own life. That experience helped turn me into a Domme. I learned to trust my own instincts and because I had been a sub, I knew limits so I could play with confidence, knowing that I had been there and how far I could go."

Amy nodded as they both picked up their sandwiches.

"So here I am," Jordan said.

"Yes. Here you are. What did your sister say?"

"Basically, she just told me to get it together and stop wasting everyone's money and time. Of course, I never told her everything. We live very different lives now. Did you know she's a Texas Ranger?"

"Really?"

"She got wounded in an arrest shootout four years ago, so she mostly just does desk work now."

"Yikes. How badly was she hurt?"

"I'm not sure. My family doesn't talk to me much. I'm not a Texan anymore. I didn't move back home after I graduated. I'm on my own."

"Are you kidding me?"

"No. When I didn't move back to Texas, they all but disowned me. I get birthday and Christmas cards."

Amy shook her head. "I'm in Colorado."

"Boy, we moved around, didn't we?"

"Yes, a lot of things changed. We need to be in touch more often."

They talked while they ate, sat there with coffee, and exchanged addresses. It was after two before Jordan got back to her hotel room.

She quietly opened the door to the room and found Morgan sound asleep in the bed. She took off her clothes and shoes and slid under the covers, next to the warm sleeping beauty. Jordan sighed. It was nice to be in bed with her lover.

Morgan stirred sleepily and turned to face her. "Hi, baby. How was your lunch?"

"It was all right, the same old questions everyone has been asking for two days. I'm tired. I just want to sleep in your arms." Jordan said as she snuggled closer into Morgan's side.

"Will you keep in touch with Amy?"

"We exchanged addresses, but I doubt I will contact her. She asked about getting some of my arrangements published...the ones I left in California. I don't know, I'm not ready to think about all that. I just want to sleep now."

"All right, baby, you rest. I'll be right here."

Chapter Twenty-two

The rest of that afternoon, Morgan and Jordan slept and then got ready for the concert. They were both nervous, Jordan more than Morgan, but they got ready and helped all the others with their makeup and getting dressed.

At 7:59, they were across the street in the Performance Center, Jordan in her tight red jumpsuit, Morgan in cobalt blue and black. Lori had a bright yellow shirt with brown slacks, Robbie a light blue outfit, and Blaine a dark green top, with Janis in a lighter green, both with black slacks. They were all standing onstage behind the closed curtain, ready to begin. The lights were off backstage, but they could hear the crowd as they settled into their seats. There was intense energy in the air. All six were ready, nervously shifting in place from foot to foot.

Morgan turned to the group and mouthed, "Let's do this."

Morgan looked over at Jordan and blew a soft kiss her way. Jordan smiled back and blew one to her, too. Morgan was beaming at the thought of Jordan being centerstage. She knew that her voice was going to blow the house down. She had been waiting for an opportunity like this for a long time, and now it was here. Now it was time to shine, to make Jordan shine.

The house lights dimmed. Silence filled the hall, the curtains parted, and one spotlight lit onstage left. Janis started her sax rift and sent it wailing into the night. Jordan answered with a long solo. Another spotlight picked her up and followed her across the stage. Her series held for almost twenty seconds. Robbie counted them all in, and the concert began. The first song was lively and showed all their talents. Jordan showed every bit of her expertise by using her eyes to focus on audience members to sing to and lifting her hand to crescendo notes to their fullest. Her body flowed across the stage, allowing every part of her to be seen by the crowd. It was what they wanted. To have the star singing directly to their soul. The crowd went wild. They were hooked. The auditorium wasn't completely packed, but there were very few empty seats. The cheering couldn't have been louder.

As Jordan strutted from one side of the stage to the other, stopping to share a segment with one of her bandmates, the audience was with her. They soaked up every note the band played. When they at last got to the final song of the first half, Jordan announced, "We're gonna play one more song, then take a break for twenty minutes, but we'll be back because this is the best audience we've ever played to. Please don't go away. Thank you, thank you."

Robbie counted in again. After that piece, Morgan was sure the applause could be heard clear across Lake Michigan. As the curtain closed, and everyone set her instrument down, Jordan fell into Morgan's arms. Her body was tense with excitement, but Morgan bet her mind was trying to wrap around all the power she was receiving from the audience. It was more than she could have ever imagined.

"Wow," seemed all Jordan could say.

"You are the most beautiful woman who ever walked this stage," Morgan whispered.

"Shut up," she replied.

They all went into a backstage room to relax. A tall, handsome black man walked into the room and went over to where they were standing and sipping the water the crew had just handed them.

"Ms. Phelps?" he started. "I was completely blown away by your performance. I was told by *several* people that I had to see you, and I'm glad I took their advice. I'm Clyde Barron."

"Yes, Mr. Barron," Jordan exclaimed, her eyes wide. "I know who you are." Then Jordan turned to introduce Morgan.

"I understand you are the arranger and leader of this group," he said. He reached into his pocket and pulled out a business card.

"Please, call me this coming week. I think we can do each other quite a lot of good." He handed a second one to Jordan.

"Thank you, Mr. Barron, I will," Morgan said. She read it and slipped the card into her back pocket. She hoped her own eyes weren't too wide.

"Unfortunately, I can't stay for the rest of this, but I'm sure you'll wow them even more than you did in the first half." He shook their hands and walked away.

Jordan looked at Morgan. "Do you know who he is?"

Morgan nodded. "You may be on your way, honey."

"*We* may be on *our* way. I'm not going anywhere without you. You've given me the chance to sing with the band, and I am damn sure not going to move forward without you. You're the reason I'm where I am."

"Who was that?" Robbie asked. All others had gathered around.

"Clyde Barron, head of Absolute Records. He liked us."

"Don't get too excited until I get a chance to talk to him," Morgan warned. "We still have another half concert to do. Are we all ready?"

A backstage crew member walked up. "Two minutes, ladies, okay?"

Robbie and Lori looked at the others and laughed. They went back onstage and waited. The curtain parted, and the lights came on. They started the next half. The audience was even more rowdy than they'd been during the first half. The band's energy was just slightly higher as Morgan played with a lighter tempo; the thought of the record company played in the back of her mind Some of the younger members of the audience crept up to the stage, forming their own romp pit.

After the first song, Stan walked onstage and took the mic from Jordan. "Aren't they wonderful?" he asked. It took almost a full minute to get the audience quiet again. "And to think this was almost silenced by one bigoted woman. No one should have that much power."

The entire audience booed Mrs. Sumner. Jordan seemed a little sad. Morgan knew she was still angry at what had been done to wreck her life, but a little empathy no doubt flowed through the anger for her as the audience showed so much hatred toward Mrs. Sumner.

It must have been hard to see the same hatred being magnified by hundreds. Morgan was glad Mrs. Sumner wasn't here to witness this. Jordan probably considered it worse than those children who taunted her in California. But then again, Jordan had to take it. Morgan guessed Mrs. Sumner could take it even though she wasn't there.

"The board of directors of ILC voted this afternoon to establish a fund to help people like Jordan who are facing legal or monetary problems because of something in this lifestyle. We'll also be compiling a list of lawyers and law offices around the world who will work at a reduced rate or pro bono for these causes. It will be called 'Jordan's Fund,' and we'd like to start it this evening. You'll notice there are ushers up and down the aisles with buckets who will gladly accept any contribution you'd like to give, whether it's a dime or a dollar. It will all help someone. If you want to make a larger donation that will be tax-deductible, there will be envelopes available in the lobby after the concert. They'll be around for the rest of the weekend. Jordan?"

She stepped up. "Thank you, everyone, this will be a big help to a lot of people who shouldn't have to endure the degradation that being put in jail brings. It will all help." She turned back to the band. "What did we always say about money?"

Morgan and the band hit an opening chord progression into the money song.

"You want my body, you want my soul," Jordan sang. "Accept my offer and you can have it all."

"I want money," the band responded. "Give her money, lots of money."

"Give me money."

"Yes, just money, money, money."

"A penny or a dime or a dollar is good, but a twenty will make me do more than I should."

There was a musical interlude.

The audience started reaching into their pockets and calling for a bucket-carrier. People helped each other deposit the donations.

The band took over. With this crowd, Morgan knew they could get a little more risqué, so she'd added a couple new raunchy lines for

Jordan. The audience was really getting into it. *Jordan* was getting into it and moved to interact with the audience.

"There's a time when you think that you're just out of luck, but pay me enough, and I'll save you a—" She slammed her hand over her mouth, but the audience cheered her on. "I want money."

"Give her money, lots of money."

"Give me money."

"Yes, just money, money, money."

"A penny or a nickel or a quarter will do, something made of paper would make me really love you."

It lasted a good five minutes. Blaine and Janis seemed to be having a ball switching responses with their instruments. They each took a solo verse while Jordan strode across the stage from one side to the other. She looked like she was having a blast doing this song. Those who were listening in addition to reaching for their money seemed to get every line.

"Gold and silver and diamonds are nice. It will take a lot of paper to buy some vice. 'Cause I want money."

And the song continued again and again. They repeated the last chorus, and the sound grew into a big ending. The crowd was on its feet. As it ended, Jordan walked to center stage. Robbie didn't count into the next song. Morgan frowned, wondering what was going on.

"Thank you for your generosity," Jordan said. "It's quite frightening when they put you in jail, and you think everyone has abandoned you. That money will help a lot. Now." She took a deep breath. "We're going to deviate from our original program and offer something new. It's a new song entitled 'Just.' Even Morgan hasn't heard this song because it's dedicated to her." She looked back at Morgan and smiled.

Morgan looked at her and shook her head. *This wasn't in the set. Dedicated to me?* Blaine stepped up and started an intro on her twelve-string guitar. Lori stood behind them and entered with her bow on the string bass. Janis stepped up to add a sax part.

"It was never just a fling to me," Jordan said. "I was hooked from the beginning. It wasn't just the way you looked..."

It went on to extol all the things Jordan said she admired about Morgan, all the reasons she stayed. Blaine's finger work on her twelve string was absolutely beautiful. Lori's string bass and Janis's soft echoes and counter melodies added even more. It was a beautiful love ballad, soft, loving, hot, and very suggestive. All through the song, Jordan seemed to sing to Morgan, leaving only to include the audience so she wouldn't lose them. It was clear, though, that this song was totally for Morgan. She sat on her piano bench gazing into her lover's eyes as she was swept into the expression of the love Jordan sang to her.

The ending line was, "So it was never just this and never just that. What I want for the rest of my life is just you."

Morgan had tears in her eyes. Jordan hurried over and pulled Morgan up into a deep, deep kiss. The audience cheered and cheered.

"Just wait till later, Ms. Phelps," Morgan warned softly.

"You betcha," Jordan quickly replied as she turned to centerstage and bowed to her audience. She then turned to Morgan, and the audience clapped louder. Once again, Jordan bowed and then took a few steps to acknowledge the band. The band members nodded or took their bows, and then Morgan got their attention, put herself back in charge, and the concert continued.

The remainder was smooth all the way through. Every note was perfect, and the crowd loved it. When the curtains finally closed for the last time after three bows, they all let out a big cheer, and Jordan ran up to Morgan to give her a hug. Morgan responded with a deep, deep kiss. The rest of the band gathered around them to share excitement about the concert, but Morgan got them silent.

"If I'm going to be the entertainment Domme, I have to be told about *every* piece," she groused rather loudly.

"Yes, Ma'am, every piece, every time," Jordan promised.

"Or I'll spank all of you."

The band and the entire backstage crew broke into laughter.

Morgan reached for Jordan and pulled her over to her. When Jordan slid closer, Morgan wrapped her in her arms and planted another deep, strong, lasting kiss on her mouth. The rest of the band grinned and finally started to put their instruments away.

"Thank you for the song," Morgan said, as she pulled back. "I've never had anyone write for me, or should I say, about me. It was beautiful. How did you get the whole band together before this event?"

"I just used a little magic." Jordan blushed. "I was going to give you something else, too, but I didn't want to put you on the spot in front of the whole audience." Jordan seemed nervous, as if she had been anticipating this moment for weeks, but she wasn't sure where she wanted to do it.

Morgan looked at her askance.

"Would you accept the ties that really bind?"

Morgan looked at Jordan with curiosity and bewilderment. "What?"

"Will you marry me?" She seemed to be holding her breath.

Morgan stared at her, frozen in place. Jordan had never mentioned asking anyone to marry her, and Morgan had never been asked. This was the biggest step of her lifetime. What if things didn't work out? Where would the relationship go if she said no? Could they live as just lifestyle partners?

No.

"I want us to be married," Jordan said. "I love you, Morgan Sparks. Please say you'll marry me."

"Yes," Morgan said with a big smile. "Of course I'll marry you."

Jordan reached into her pocket. "I didn't have enough to buy you an engagement *ring*, but would you accept this in the meantime?" She unwrapped and presented a gold tie clip with a diamond chip in it. As Morgan smiled, Jordan reached up and slipped it onto her shirt collar.

Morgan glowed inside. "Just wait till later, Ms. Phelps," she said again.

"You betcha."

Morgan leaned down and kissed Jordan again.

"I'd tell you to get a room, but you have one just across the street," Robbie called from the hallway. "You ready to go back to the hotel? Can't you two wait?"

"Not this time. That was a special moment. Morgan just agreed to marry me," Jordan announced. She turned to Morgan, hand over her mouth as if fearing she'd spilled the beans too early. "It is all right that we tell everyone, isn't it?"

"Well, not everyone, but our friends should know."

"Wait! What?" Robbie asked, rushing over to them, bouncing around in her usual overly excited self.

"We're engaged," Morgan said. She flashed the diamond at her.

Robbie leaned forward and stared at the tie clip. "Congratulations!"

Morgan stood hand in hand with Jordan, beaming at the thought of being married to her love. Jordan had just finished performing her first big show, revealed her past to the world, and now, asked Morgan to marry her. What more could either of them want?

Jordan seemed to know and quickly said, "Let's get back to the hotel."

Chapter Twenty-three

S unday morning was incredible. When the band walked into the big breakfast gathering, everybody stood and cheered them. Morgan and Jordan couldn't pass one person without getting praised for the concert. It was a bit overwhelming, but they both were enjoying the attention. Jordan had said that she hoped she wouldn't be bombarded with question about her past. She was done with her past. It was time to move forward. Morgan agreed.

Harry had saved them a table. "Wow," he said as he greeted them. "I've never heard anything that good. That was a wonderful show."

"Thanks, Harry. This is just the right mixture of musicians," Morgan said. "So far, we all get along."

"Most of the time," added Robbie. Everyone laughed.

"I don't think your old band would have ever been half as good," Harry said.

"And now they don't have Jordan and me," said Blaine.

"And the only person I miss from that band is Max," Jordan said, "and he didn't make a sound."

They all sat down to eat although there were constant interruptions of people asking for autographs. "They're treating us like celebrities" Jordan whispered to Morgan. "It's a bit uncomfortable. I'm not used to all this attention, except from you."

Many people flirted with the two unspoken-for members of the band. One person even came up and asked if she could get a picture of Morgan and Jordan kissing because she hadn't been able to catch it from her seat which was so far back. They graciously kissed for her, and then Jordan kissed the woman softly on the cheek. The girl walked away with her head in the clouds.

At one point, Jordan whispered into Harry's ear. Morgan could only guess what Jordan was telling him. He was one of her closest friends, so she supposed he *could* be included on their big secret.

"Really?" he said. "That's fantastic." He reached out to shake Morgan's hand.

"What's fantastic?" Blaine asked from across the table.

Harry looked at Jordan.

"Our engagement," Morgan announced. The entire table now was abuzz.

Stan came up to the table, too, to thank them for last night. "I also had another contribution to Jordan's Fund last night. There's a law firm in San Francisco who's willing to sue Mrs. Sumner for everything she did to you. They feel you could get up to a million dollars."

"Well, I'd have to think about it. She *is* my ex's mother."

"But you went through a lot. At the very least, it could set a precedent that this cannot be done, that our community cannot be trifled with. Can I give them your phone number?"

Jordan looked up at Morgan.

"It will show her how wrong she was," Morgan said. "She really hurt you and almost destroyed your life. Fortunately, she didn't, but who knows what another *Mrs. Sumner* could do to another Mistress, or submissive, for that matter."

"All right," said Jordan. "The least I can do is talk to him."

"Her," he corrected. "Victoria Walker."

"Of course, I'll talk to her."

"Thanks, Jordan. I told you this weekend would change your life, and it already has in a lot of ways. I understand a certain record company spoke with you last night."

"Yes." She grinned. "But even more because Morgan agreed to marry me."

"Really? I hadn't heard that, just about Absolute." He gave her a hug and then gave a hug to Morgan. "Congratulations."

"Thank you for everything, Stan," Morgan said.

They said good-bye to him as he left. "What time is your flight back?" Harry asked.

"Blaine and Janis are taking the truck back as soon as it's loaded. Mel and Lori are staying another day or two. The rest of us are flying out late tonight."

"Are we still going to Suzanne's?" Jordan asked.

Morgan nodded. "I think we should." Morgan felt a pit in her stomach. This was going to be a tough visit. She really didn't want to go back to that dark place she had lived in so long ago. She was happy now and wanted to remain here.

"Where are you going?" Harry asked.

"I promised to visit an old friend while we were here. Suzanne Rhapsody?"

Harry looked shocked. "*The* Suzanne Rhapsody?"

Morgan nodded and Jordan added, "Morgan used to play with her."

"Play? As in piano?"

Jordan chuckled as she glanced at Morgan. "Yes, that, too."

Harry laughed. "Wow," he said.

Yes, she was The Suzanne Rhapsody. The famous singer who belted out music as if the gift of sound was plated on her tongue. It was plated all right, like silver. Like quicksilver. Ready to pull you in.

"We'll only be there a few minutes," Morgan said with finality. She was surprised at how in control she sounded. *I am no longer her submissive. I will visit with her and walk away, just as I did before, on my own terms.*

Harry looked over at Jack as if asking a question that was just between them. "Listen, we have a rental car. Jack is from Fort Wayne, and that's only a couple hours from here, so we're visiting family and friends while we're here. Why not let Jack drive you? That way, you won't have to pay for a cab, and you won't have to go through all the hassle of trying to find one when you want to come back."

"Really?"

"Sure. I have to be in a meeting this afternoon, and Jack has nothing planned. Do you, Jack?"

"Nope. I was just going to hang out. I can drive you."

"You're sure?" Jordan asked.

"Sure. Anything for you, Mistress Jordan."

"You're sure you still want to do this?" Jordan asked Morgan.

Morgan turned to Jordan and took her hands. "Yes, as long as you're beside me. I am a lot stronger than I was back then."

"Honey, I'll always be beside you, and it will be a strange thing for me to meet the great Suzanne Rhapsody." She lowered her voice. "Part of me wants to hate her for what she did to you, but I still adore her as an artist. I always have."

"I know. I feel the same way.

"Do you know where this place is?" Morgan asked, handing him the piece of paper she'd had in her pocket.

He looked at it. "Easy. It's not that far from here."

"All right. Shall we say one o'clock?"

Jack nodded. Morgan rose from her seat. She knew she had Jordan by her side, but she also knew that Jordan idolized Suzanne. She wasn't going to let Suzanne draw them in again, either her or Jordan.

"Do I look okay?" Morgan asked. She had on a bright green silk shirt and a gray blazer with her black slacks and boots.

Jordan appraised her. "Very handsome, stud."

Harry and Jack laughed. They didn't know the reference, but it clearly wasn't what they thought they'd hear. Jordan had been using that term since Morgan had admitted what had happened, just to take the sting out of it. Morgan had begun to feel better about the situation, although she was still angry and nervous.

Later, after finishing lunch and talking to everyone, it was time to leave. Rather than calling, as Suzanne had requested, Morgan had sent a text saying, "We'll stop by early Sunday afternoon." She felt more in charge setting her own schedule and definitely didn't want Suzanne to have any control over her.

Jack drove several blocks to a more residential area and pulled up to a row of connected houses. "This should be it," he said as he set the brake.

He quickly got out of the car and ran around to open the door. Morgan got out and held her hand out for Jordan. She checked the address again. They walked up the front steps, and Morgan rang the bell. Her stomach churned as it took longer for someone to answer the door than she expected. A few minutes later, she heard the lock turn, and the door opened.

Suzanne Rhapsody stood there...an older Suzanne Rhapsody, but still *the* Suzanne Rhapsody. She looked a little shorter, and her hair was almost completely gray. She had definitely aged since Morgan had last seen her. In fact, she looked a little weaker than when they'd lived together. Morgan felt her stomach ease as she slowly stretched her back to make herself look taller.

"Well, well, well," Suzanne said, scanning Morgan. "Haven't you grown up?"

It took all of Morgan's reserves not to respond with a negative rejoinder, but she couldn't bring herself to start the visit with an argument. All she said was, "Hi, Suzanne."

Suzanne scrutinized Morgan for a moment and then seemed to notice Jordan behind her. "And who's this vision?"

"My fiancée, soon to be my wife," Morgan announced. It felt good to say that. It was also her version of the dig that Suzanne had started.

"Well, then, come on in." Suzanne stepped back to let them in. "I assume you have a name, sweetheart," she said as Jordan passed her.

"Yes, I'm Jordan," she said putting her hand out.

Suzanne shook it while she looked at Jordan from head to toe.

"Very nice," was her appraisal. As she drew Jordan into the living room, she asked. "Do either of you want a drink...or anything?"

"No, thanks," Morgan said. She didn't want her or Jordan under the influence of anything while in the presence of *this* woman. She walked in, looked around the room, and sat on the sofa without an invitation. "We can't stay very long. We're flying out in a little while." She looked around. This living room was much the same as the one in New York had been but with better colors and fabric.

Jordan slid in beside her. "Nice place you have here."

"Thanks. Manhattan is going downhill. There's too much noise and graffiti all over the city."

"There's construction and graffiti everywhere these days," Morgan noted. "I would have thought you'd have moved to somewhere warmer."

"No. Chicago is fine. I have friends here."

"Good."

"So what have you been doing these past few years?"

Morgan adjusted her attitude. She didn't want to start this angry. "After I left, I stopped playing for a while and got into real estate. I'm part of a big agency now, at least for the time being, and I love it. It provides well for me and Jordan."

"Real estate? Maybe you could have gotten me a better deal on this place. Think a million three was too much?"

"I'd have to see the whole thing. What is this, three floors with a basement? I'd need to check the value of the other houses around here. Of course, I think having Suzanne Rhapsody living next door would raise all the prices."

"You're definitely a real estate agent with that golden tongue of yours." Suzanne smiled as she settled into her big easy chair. "It's a shame you dropped off the radar. I could have gotten you a lot of jobs if I knew where you were."

"I didn't think you cared for my playing that much." *In fact, the way I remember it, you belittled me every day for months on my playing.*

Suzanne closed her eyes. "I'm sorry you thought that. You were very good, and your arrangements were excellent. I'm just not sure I was the right"—she glanced over at Jordan—"singer for you."

Morgan wanted to say something about Suzanne's criticisms, but now wasn't the time. She should have said it years ago. That time was long past. "Do you still hear from Jasper?" She had to change the subject before they got into something that wouldn't end well. Jasper was the bass player they'd been on tour with. Morgan had always admired him.

"Yes. He's still playing when his arthritis lets him. We're all getting old, I guess."

They discussed some people they both knew. Mostly about their ailments or about Suzanne having to move on to other things. "I thought we'd have a little time to talk in private," Suzanne finally said.

"You can say whatever you want. Jordan knows everything about me. I'd never hide anything from her."

Suzanne looked over at Jordan, then back to Morgan. "Well, then." Suzanne took a deep breath. "It was quite a surprise to come home to your note."

"I'm sorry. I didn't know what else to write."

"Why did you leave like that?"

"Because you didn't want me there."

"Where did you come up with that lame idea?"

"You'd been yelling at me and telling me how stupid I was for months."

Suzanne's mouth dropped. Morgan knew the look on her face had turned from sociable and placid to one that could have fried eggs. She had to stop this before it became a shouting match. She didn't come here for that.

"And that's why you ran away?"

"If I had stayed, I'd have been dead by now," Morgan continued softly. "If I listened to you, I would have put a bullet between my eyes."

"You weren't that weak."

"Maybe not, but I listened to everything you said…and I believed most of it."

"You did not."

"Yes, I did. I was just a kid, barely twenty-two. You were the great Suzanne Rhapsody. How could I compare with you? You'd been out in the world for years. I was only three years out of high school. I adored you. You were a goddess."

"That was your first mistake. No one's a goddess. They went away centuries ago."

"You sure acted like one."

"And that's all it was, an act."

Morgan had no comeback for that. They stared into each other's eyes. Morgan felt tears welling up and burning her nostrils. She held them back as she didn't want to show weakness. She was angry, angry as hell.

"I loved you," Morgan confessed.

"I know. I loved you, too, but not in the way you needed."

They stared in silence.

"I'm sorry you felt you had to run. You could have been the best in the business. I think you were better than Quincy in some ways. You could have been great."

"But you stopped me," Morgan said.

"Then I'm sorry."

"I couldn't compete with you. I wanted to be like you, admired by everyone, sophisticated and loved. I tried everything to please you, and you just kept tearing me down."

"You shouldn't have tried. I was already on your side. I meant to toughen you up so you could vie with the competition."

They were both silent for quite a few minutes, just studying each other. This had to stop; it was growing into a fight.

"How did your concert go last night?" Suzanne finally asked.

"It went very well."

"I read all the publicity." She turned to Jordan. "That was all about you?"

"Yes, it was. But I've come through it all, thanks in part to Morgan."

"She saved you with her proposal?"

Jordan smiled at Morgan. "No. She believed in me. I proposed to her."

Suzanne smirked back at Morgan. "Did she beat you to the punch?"

Morgan nodded. "Yes, she did, but that's okay."

"Good for you, Jordan. Get what you want."

Jordan couldn't seem to hold back any longer. "Why did you retire? You're not old." Maybe she wanted to hear that Suzanne would be coming back for a big return. She'd already said that she loved Suzanne's music and had a difficult time understanding how she had been so hard on Morgan.

Suzanne snorted. "Tell that to my body. My diabetes was running rampant. My counts were all over the place. There were some nights I could hardly get onstage. My eyes are going, too. I can barely read music anymore, and the stage lights give me a migraine. It's shit getting old."

"I'm sorry."

Suzanne shrugged and grinned at her. She turned back to Morgan. "What have you done since then? You said you're doing real estate *and a band*?"

"We started up another band about six years ago. We play somewhere every week," Morgan said, skirting the issue of where it was. "Jordan sings with us."

Suzanne looked at Jordan. "Ah. My Morgan always loved to take her work home with her."

My Morgan?

Suzanne turned from Jordan to Morgan. "Is she as good as me?"

What was Suzanne referring to? The voice or the sex? She cringed at the thought of both. Hearing her yelling at her every day, belittling her for no reason, and the sex, she never understood why she kept going back to make love to an older woman. Older women were not her scene. It must have been the drugs. It just had to have been.

"I've never made the comparison," Morgan said. She wanted to say "better," but there was no use now. "*My* Jordan has a beautiful voice."

"Let me hear it, then." Suzanne gestured toward her piano.

"We didn't come here to—"

"What? You won't let me hear my replacement? I'd love to hear you, Jordan. I'm sure Morgan remembers something you sing."

"Well," Jordan stood and turned to Morgan.

Morgan rose and gestured Jordan toward the piano. Was this a way to show Suzanne what she'd lost? *Yes, let's give her a taste.* "We can do one of your slower songs from last night, something that doesn't need drums." She wasn't going to let Suzanne's animosity ruin the entire afternoon. She sat at the piano.

She tried a few chords. The piano was a little stiff and slightly out of tune. It hadn't been played in a while. Then she started the tune Jordan had sung in the first half of the concert.

Jordan's voice was perfect, as always. She let it soar, and then she cradled it back to caress the sounds, and then let it fly again. She was performing as if to show Suzanne Rhapsody what Morgan had now. She seemed well aware that Suzanne's eyes were watching her very closely. Suzanne kept a close eye on Jordan as she sang out the song in perfect pitch and rhythm. *You see, old woman, you lost me, but I gained this, this wonderful piece of heaven.*

When the song finished, Suzanne clapped. She actually looked impressed. "*Very* nice. Was that one of yours?" she asked Morgan. When Morgan nodded, Suzanne said, "I guess you really have grown up."

"Yes, and I've learned to make better decisions."

Suzanne licked her lips. Morgan hoped she was thinking that yes, she had been a bit strict, even if she only wanted Morgan to succeed. "Are you recording?"

"We're talking to Clyde Barron."

Suzanne nodded. "Absolute is a good label."

"When are *you* going to record again? Everyone's waiting," Jordan asked.

Suzanne shifted her weight. "I'm retired, honey. It's up to you youngsters now."

Morgan could see the loss in Suzanne's eyes. Yes, she really knew she was in the downside of her career. Jordan no doubt wished she could get her to sing for them, just one private performance. For Jordan, it would be a dream come true. But she didn't ask, thank God.

"You'll never go out of style, Suzanne," Jordan said. "Everyone knows and loves your voice."

"Well, when you get famous, I'll do a duet with you. How's that? What do you think, Morgan? Can you handle both of us at once?"

Morgan grinned. "One with each hand?"

Suzanne laughed out loud. "One with each hand." It was the first genuinely relaxed smile she'd had all afternoon. "Well, if anyone could do it, it would be you."

Morgan looked at her hands. She stared at Suzanne for a moment, then closed the keyboard cover and stood. "We should get going. We're flying back tonight."

"You can't stay a little longer?"

"I'm sorry, Suzanne. We have a plane to catch."

"Do you need to call a cab?"

"No, thanks, we have a friend driving us. He's waiting in the car."

"Your own chauffeur!"

"Not yet. Just a friend."

Suzanne stood slowly. "It was nice meeting you, Jordan, and you have a very special voice. You're going far."

"Thank you." Jordan pressed her hand as she went past her to the door.

"It was nice seeing you again," Morgan said as she also went to the door. Maybe that wasn't totally true, but it was the right thing to say. Morgan was ready to walk out the door. There was not even a spark for Suzanne any longer. She just wanted to get away from Suzanne and to block her completely from her past.

"Yes," Suzanne said. As Morgan walked out, Suzanne took her hand and stopped her. "Treat her right, Morgan. You've struck gold there."

"I always had gold. This is just a new vein."

Suzanne smiled and grabbed Morgan's lapel to pull her closer. She gave her a soft kiss on the lips. They looked into each other's eyes, all the what-ifs and the why-nots streaming between them. Then Suzanne stepped back and closed the door.

Morgan hurried down the stairs and got into the car.

"Are you all right?" Jordan asked.

Morgan nodded. "She's not the same." She wiped away a tear. Jack started driving toward the hotel.

"She was nervous," Jordan said. "She still loves you."

"No, she loves the past."

"It's all she has left. You can see that in her eyes."

Morgan nodded.

"When we walked in and she said, haven't you grown up, I wanted to slap her," Jordan said. "I know I shouldn't have any negative feelings toward her because what happened between you and her happened long before you met me, but I just got so angry when she acted like you were still a child and still needed to be told what to do."

Morgan let out a burst of air. "I almost said, haven't you gotten old, but she knows that, so I decided to take the high road. There were a lot of things I wanted to say, but those words should have been said years ago."

Jordan took Morgan's hand and squeezed it to her cheek. "I think she saw what she had forced away. You're right, though. It doesn't make sense to fight about it now. You would have ended right back where you used to be." Jordan patted Morgan's thigh. "And now she's dealing with her health."

"She's not that old. She's not out of her sixties yet. She's sick. I think it took her self-confidence away, too. She used to be more outspoken. She would have critiqued you a lot more. She was being truthful and not just comparing you to herself and what she could do."

"She may have lost her belief in what she can do. I expected her to be much more...you know...more...Suzanne Rhapsody. She was nicer than I was prepared for."

"Yes. I felt that, too." Morgan squeezed Jordan's hand. "I'm glad we came, though. I saw what I needed to see. I can get past it now. I have a long life in front of me...and I have you."

"We have each other," Jordan said as she brought Morgan's hand to her lips.

"Yes." And from here on out, the past was just that, the past.

They both sat back in the car and enjoyed the ride back to the hotel.

Chapter Twenty-four

L ate Sunday night, their plane touched down at Logan, they grabbed their carry-on luggage, and walked to where they could catch a taxi. Their suitcases and other stuff were in the truck, which wouldn't be back until tomorrow night at best. They were all exhausted from the trip and glad to be on the last leg home. Morgan, Jordan, and Robbie grabbed a taxi to take them first to Allston, then on to Brookline. Robbie hadn't smiled all the way home. Something was weighing on her mind. Jordan noticed it and squeezed her hand. "Everything okay?" she asked.

"Yes, I think. I had a decision to make." She smiled at Jordan.

"Do you want to talk about it?"

"Nope. I've made up my mind. It's gonna be fine."

"Good luck," Jordan said. Robbie merely nodded.

The cab slowed down outside Robbie's address, and Robbie got out with her bag. She waved good-bye to Jordan and Morgan, and then walked into her apartment building with determination.

Robbie burst into the apartment. "I'm back," she cried.

"Finally." Chelsea came out of the bedroom to greet her. "How did it go?"

"Oh. Honey! It was fabulous," Robbie said as she hugged Chelsea and gave her a big kiss. "Everybody adored us, *and...*" Robbie was so excited. "The head of Absolute Records was there, and he loved us. He gave Morgan his card and asked her to call him this week."

"Really? Absolute?"

"Yes. We may be on our way. Morgan should find out this week."

"That's wonderful. I'm so proud of you."

"And." She paused again.

"There was more?"

"Yes. Jordan had been rehearsing a new love song that she wrote with Blaine. Morgan didn't know about it. Jordie sang it in the second half and dedicated it to Morgan…then, right after the concert was over, she proposed."

"Proposed? Marriage? Right there?"

"Yes. And Morgan said yes."

"Wow. Backstage? Jordan had to be nervous in front of all the band and backstage crew. What if Morgan had said no?"

"Well, it was sort of private, and she didn't say no. Things were getting better between them. I know Morgan has been more relaxed since she came back from her little trip."

"Did they set a date?"

"No, not yet, but I had an idea. I missed you a lot this weekend, and you know I've been falling more in love with you, so when they get married, do you want to join them?" She took a deep breath, having got that out as fast as she could.

Chelsea stepped back. "Did you just ask me to marry you?"

Robbie looked around the room. "There's nobody else here, so if someone did, it must have been me."

"Roberta Elaine Nelson, are you in your right mind?"

"I thought I was. Do you think that was a crazy idea?"

"No. It's a beautiful idea. I missed you this weekend, too."

"Then will you?"

"I may need to be convinced. Why don't we go into the bedroom and see how you can persuade me?"

"I would love to persuade you. Watch this." She drew Chelsea into her arms, planted their lips together. and walked her back into the bedroom without breaking the lip lock. This would be a fabulous homecoming…and another Sunday night she wouldn't get any sleep.

❖

Morgan called Clyde Barron on Monday afternoon. "Are you still in Chicago or back in Boston?" he asked.

"We're back in Boston, Mr. Barron."

"Let's cut this Mister, Morgan. Call me Clyde."

Morgan chuckled. "That's easier."

"All right. If you're in Boston, I'll call a recording studio there. I want you to do a demo," he said. "Your original music, maybe one oldie if there's something special about the arrangement. Do you all write?"

"No. Robbie, our drummer, and Janis, on sax, don't or haven't." *I guess this means he wants the whole band. Wow. Wait till I tell them. This is what we've all been waiting for.*

"I don't usually ask, but are all of you college trained?"

"Robbie and Jordan graduated from the University of Illinois in Urbana, so they have a solid music background. Janis graduated from Berklee. I'm not sure where Blaine, our guitar player, or Lori, on bass, studied."

"What about you?"

"I grew up playing piano. I then took three and a half years at Berklee here in Boston. I accepted a job with a band in New York before I graduated."

"Did you play with any of the greats?"

Morgan paused. "Suzanne Rhapsody?"

"Really? Good for you. I wish she'd come out of retirement."

Should I let him know about the promise she made with Jordan? I thought our visit would be the last time we would ever see each other. "She promised to do a duet with Jordan if we ever get famous, but I really doubt it."

"That she'll sing or that you'll be famous?" he asked.

"I think there's more of a chance that we'll get famous than that she'll record again."

"Really? I wish she would. That's something to shoot for, though."

"I doubt that will happen."

"No, probably not, but it is a nice thought."

"Yes," Morgan said softly. *I don't want anyone to think we're hanging on to her coattails, even though it would be a big coup for Jordan to sing with her.*

"Have you seen her lately?" he asked.

"We were over at her house yesterday afternoon. She wanted to hear Jordan sing."

"What did she think?"

"She was impressed. I think she was jealous that Jordan's at the start of her career, and she's at the end."

"It's a great loss to the industry." Clyde paused a minute, then launched into a new subject. "Now, just the bass player is married?"

"Jordan and I are engaged."

"Really? Congratulations."

"Thanks."

"I'm looking at potential dropouts due to personal commitments."

"Robbie, the drummer, has been living with her partner for almost six months, but I don't think there'll be a problem there. Janis and Blaine are very single. But that can change in a heartbeat, can't it?"

They discussed the band for almost an hour. He wanted to know everything about them so he'd be prepared for any problems. *Such invasive questions. You'd have thought we were going to work for the CIA or FBI. I'm surprised he doesn't ask me what brand underwear we each wear.*

"Now, eventually we'll have to find a manager for you. I understand you've been doing all the managing, negotiating, payroll, etc. Once we really get started, you won't have time to do any of that. You'll need someone to do all the calling ahead to make sure hotels and venues are ready. You'll need someone to make sure all the equipment is packed, and everyone is on the bus. You'll need someone to make sure the bills are paid, and everyone is fed and happy. You don't need to hire him now, but look for someone you trust. We'll supervise at the beginning, but we want you taken good care of. Look for someone you *really* trust."

"Does it have to be a him?"

"No, but it has to be someone who won't be afraid to fight if the rooms are inadequate, or one of you is unhappy with the food or if the bus breaks down. It has to be someone who will step right in and take charge. It'll be someone who'll be like a mother to you all."

"I understand. How much will that job pay?"

"It depends on how many jobs you get in a row, anywhere from a couple thousand for one concert to about fifty-K for a full tour of about fifteen to twenty shows, but it will go up as you get more jobs."

"All right, that gives me some idea about who to look for."

"Check with your band. If you record three songs, we'll release the two we think will sell, and if they make the cut—that is: sells a million in six months, which I'm sure they will—you'll record the rest of a full album, and we'll release it and schedule a tour."

"Good, Clyde," Morgan said. "I'm pretty sure they'll all be ready for this." Her train of thought switched to Lori, who was collared and also married. Her partner had always been overbearing and controlling with her, and she really wasn't sure Lori was going to be able to get permission from her wife to travel and be away for so long. "The only one I'm worried about is Lori, our bass player. Her wife isn't a big fan of the band, but the reception we got in Chicago might have turned her around. She was there with us."

"Will that be a problem when we go out on the road?"

"I'm not sure."

"Tell Lori how much I said the first recording would bring you. Maybe that will turn her wife's head."

"I hope so. They just bought a house."

"Big mortgage?"

"Two-hundred-K."

"It can be paid by next Christmas."

"I'll tell her."

"What about yours."

"Still owe sixty."

"Nothing to worry about. If two of those tunes are yours, you'll be paid off by Easter."

"Wow." *This is just too much. It's moving so fast and all because of Jordan. She really put her life out there for all of us. I can't believe I'm going to become her wife. This is all just too real.*

"Any other problems?" he asked.

"I don't think so."

"Then we have a start."

"Thank you, Clyde for this opportunity. I can't wait to share it with the band. Talk to you soon." The phone went silent, and Morgan sat back in her chair, letting all the thoughts of the discussion float around in her head. Getting married, going on tour, and getting the house paid off. *And don't forget, recording our own records.* She reached for the diamond clip Jordan had given to her as her engagement symbol. It was all because of Jordan. "All because of you, my love," she said softly as she closed her eyes.

❖

On Tuesday night, when Jordan got back from work, they discussed everything that had happened that afternoon. Jordan reported that she'd called Victoria Walker at Stanberg, Wandelle, and Walker in San Francisco. "We talked for almost an hour. She wants me to write the entire thing as I remember it and send it to her. She thinks she'd like to start with a couple million in damages. Not that I think we'll get it, but at least we'll make a statement. I probably should have done it months ago. I let Lacey's mother spew her hatred, and I ran away. Not that I thought I could have done anything else, but at least I should have said something. I didn't know what else to do. I was terrified and felt betrayed and alone. I just wanted to get the hell out of there."

"Honey, it all came down on you at once: those stupid students with their signs, having to leave your job, Mrs. Sumner and her accusations and hatred, that recording company that ran out on you because they didn't like the way people were reporting on you. That was a shitty day for you, an entire shitty month. I would have run away, too."

"Well, maybe if I can just kick her butt once and make her see what she did, it'll be worth it."

Morgan reached over and wrapped her arms around her. She explained all that Clyde had told her. Jordan explained what Amy had told her about publishing.

"My heavens," Morgan said. "We're getting all this at once. That's phenomenal."

"Yes. A recording contract, getting our music published, and getting my arrangements for choruses published as well."

"And on top of that, maybe some money from Mrs. Sumner for trashing you and making you lose your job."

"Which, looking back, I should thank her for that. I would have never met you. You were the icing on a very tasty cake," Jordan said.

"There is that to thank her for."

"What do you think about the record deal?" Jordan asked when they got ready for bed. "Think we'll make it?"

"I'll have to see the contract first. I should have it tomorrow."

"It will be amazing."

"Everyone's going to be scared but excited, if that makes sense," Morgan said.

"I know Blaine was ready last year, but she was disappointed when that fiasco happened."

"Understandable." Morgan glanced at her computer. "Look. Stan's forwarded a review from a Chicago newspaper." She began to read aloud.

New group bursts onto the scene at the ILC convention. Stone Cold Perception, out of Boston, was highlighted at this year's international convention here in Chicago. They lifted the roof from the Performance Center from the very first song and had the entire place jumping by the end of the concert.

After intermission, Stan Weltz, current President of ILC-International interrupted the music to announce the formation of "Jordan's fund," to provide legal and educational-aid assistance to any person or company who incurs legal debt because of its involvement in the Leather Community.

This fund was named for Jordan Phelps, singer with Stone Cold Perception, who was jailed in Southern California when fire broke out at the Furies Loft, a BDSM play club, and left a person seriously injured. Ms. Phelps was eventually cleared of any wrong-doing but lost her job and a recording contract because of the backlash. She subsequently moved to Boston. After the announcement, over thirty-five hundred dollars was collected with promises of an additional hundred and fifty thousand more. Weltz says he expects the fund to bring in close to a quarter of a million dollars.

Shortly after the collection, Phelps debuted and dedicated a new love song to the pianist and leader of the group, Morgan Sparks. Both that song and the rest of the concert was magnificent.

Phelps, Sparks, and the other musicians provided an outstanding collection of songs, and hinted that they will soon release a recording. To say they rivaled others already in the field would be foolish. They are as good, if not better, than many groups that have been making records for years. We can't wait to hear their first offering.

Jordan looked deeply into Morgan's eyes. She stepped forward and took Morgan's hand, pulled them together, and kissed her.

"That's a good start for the evening," Morgan whispered.

"How's this for a segue?" She pulled Morgan out of the chair, walked her to their bed, and gently pushed her back onto the comforter. She leaned down to take Morgan's shirt off, leaving only her panties. "I'll get that off you soon enough," she said and leaned forward to cover Morgan with herself. As she slid up and down Morgan's body, their breasts rubbed back and forth against each other.

"No foreplay tonight," she said as she rolled off. She kissed her and reached into Morgan's underwear and felt the warm, slickness already there. "I love you, Morgan," she said.

"As much as I love you?"

"More."

"Not possible."

Jordan slid her fingers into Morgan, reaching in as far as they'd go, curling to meet that spot that sent her overboard. She then brought her lips to Morgan's left breast and started to tease it with her tongue and teeth while squeezing her right nipple.

Good God. I love this woman. Where has she been all my life? The entire world was mediocre-to-horrible until I walked into the club and saw her playing. Now everything is exploding, including me.

Jordan could feel Morgan's body tightening up and down her spine as her fingers slid in and out. She inched down to plant her lips on Morgan's clit. She lapped up the saltiness collecting there. This was what she wanted. It was more valuable than the record, the tour, the fame or even the money that fame would bring them. Her teeth pressed into Morgan's clit.

Morgan's back arched, and she ran her hands through Jordan's hair, her fingers getting straighter and straighter as her whole body began to stiffen in climax. Jordan wrapped her arms around Morgan's legs and continued to feast on the banquet Morgan was giving her.

"Jordan," Morgan screamed as her body exploded in waves of release. Jordan crawled up and planted her lips on Morgan's and kissed her hard and deep. It was many minutes before Morgan's breath settled, and her body relaxed.

"My God, Jordan. No one's ever made me come as deep as you do. Never."

"Sometimes, you need the good old-fashioned direct approach," she said with a big smile. "Being able to bend your finger to the side also helps."

They both laughed.

"I love your fingers, too," said Jordan. "They do such wonderful things, too."

Morgan giggled. "Like play well enough to get us a recording deal?"

"Yes, you make me sound so much better than anyone else has. Until now, no one has ever brought out the true me and my singing ability."

"Oh, I don't know…you and Blaine really blasted that love song. By the way, who wrote that?"

"Blaine and I, about three years ago, but we hadn't finished it. We'd been working on it while you were at work. We brought Lori and Janis in on it at Lori's house one night, too."

"It was beautiful."

"Do you want to do an arrangement for the whole band?" Jordan asked.

"Should I? It was wonderful with just you four."

"We could do the first verse by ourselves and bring you and Robbie in little by little?"

"Let me think about it."

"Think about this," Jordan said as she leaned in to kiss Morgan. It was her turn again. She slipped down Morgan's body, all the way until her knees touched the floor, and her face was level with Morgan's crotch. She opened her mouth as if to take a big bite, but instead, she nuzzled in and took that clit with her teeth again.

"I love you," she said. "I love this, I love being with you. I love everything about you." As she started up Morgan's body, she named each part. "I love your feet, your ankles, and your calves. I love your knees, your thighs, your clit, and I adore your hips and your pelvis, and your butt. I love your waist, your belly button, your ribs, your breasts, and these delectable nipples on top of them." She ran her tongue all around Morgan's breasts. "Good God, I love all of you, Morgan Justine Sparks who hates being called Sparkie."

Morgan burst out laughing. "Where did you hear that?"

"On the grapevine," she said. "Don't you?"

"Yes, I was called that all the way through grade school, and I hated it."

"Do you prefer stud?"

"Given just those two, yes, I prefer stud," Morgan said.

"I prefer you being a stud, too. I've had far too many sparks and fires in my day."

"You don't want any sparks?"

"Show me that stud. Show me Stud Sparks."

Morgan reached around Jordan and twisted her down to the bed. Her hand slid between Jordan's legs. She took Jordan's mouth with her tongue and her pussy with her hand. That lit more sparks than Jordan ever imagined.

CHAPTER TWENTY-FIVE

A week later, Morgan called a meeting of the band at her house on Monday night. Everyone arrived and settled in with their drinks. Morgan had delayed the meeting until everyone could be there, and she was still worried about Lori. She needed to know that Lori was on board and could do this without question. She didn't want to have to exclude her or replace her in the middle of a tour.

"Okay. Are we going to be famous?" Robbie was the first to ask.

"It seems we already are." She handed out copies of the review Stan had sent her.

"Wow. I guess we were good," Lori said, scanning the page.

"We need to talk about this. It will mean a big change in our lives." Morgan sat and related everything Clyde had told her.

"So if we burn a record, we could make over fifty thousand apiece?" Robbie asked.

"Well, if it's a good record, but then we'd be expected to go on tour, which would mean being on the road for a while. It could be as long as six months. So it's up to you."

Lori immediately spoke up. "Damn, I like the sound of it, but I doubt Mel would."

"Tell her about all the money you'd be making," Robbie suggested. "That might persuade her. You could have your new house paid for by Christmas of next year."

"We'll see."

"I want all of you to think about what you can do," Morgan said. "Playing in the band is one thing, and it will get you paid well. Composers get a lot more, so if you want to work on something, do it."

"I'm in," Blaine said.

"I'm ready, too," Robbie said.

"Let me make sure I have this straight," Janis said. "We do a recording here and let the folks at Absolute release it. It could fly, or it could sink. If it flies and sells a million downloads in six months, we record more to make a full album, which they will release, and we get a tour scheduled. We can't tell right now how long the tour would be. It could be as long as six months on the road, playing two or more times a week." She looked around as the others nodded. "We could get quite a lot from the recording but a lot more if we compose one of the pieces on it. The tour will be even more, but we won't know until we start. The start is to make the demo recording. Then, we take it step by step."

"How much will we make on a tour?" Blaine asked.

"Well, first, all the expenses have to be covered: hotel, the price of a tour bus, food, advertising, all of that, then our extras are paid, and we'd split the rest. It depends on how well the show sells, how much it costs to get there and back, and all the other expenses. So don't quit your day jobs yet. You don't have to commit to a tour until after the first recording is out, and the tour is scheduled. That would probably be next spring." Morgan was beginning to feel the pressure of trying to make this sound good and yet divulge all of the cons.

"You think we can really do this?" Janis asked.

"We can try. It's always a gamble, but if we don't try, we'll never know what could have been." Morgan looked at each of them.

"Let me talk it over with Mel," Lori said. "Answer me this, though. If I make the record but don't go on tour with you, would I still get the money?"

"Of course," Morgan said right away. "You wouldn't get anything from our tour, but you would get the record money. Of course, if we made a second record, we'd have to use the new bassist."

"That's understandable. I'll talk with Mel."

"All right. We're golden with Jordan, Robbie, Blaine, and me. We still need to wait on Janis and Lori to make the decision. Correct?"

"How soon does Clyde want to know?" Lori asked.

"Well, as soon as we say yes, he'll put everything in motion."

"Why don't you two say you'll do the initial demo," Lori said, "then you'll have a few months to decide on the record and the tour. By then we'll also know how successful we might be, how long the tour would go, and also how much we'll be making on it."

"That could work," said Janis.

"That will give me more time," Lori said.

"Which songs do we want to do first?" Morgan asked.

They sat down to discuss that. It took several hours as they all had their favorites with solos they either wanted to play or were afraid of.

"Second problem," Morgan said, "we'll need a tour manager, someone to call ahead and make reservations, make sure we're all on the plane or bus, that all our equipment is with us, and we're all fed and watered. I would say the beginning salary is around two thousand a concert, but it'll rise as we get more gigs. As Clyde described it, we need a mother, although most tour managers are men. We need someone to take over if the tour bus breaks down."

"Mel works for a company that does different seminars all over the world," Lori said. "She's used to making hotel and bus reservations and planning banquets for two to three hundred people at a time. Let me talk to her. She might be interested, or she may know someone who might be."

"Well, we don't need anyone right away, but if we go on tour next spring, we will. It's also a 'maybe' job. We can't guarantee how long it will be or how many shows it will cover. We may have ten shows over three months, and that's it, or we may have a hundred shows over six months or two hundred throughout the year." Morgan tried to keep reality in perspective but also threw in a little boost to bring in some enthusiasm.

"It's something to think about. Of course, before that even happens, we have to cut that demo."

They looked around at each other. "Which three songs do we want to do?" Morgan asked.

"Your 'Saturday Night' is always a big hit," Robbie said.

"Yes. That could be one." They all agreed. "What else?"

"How about 'Midnight Blue'?" Lori said.

"That's a good one. Everyone in Chicago loved it."

"And 'Mistakes'?" Blaine said.

"Or 'Just,'" suggested Robbie. "I loved that one."

"Morgan's going to arrange it so we can all play on it," Jordan said.

"Let's save that for the full album. I think we need three up songs so we set our style. The slow ballads can be the surprises on the album." Morgan wasn't ready to give up *her* song just yet to the world. Besides, she just might want it played at her wedding.

"That's what you did on Suzanne's Blue Moon album," Robbie said.

Morgan looked up. "How did you know that?"

"I found your name on the back of the album."

"What's this?" Janis asked.

Morgan gritted her teeth. She'd have to explain. *Can't Suzanne for once just crawl back into whatever dark place she came from? It's my time to shine, not carry her along like an old piece of sheet music.*

"I used to play for Suzanne Rhapsody," she said softly.

"What?" Lori asked. "Why didn't we know that?"

"Why didn't anyone tell us?"

Morgan felt embarrassed. "I don't usually tell people about it."

"Why not? I'd be bragging all over the place," Blaine said.

"Well, it was years ago."

"Do you still talk with her?" Janis asked. "I heard she was retired."

"Yes, we visited her when we were in Chicago," Jordan said.

"You did? And you didn't let us know?" Robbie said.

"It was Sunday afternoon. You'd already left," Jordan said

"She's older," Morgan said. "She doesn't see many people."

Blaine, Robbie, Janis, and Lori had question after question. "What was she like? Does she still play? Is she still recording?"

Morgan tried to politely answer their questions, but all she really wanted to do was get back to the recording meeting. "She's completely gray. Almost white," Morgan said again.

"Did she ask to hear some of your music?"

"Did she ask to hear you sing?"

"Yes," Jordan said. "I sang 'Midnight Blue,' and she said I had a good future ahead of me."

❖

Jordan saw the look on Morgan's face. She knew that Morgan was getting frustrated with all the questions. She knew the girls didn't mean anything by it, but Morgan had had enough. It was time to shut them down. "Anything else?"

"Well, I have an announcement," Robbie said. "I asked Chelsea to marry me."

"Robbie!" Morgan said.

"You?" Lori asked.

"Are you serious?"

"Were you drunk?"

"Did she say yes?"

Robbie grinned shyly. "Not yet, but she asked me to persuade her."

"And have you been?" Morgan asked.

"We haven't slept all week."

Everyone laughed, but Morgan still looked worn out, especially as the conversation began to turn toward Suzanne again.

"That's enough for tonight," Jordan said. "If we ever go back to Chicago, we'll see if she'll meet with you, but Morgan's right. She's really into her retirement. She looks older. She wasn't that well." Jordan studied Morgan. She didn't want her to close down again, and she would if pushed to rethink the visit.

"I'm not ready to talk about it," Morgan said. "It was a tough time in my life. I was living in New York, and there was a lot of drug use and other stuff there."

Everyone looked at her but didn't ask anything else. "Are you okay?" Jordan asked.

Morgan nodded. "Okay, so we decided on 'Saturday Night,' 'Midnight Blue,' and 'Mistakes.' Right?"

"Yes, that's it," Robbie said.

"And we'll think of someone for manager," added Lori.

"Anything else?" Jordan asked abruptly. *Let's end this meeting.*

No one seemed to have anything to add. "I'll email the contract back, and then I'll call you when Clyde sets a recording date," Morgan said.

"Sounds good to me." Lori said as she got up and headed for the door. "See you later."

"Me, too," Janis and Robbie said at the same time. Robbie eyed Jordan with a questioning look.

Jordan turned to look at Morgan, who was just sitting there, not really looking at anything. Jordan walked the two to the door and stepped outside. "It was hard for her to see how far Suzanne had slipped," she explained softly. "She'll be okay."

Janis patted Robbie's shoulder, and Robbie nodded as they went down the front steps to get into their cars. When Jordan walked back into the house, Blaine wanted to talk.

"If we're going to continue with this band, I should start looking for my own place," Blaine said.

"I've been thinking about that," said Jordan. "I still have that room in Cambridge. I never gave it up. You could move in there, I think. You'd just have to meet with Carole, Kathy, and Bob. It's a comfortable place, and you won't need to buy any furniture or cooking stuff. It will give you time to look around. You might decide to move here, or you could commute back and forth to California. It's not expensive here, and you could afford to buy a car."

Blaine thought about it. "I'll have to meet them."

"I'll bring you over this weekend, and we can go looking for a car any morning this week."

"If you need it, I could loan you the money for the car," Morgan added as she walked into the room.

"It doesn't have to be a new car. I'll get that when we make it big."

CHAPTER TWENTY-SIX

That same week, Jordan decided to email Principal Wright to say hi and check in. She knew it was summer vacation break but expected there'd be someone in the school. She wrote:

Dear Principal Wright, Ethyl, how are you? I hope the school year went well there. I have settled in Boston and am very happy here. I didn't look for another teaching job for this past year, but I have a good job at a restaurant greeting customers Tuesday through Thursday and performing with a band there on Friday and Saturday. If I decide to apply for a teaching position, next year, would you still write me a reference? Hopefully, a good one? Also, can I get copies of the arrangements I made for the choruses? They are all in my handwriting. I think there were about twenty of them. I've had an offer to have them published. Of course, your schools can use them as much as they want. Oh, and I'm engaged. I'll marry Morgan Sparks, the pianist with the band here. She had a wonderful career in music. She played with Suzanne Rhapsody for a few years. She introduced me to Ms. Rhapsody last week and had me sing for her. We're also talking to Absolute Records about recording a few tunes this year.

Wishing all of you a good year, Jordan Phelps

She got a reply that afternoon:

Jordan! It's good to hear that you found some place to settle and that you're happy. I was always so regretful to see you leave. Your life there sounds wonderful, and I wish you all of the best. Everyone here sends their good wishes. The new music teacher we hired in your place can be a little pedantic at times, but his results are good, although the concerts are not as much fun as yours were. Of course I'll send your arrangements. They will be in a package to your home, if you send the address. I'll also include a reference letter. I hope you get a good teaching position, if that is the road you wish to travel. Congratulation on your betrothal. We wish you and Morgan the happiest and most successful life together. Please let me know what else you are doing from time to time. We think of you often.

Best wishes for your success.
Ethyl Wright

Jordan sat back in her chair and closed her eyes. Ethyl Wright was true to her word. *She is proud of me and missed me. It's one part of California I do miss. Probably the part I miss the most. I'm glad I wrote her, and yes, we will keep in touch. She is one person from my past that I want to remain in my future.*

She turned back to the computer and composed a second letter to Ms. Wright, sending her address.

Friday night went very well at the restaurant. The crowd was happy that the band was back after their short vacation. The place was filled. Even though a complete week had passed, word had gotten out that they were back, and everyone wanted to see them.

After they closed the final set, a tall black woman walked up to Jordan. She was dressed in a two-piece, navy blue, pinstriped suit with a cream silk blouse. Her shoes were semi-flats, and she carried a mahogany lawyers' brief case in one hand. Her makeup was light and very professional. "Jordan Phelps?" she asked, holding out her hand. "Victoria Walker."

"Really?" Jordan didn't know what to say.

"Yes. I had to meet you. I'm in Boston for the weekend. Can we meet for a while tomorrow?"

"Of course. I'd be happy to."

"You know this place better than me. Where do you suggest?"

"Let me just doublecheck it with Morgan." She turned and saw Morgan still sitting at the piano, going through some music. She hurried over to her. "Victoria Walker is here…the attorney who's going to take my case? Where do you suggest we meet her tomorrow?"

Morgan got up and walked over, and Jordan introduced them. "Why don't you come to our place tomorrow?" Morgan asked. "Come for dinner. We can relax, and there's no time restraint."

"That sounds great."

"Do you have a rental, or will you be in a taxi?"

"Probably a taxi. I'm at a hotel nearby."

"I'll pick you up," Jordan suggested. "In fact, stick around for a few minutes, and we'll drop you off tonight."

"You don't have to," Victoria said.

"It'll be nice getting to know you."

"All right," Victoria said. "I understand you two live together."

"Yes. We do."

Morgan smiled. "Let me get my music put up, and I'm ready."

The next afternoon, Jordan and Victoria entered the house through the back door into the kitchen at around three p.m.

"Something smells wonderful," Victoria said.

"Don't look at me. I was just watching it. She made it earlier. I don't cook." Morgan wistfully blurted. She took a look at Victoria and almost fell off her stool. She had completely transformed from the upscale lawyer to just an ordinary, working-class woman.

"No. For such an accomplished woman," Jordan said, "the best she can make is a call for delivery or reservations."

"That's not true. I'm not bad at breakfast," Morgan protested.

"If you like toast and coffee."

"Who doesn't?"

Victoria laughed. "And you're going to get married?"

"Yes. I'm saving the world," Jordan said. "Come sit down in the living room." She led Victoria into the front of the house, and Morgan fixed her a drink. Jordan went back to check her roast before they all got down to business.

"I read through your entire narrative of that night," Victoria said. "Good God, Jordan, how could you survive that?"

"Because the opposite was unthinkable, and I did what I had to do."

"If Mrs. Sumner hadn't pressured the police, they wouldn't have done anything?"

"No. I went home that morning thinking that Lacey's injuries were all we had to worry about. When the police showed up at my house, I was completely floored. I mean, I was scared because I had never been arrested, but what I couldn't understand was the charge."

"And Lacey was your lover at the time?"

"Sort of. We were more playmates than anything. We weren't romantic with each other. I mean, I felt close to her, and I cared about her, but we weren't in love."

"But you wouldn't have hurt her."

"Harm, no. You have to remember that in the Leather community, hurt and harm are two very different concepts."

"I'll remember that. Now, what you lost was your job, your contract, your honor, and you had to give up your home."

"That's right."

"And your teaching salary?"

"I was making fifty-four thousand."

"And the contract?" Victoria asked.

"There was no amount stated."

"No," Morgan said, "the one we have now depends on the two recorded demos we make. If it sells a million downloads in six months, then we'll make a record and sign for a tour. It's all contingent on the demos."

"Which you hadn't made yet," Victoria said.

"No, but we've been told that we'd each make around twenty-K within the next six months on this one."

"And besides your teaching," Victoria asked, "was there anything else you lost?"

"Well," Jordan said, "the year before, I was asked to conduct the all-county festival chorus."

"So your music teaching was well-known around the area?"

"Yes. I was hoping to conduct the all-state chorus in a couple years."

Victoria wrote this all down.

"My high school chorus won awards three years in a row during the all-state competitions," Jordan said.

"You were a well-respected music teacher there."

"Yes. I'd been asked to run for the board of the Music Teachers Association, but I didn't."

"Would that have brought you more money?" Victoria asked.

"Probably. I never checked to see how much."

"And you said Ethyl Wright was the principal of your school."

"Correct."

"Did she ask you to resign?"

"No. I offered, and she didn't want to accept it until the parents started calling. We really didn't have a choice."

"So if Mrs. Sumner hadn't interfered in police business, it would have been reported as an unfortunate accident."

Jordan nodded.

"Do you think Jordan has a case?" Morgan asked.

"I do. Not only did Elizabeth Sumner interfere with police procedure, she slandered Jordan and caused her to lose a minimum of ninety thousand dollars that year alone. If Jordan hadn't resigned, she might have been making sixty thousand a year at the school, plus all that would come from the recording. I want to sue for one million and settle for five hundred thousand."

Jordan sat back and looked at the ceiling. "I'd settle for a public apology. I had no idea I had lost so much money."

"We'll get that anyway."

"All right, Victoria. Thank you. Let me get dinner on the table, and then we can keep talking."

❖

Two months later, Jordan flew to California for the first case hearing. She had forgotten how much she missed the traffic and buildings here. She stepped out of the cab and walked the towering steps into the courthouse. Victoria was waiting. A small crowd of people had gathered outside the courtroom, some witnesses in upcoming cases, some just spectators. Jordan wished that Morgan had been able to come stand with her. She felt naked without her.

"Are you ready to do this?" Victoria asked.

"I'm as ready as I'll ever be. I'll just be glad to put this all behind me."

"I'm sure you will be."

Just as she started to ask Victoria a question, she felt a tap on her shoulder. She turned only to see an old but familiar face standing before her.

"You didn't need to do this," Elizabeth Sumner growled.

"Neither did you," Jordan replied.

Victoria frowned at Jordan and pulled her away. They walked into the courtroom and to the complainant's side of the table and took a seat. The judge entered, and the whole room stood. The judge was seated and Jordan's case presented.

Jordan reiterated what had happened that night. There were affidavits from Harry, Principal Wright, and several other people who knew her. She was presented as a promising teacher and an asset to the community.

William Sumner testified that he supported his wife's actions. The original recorded deposition Lacey had offered during Jordan's "trial" was presented, too. She hadn't been called to testify as she would have been a hostile witness, wanting to back Jordan but not wanting to be against her parents.

Mrs. Sumner testified how disturbed she'd been to see her daughter possibly burned to death. When Jordan heard her testimony, she wanted to run from the courtroom. Was what she was doing right? She did cause the fire that had burned Lacey. She couldn't imagine seeing her child go through the recovery after being burned. It must have been horrible.

The case didn't last long, but the judge said he needed to take it into consideration and would rule the following week.

"I think it's going well. The Sumners didn't offer much of a rebuttal," Victoria told her as she dropped Jordan off at the airport. "I'll be in touch. I don't think you'll be needed at the next hearing."

"I still don't need any money. I'll be satisfied if she clears my name."

"You'll definitely get that. I'll let you know as things happen."

"Thanks so much, Victoria. I really appreciate all the work you've done on this."

"Just relax, record your record, and give my regards to Morgan."

On the plane home, Jordan looked out of the window as she took off from the airport. The buildings got smaller and smaller as the plane rose in the air. Her mind drifted once more to the words Mrs. Sumner said during her testimony. Then Jordan watched as the buildings disappeared beneath the clouds. She closed her eyes and quietly congratulated herself on standing up and fighting for her dignity and self-worth. When this was over, she would always be known in the Leather community as the woman who began the fight for those discriminated against and hurt in this lifestyle. Her name would always be one of firsts and leadership. All because she chose not to let someone take her life from her.

CHAPTER TWENTY-SEVEN

Today was a slow day. Yesterday, Morgan had sold a house but had no appointments today. Twelve weeks had passed since their recording, and there was no sign their band was going anywhere. She was still sitting at the piano playing the usual songs, and Jordan was still singing and playing host at the restaurant. The band members were beginning to think the music contract had all been just hype to get their hopes up.

Morgan's phone rang. The name of the incoming caller was Absolute. "Hi, Clyde. What's up?"

"Three months, Morgan. It's been on the market for three months."

"Yes. I know. What's up with it?"

"It sold! You're over the million mark."

Morgan was too surprised to respond. Her hand trembled as she tried to hang on to the phone. *Is this really happening? Did he just say a million?*

"Are you still there?" he asked.

"Uh, yuh. Is today April first?"

"Not yet. It's only January fifteenth."

"Then why are you playing an April Fool's joke on me?" She tried so hard to believe this was real, but she just had to ask if he was fooling her.

Clyde laughed heartily. "This is no joke, Morgan. No one has sold that fast since that boy band from South Korea. You'd better get into the studio and finish the album. I'll call the recording studio and set up some time for you. Tell the band that they've each got about twenty-three thousand coming. But you personally have around thirty-six thousand dollars waiting for you, and it's still selling."

"Are you sure?"

"Yes, Morgan. Now, will this interfere with your wedding?"

Oh my God, Jordan and our wedding. The wedding was planned for Valentine's Day. *We have to tour. We have to buy clothes and pack. We need a manager, a bus, and food. Keep well, stay healthy.* "I'm going to have to sit down and think this through. You've caught me completely off guard."

"Well, tell your bride that she's a superstar and hurry back into the studio. Do you know what you're going to record?"

"I think we do. We've been working on some."

"Well, then, get back into the studio."

"You're sure? It's only been three months."

Clyde laughed loudly as the phone went dead. She stared at the machine that only made beeping sounds.

What time was it? Just after eleven? Jordan wouldn't have left for work yet. She could get home in time. *Oh my God.* Morgan danced around the room, laughing and singing bits of 'Just.' *She's never going to believe this.*

"I'm going home for a little while. I don't have any appointments. I'll try to get back, but if I don't, I'll see you in the morning," Morgan told her secretary as she walked past. She thought her secretary responded, but she wasn't certain of anything at the moment.

She got into her car and started toward home. She wasn't sure how she got there and couldn't remember any of the drive, but she pulled into her driveway. Jordan's car was still in the garage.

When she walked in the back door, no one was in the kitchen or the living room, so she went upstairs. Jordan was in the bedroom getting dressed. "What are you doing home in the middle of the day?"

"I had to kiss you to get a reality check."

"Well, that's easy." She walked over, threw her arms around Morgan's neck, and gave her a long hard kiss. "What are you checking reality for?"

"Clyde called to tell us we've reached the million-download mark."

Jordan's eye went wide. "For real?"

"That's what he said. He said the only ones who've gone that fast was that boy band from South Korea. He's making arrangements to get us back into the studio."

Jordan sank down onto the bed. "Oh my God," she moaned. "I can't believe it."

"Now we've got to tell the others. Tonight's Wednesday. Robbie and Lori will be at the restaurant. Let's tell the others to meet us there. We'll have a bottle of champagne waiting."

"Paul will not be happy."

"Well, we're not quitting yet."

"I can't believe this."

"No, me either."

"Let's take a moment before we tell the others. It's only one thirty. We have time to do our own celebration."

"I was hoping you'd say that."

Jordan reached for Morgan's belt and started undressing her. This was going to be one celebration that she'd never forget.

❖

That night at The Dam Restaurant, they had a celebration unlike any that had been there before.

Jordan had called and asked Paul to put a dozen bottles of champagne on ice but didn't tell him why. Morgan asked Blaine and Janis to bring their instruments and asked everyone in the band to meet a half hour before they were scheduled to begin and to bring their significant others.

When they got there, Jordan met with Paul and told him what was happening. He was ecstatic for them but unhappy that he'd now have four months to find a new band for the restaurant. That evening, he said he'd act as host so Jordan could celebrate with her friends.

When the band arrived, a table was set up for them with bottles of champagne on ice and flutes for them to drink from. "Is this what I think it is?" Robbie asked. Chelsea had come with her. Mel was also there with Lori.

"Well, gang. It's only been three months, but today we went over the one million downloads mark," Morgan said. They all whooped with joy. "I talked with Clyde this morning. He wants us in the studio as quickly as possible." She told them what he had said about the quickness of their sales. "This will mean we'll probably start a tour in May, or June, sometime around then. Don't quit your day job just yet, but get yourselves prepared to take that step."

Jordan popped the cork on one of the bottles and started pouring. Robbie popped the second one. "Here's to us, guys. We're taking the second step on our journey." Jordan toasted and held her glass up and took a sip. "And this is happening before the wedding."

The cheers and happy laughter filled the room. "And here's to Morgan for pulling us all together," Lori added.

"And to Jordan for making us the hottest band in the nation!"

"You'd better make an announcement before the whole restaurant starts asking questions," Jordan whispered to Morgan. Morgan nodded, then went up to the stage and flipped the sound system on.

"Ladies and gentlemen," she started, "the band will be a little late starting tonight, but you'll hear a lot more than you bargained for. Tonight, we're celebrating because our demo record has sold over one million downloads in just three months. Because of that, we will be going back into the studio to record the rest of a full album that will be released by Absolute Records in Chicago. Many of you know that we took a week off last summer to perform in Chicago, and the president of Absolute heard us. We signed with them and released two tunes in October. Today, we were notified that they've met their mark, so we got the go-ahead to finish our first album. Tonight, the other two members of our band, Blaine Jones and Janis Lynkowski will join us for a few tunes while we celebrate. Thank you all."

There was cheering and applause throughout the restaurant.

Jordan took over the microphone. "And because this restaurant and its patrons have supported us for almost five years, tonight, we'll buy everyone here a glass of champagne so you can help us celebrate." She'd already cleared it with Paul, and the servers were starting to go around the room making sure everyone had a glass of the bubbly. It seemed overwhelming to be able to finally share something good with people. Everyone was laughing and having a good time. Jordan looked over the room and then back at Morgan. She nodded as if to say, *I am happy.*

"Let's start something before we get too loaded to remember how to play." Morgan got everyone up on stage and tuned. "Our first demo, something we hope we don't make a lot of, 'Mistakes.'"

Robbie counted off, and the celebration started. Everyone there was fully engrossed in the music, and it became one monster party.

As they settled into the car to drive home, Jordan pulled out her phone to find a long email waiting. "Morgan, listen to this. I got an email from Victoria."

Knew you were working and didn't want to disturb you, but I hope you sleep well tonight. I told you two weeks ago that the courts awarded you damages of a half-million dollars for your complaint against Elizabeth Sumner. The Sumners, of course, protested, tried to file a counter charge, and protested the ruling, saying they'd need to sell their house and property. We signed the agreement with Mrs. Sumner this afternoon to reduce the amount to one-fifth. I know you said you didn't care about the money as long as she apologized, but I couldn't let her off that easily. We agreed to settle for a lesser amount so they can remain in their home, although they will have to sell other property. Mrs. Sumner will write a full and solemn apology to you. So you'll be receiving the money very shortly and the apology, which will be sent to newspapers and other news outlets around Southern California and neighboring states. She will make it her concern to elevate your reputation within the entire community. I'll send you a copy as soon as it's released. Give your honey a hug from me and start planning a dynamite honeymoon.

Best, Victoria Walker

"Jordan!" Morgan sighed. "Now we have even more to celebrate tonight. I hope you don't have anything planned for early tomorrow."

"What time is it now?" Jordan asked as they drove into the driveway, "Because if it's past midnight, I have a hell of a lot of things planned for early *this* morning."

"You do?" Morgan asked as they arrived home, and she closed the garage door. "Anything that includes me?" They walked into the house.

"A lot of things that include you, my exquisite good luck charm. My whole world changed for the best when I met you, and I'm never going to let you go." She turned and locked the kitchen door behind her. "Now, get your sexy little butt upstairs where I can give it the attention it needs."

"Is this where I'm supposed to say, yes, Mistress?"

"No, but soon you can say, yes, Missus."

"I can hardly wait." She turned and lifted Jordan in her arms and carried her up to the bedroom.

"Isn't this what you're supposed to do after we're married, stud?"

"Just practicing." She threw Jordan onto the bed and started taking her clothes off, only stopping to kiss her. "I can't wait to get into the studio, either."

"And we haven't heard from Amy about publishing our music."

"You should call her and tell her about the record. That will make those arrangements and our music much more valuable next year."

"I'll think about doing that tomorrow...or later today. I have much more important things to do right now."

Jordan reached up, pulled Morgan down onto the bed, and kissed her with all her strength.

As they both wanted, there was no leader, no follower, no Mistress or sub, just the two of them. Soon they would be Mrs. and Mrs., bringing new music to the world as only they could.

About the Author

Nanisi had a successful music career as a pianist and conductor and performed and traveled around the world. She has lived in New England, Washington State, and the central south U.S. She now lives on thirty acres of wooded land in south central Oklahoma with her partner of over twenty years.

When MS curtailed travel and performing, she turned to writing. She has written mysteries, romances, and erotica in both novel and short story form. Her novel *In Helen's Hands* is a finalist for a Golden Crown Literary Award.

Books Available from Bold Strokes Books

A Different Man by Andrew L. Huerta. This diverse collection of stories chronicling the challenges of gay life at various ages shines a light on the progress made and the progress still to come. (978-1-63555-977-4)

All That Remains by Sheri Lewis Wohl. Johnnie and Shantel might have to risk their lives—and their love—to stop a werewolf intent on killing. (978-1-63555-949-1)

Beginner's Bet by Fiona Riley. Phenom luxury Realtor Ellison Gamble has everything, except a family to share it with, so when a mix-up brings youthful Katie Crawford into her life, she bets the house on love. (978-1-63555-733-6)

Dangerous Without You by Lexus Grey. Throughout their senior year in high school, Aspen, Remington, Denna, and Raleigh face challenges in life and romance that they never expect. (978-1-63555-947-7)

Desiring More by Raven Sky. In this collection of steamy stories, a rich variety of lovers find themselves desiring more, more from a lover, more from themselves, and more from life. (978-1-63679-037-4)

Jordan's Kiss by Nanisi Barrett D'Arnuck. After losing everything in a fire, Jordan Phelps joins a small lounge band and meets pianist Morgan Sparks, who lights another blaze, this time in Jordan's heart. (978-1-63555-980-4)

Late City Summer by Jeanette Bears. Forced together for her wedding, Emily Stanton and Kate Alessi navigate their lingering passion for one another against the backdrop of New York City and World War II, and a summer romance they left behind. (978-1-63555-968-2)

Love and Lotus Blossoms by Anne Shade. On her path to self-acceptance and true passion, Janesse will risk everything—and possibly everyone—she loves. (978-1-63555-985-9)

Love in the Limelight by Ashley Moore. Marion Hargreaves, the finest actress of her generation, and Jessica Carmichael, the world's biggest pop star, rediscover each other twenty years after an ill-fated affair. (978-1-63679-051-0)

Suspecting Her by Mary P. Burns. Complications ensue when Erin O'Connor falls for top real estate saleswoman Catherine Williams while investigating racism in the real estate industry; the fallout could end their chance at happiness. (978-1-63555-960-6)

Two Winters by Lauren Emily Whalen. A modern YA retelling of Shakespeare's *The Winter's Tale* about birth, death, Catholic school, improv comedy, and the healing nature of time. (978-1-63679-019-0)

Busy Ain't the Half of It by Frederick Smith and Chaz Lamar Cruz. Elijah and Justin seek happily-ever-afters in LA, but are they too busy to notice happiness when it's there? (978-1-63555-944-6)

Calumet by Ali Vali. Jaxon Lavigne and Iris Long had a forbidden small-town romance that didn't last, and the consequences of that love will be uncovered fifteen years later at their high school reunion. (978-1-63555-900-2)

Her Countess to Cherish by Jane Walsh. London Society's material girl realizes there is more to life than diamonds when she falls in love with a non-binary bluestocking. (978-1-63555-902-6)

Hot Days, Heated Nights by Renee Roman. When Cole and Lee meet, instant attraction quickly flares into uncontrollable passion, but their connection might be short lived as Lee's identity is tied to her life in the city. (978-1-63555-888-3)

Never Be the Same by MA Binfield. Casey meets Olivia and sparks fly in this opposites attract romance that proves love can be found in the unlikeliest places. (978-1-63555-938-5)

Quiet Village by Eden Darry. Something not quite human is stalking Collie and her niece, and she'll be forced to work with undercover reporter Emily Lassiter if they want to get out of Hyam alive. (978-1-63555-898-2)

Shaken or Stirred by Georgia Beers. Bar owner Julia Martini and home health aide Savannah McNally attempt to weather the storms brought on by a mysterious blogger trashing the bar, family feuds they knew nothing about, and way too much advice from way too many relatives. (978-1-63555-928-6)

The Fiend in the Fog by Jess Faraday. Can four people on different trajectories work together to save the vulnerable residents of East London from the terrifying fiend in the fog before it's too late? (978-1-63555-514-1)

The Marriage Masquerade by Toni Logan. A no strings attached marriage scheme to inherit a Maui B&B uncovers unexpected attractions and a dark family secret. (978-1-63555-914-9)

Flight SQA016 by Amanda Radley. Fastidious airline passenger Olivia Lewis is used to things being a certain way. When her routine is changed by a new, attractive member of the staff, sparks fly. (978-1-63679-045-9)

Home Is Where the Heart Is by Jenny Frame. Can Archie make the countryside her home and give Ash the fairytale romance she desires? Or will the countryside and small village life all be too much for her? (978-1-63555-922-4)

Moving Forward by PJ Trebelhorn. The last person Shelby Ryan expects to be attracted to is Iris Calhoun, the sister of the man who killed her wife four years and three thousand miles ago. (978-1-63555-953-8)

Poison Pen by Jean Copeland. Debut author Kendra Blake is finally living her best life until a nasty book review and exposed secrets threaten her promising new romance with aspiring journalist Alison Chatterley. (978-1-63555-849-4)

Seasons for Change by KC Richardson. Love, laughter, and trust develop for Shawn and Morgan throughout the changing seasons of Lake Tahoe. (978-1-63555-882-1)

Summer Lovin' by Julie Cannon. Three different women, three exotic locations, one unforgettable summer. What do you think will happen? (978-1-63555-920-0)

Unbridled by D. Jackson Leigh. A visit to a local stable turns into more than riding lessons between a novel writer and an equestrian with a taste for power play. (978-1-63555-847-0)

VIP by Jackie D. In a town where relationships are forged and shattered by perception, sometimes even love can't change who you really are. (978-1-63555-908-8)

Yearning by Gun Brooke. The sleepy town of Dennamore has an irresistible pull on those who've moved away. The mystery Darian Benson and Samantha Pike uncover will change them forever, but the love they find along the way just might be the key to saving themselves. (978-1-63555-757-2)

A Turn of Fate by Ronica Black. Will Nev and Kinsley finally face their painful past and relent to their powerful, forbidden attraction? Or will facing their past be too much to fight through? (978-1-63555-930-9)

Desires After Dark by MJ Williamz. When her human lover falls deathly ill, Alex, a vampire, must decide which is worse, letting her go or condemning her to everlasting life. (978-1-63555-940-8)

Her Consigliere by Carsen Taite. FBI agent Royal Scott swore an oath to uphold the law, and criminal defense attorney Siobhan Collins pledged her loyalty to the only family she's ever known, but will their love be stronger than the bonds they've vowed to others, or will their competing allegiances tear them apart? (978-1-63555-924-8)

In Our Words: Queer Stories from Black, Indigenous, and People of Color Writers. Stories selected by Anne Shade and edited by Victoria Villaseñor. Comprising both the renowned and emerging voices of Black, Indigenous, and People of Color authors, this thoughtfully curated collection of short stories explores the intersection of racial and queer identity. (978-1-63555-936-1)

Measure of Devotion by CF Frizzell. Disguised as her late twin brother, Catherine Samson enters the Civil War to defend the Constitution as a Union soldier, never expecting her life to be altered by a Gettysburg farmer's daughter. (978-1-63555-951-4)

Not Guilty by Brit Ryder. Claire Weaver and Emery Pearson's day jobs clash, even as their desire for each other burns, and a discreet sex-only arrangement is the only option. (978-1-63555-896-8)

Opposites Attract: Butch/Femme Romances by Meghan O'Brien, Aurora Rey, Angie Williams. Sometimes opposites really do attract. Fall in love with these butch/femme romance novellas. (978-1-63555-784-8)

Swift Vengeance by Jean Copeland, Jackie D, Erin Zak. A journalist becomes the subject of her own investigation when sudden strange, violent visions summon her to a summer retreat and into the arms of a killer's possible next victim. (978-1-63555-880-7)

Under Her Influence by Amanda Radley. On their path to #truelove, will Beth and Jemma discover that reality is even better than illusion? (978-1-63555-963-7)

Wasteland by Kristin Keppler & Allisa Bahney. Danielle Clark is fighting against the National Armed Forces and finds peace as a scavenger, until the NAF general's daughter, Katelyn Turner, shows up on her doorstep and brings the fight right back to her. (978-1-63555-935-4)

When in Doubt by VK Powell. Police officer Jeri Wylder thinks she committed a crime in the line of duty but can't remember, until details emerge pointing to a cover-up by those close to her. (978-1-63555-955-2)

A Woman to Treasure by Ali Vali. An ancient scroll isn't the only treasure Levi Montbard finds as she starts her hunt for the truth—all she has to do is prove to Yasmine Hassani that there's more to her than an adventurous soul. (978-1-63555-890-6)

Before. After. Always. by Morgan Lee Miller. Still reeling from her tragic past, Eliza Walsh has sworn off taking risks, until Blake Navarro turns her world right-side up, making her question if falling in love again is worth it. (978-1-63555-845-6)

Bet the Farm by Fiona Riley. Lauren Calloway's luxury real estate sale of the century comes to a screeching halt when dairy farm heiress, and one-night stand, Thea Boudreaux calls her bluff. (978-1-63555-731-2)

Cowgirl by Nance Sparks. The last thing Aren expects is to fall for Carol. Sharing her home is one thing, but sharing her heart means sharing the demons in her past and risking everything to keep Carol safe. (978-1-63555-877-7)

Give In to Me by Elle Spencer. Gabriela Talbot never expected to sleep with her favorite author—certainly not after the scathing review she'd given Whitney Ainsworth's latest book. (978-1-63555-910-1)

Hidden Dreams by Shelley Thrasher. A lethal virus and its resulting vision send Texan Barbara Allan and her lovely guide, Dara, on a journey up Cambodia's Mekong River in search of Barbara's mother's mystifying past. (978-1-63555-856-2)

In the Spotlight by Lesley Davis. For actresses Cole Calder and Eris Whyte, their chance at love runs out fast when a fan's adoration turns to obsession. (978-1-63555-926-2)

Origins by Jen Jensen. Jamis Bachman is pulled into a dangerous mystery that becomes personal when she learns the truth of her origins as a ghost hunter. (978-1-63555-837-1)

Pursuit: A Victorian Entertainment by Felice Picano. An intelligent, handsome, ruthlessly ambitious young man who rose from the slums to become the right-hand man of the Lord Exchequer of England will stop at nothing as he pursues his Lord's vanished wife across Continental Europe. (978-1-63555-870-8)

Unrivaled by Radclyffe. Zoey Cohen will never accept second place in matters of the heart, even when her rival is a career, and Declan Black has nothing left to give of herself or her heart. (978-1-63679-013-8)